DEAD
MAN'S
PACEMAKER

COSMIC FORGE PRESS

For information about special discounts for bulk purchases or author
interviews, appearances, and speaking engagements please contact:

www.DiakoHazhir.com

First Edition

ISBN eBook	979-8-9929927-0-0
ISBN Paperback	979-8-9929927-1-7
ISBN Hardcover	979-8-9929927-2-4
ISBN Audiobook	979-8-9929927-3-1

Library of Congress: 2025905914

Edited by Jennifer Eaton and Ezra Linehan-Clodfelter
Cover design, layout, production, and consulting by Rodney Miles

DEAD MAN'S PACEMAKER

A DR. ARMAN PIROUZI
PERSIAN MISSION NOVEL

DIAKO HAZHIR

COSMIC FORGE PRESS

To Mahsa Amini, Nika Shakarami, Neda Agha-Soltan, and all Iranian women who have never wavered in their fight for freedom. Your courage echoes through history, and your sacrifice will never be forgotten.

PROLOGUE:

A BRIEF & RECENT
HISTORY OF MODERN IRAN

i ii iii

In 1979, a rebellion of lowbrows dismantled Iran's monarchy, overthrowing a regime that had overseen one of the fastest-growing economies in the world. The so-called Islamic Revolution replaced a government focused on modernization and economic expansion with a theocratic system, reversing many of the industrial and social advancements of the Pahlavi era. Despite the Shah's efforts to modernize Iran, segments of the population—driven by deep-rooted religious traditions and leftist revolutionary ideals—rallied against what they saw as an oppressive monarchy. In the chaotic months following the revolution, over 200 of the Shah's senior officials and military leaders were executed in summary trials, marking the beginning of what Mohammad Reza Pahlavi ominously referred to as the "Great Horror"…

Between 1981 and 1982, the Islamic regime carried out one of the largest political massacres in Iran's modern history, targeting thousands of dissidents in a systematic purge. Having risen to power through a fragile coalition of socialists, social democrats, nationalists, and liberals, the regime quickly turned against its former allies, dismantling any opposition that challenged its absolute rule. With a brutal campaign of mass arrests, show trials, and summary executions, the new theocracy sought to eradicate secular voices and ideological threats. Although the exact number of victims remains unknown, some estimates suggest over 3,500 executions took place across 85 cities. Families were denied the right to mourn, and the graves of the executed were often hidden or destroyed to erase their memory. The regime's goal was not just political dominance, but the complete annihilation of any future resistance. With the opposition crushed, dissent silenced, and fear instilled in every corner of society, a tyrannical theocracy was born…

In 1988, just months before his death, Ayatollah Khomeini ordered the mass execution of thousands of political prisoners who gave "wrong" answers in hastily arranged trials. These kangaroo courts questioned prisoners on their religious beliefs and political affiliations, sealing their fate in mere minutes. Most victims belonged to the unpopular People's Mojahedin of Iran (MeK) and other leftist groups. Many had already been tried, convicted, and were serving their sentences when they were suddenly retried and executed. While some argue that Khomeini's signature on the execution order was fabricated, others present evidence that the massacre was meticulously planned months in advance. Many believe these executions served to unite hardliners while purging moderates, ensuring control of the regime's future leadership. The massacre solidified the regime's brutality...

In 1999, a peaceful student protest at Tehran University against the closure of a reformist newspaper escalated into what became known as the Kuye Daneshgah Disaster. Over the course of six days, security forces and plainclothes militia violently suppressed the demonstration, leading to the detention of approximately 1,400 people, over 200 injuries, and the disappearance of at least five protesters. At least one confirmed death was reported, though many believe the true number was higher. For the first time in two decades, ordinary citizens openly clashed with the regime's paramilitary forces, exposing deep-rooted public resentment toward the ruling theocracy. The crackdown did not end with the protests—many students faced lengthy prison sentences, exile, or continued harassment by intelligence forces. This monumental uprising shattered the illusion of reform within the Islamic Republic, revealing the true nature of a dictatorship disguised behind staged elections and hollow promises of change...

In 2009, millions of Iranians took to the streets in one of the largest uprisings since 1979, protesting the fraudulent re-election of Mahmoud Ahmadinejad. The Green Movement, born from calls for transparency, quickly became a direct challenge to the regime's authority. Chanting "Where is my vote?" protesters filled the streets of Tehran and other cities, only to be met with brutal crackdowns by riot police, Basij militias, and Revolutionary Guards. Security forces used tear gas, batons, and live bullets to silence dissent. Among the fallen was Neda Agha-Soltan, a young woman shot in the streets—her dying moments captured on video became a symbol of the movement's sacrifice. Thousands were arrested, many tortured or disappeared, but the Green Movement shattered the illusion of regime unity. Though the protests were crushed, the spirit of defiance remains alive, proving that the fight for freedom in Iran is far from over. The regime cemented its legacy as a murderer of its own people...

In 2022, the death of Mahsa Amini, a young woman beaten by Iran's morality police for improper hijab, ignited the largest uprising in decades. What began as a protest against oppressive dress codes transformed into a nationwide demand for freedom, as Iranians—led by fearless women—took to the streets under the rallying cry: "Woman, Life, Freedom!" The regime responded with ruthless force. Security forces opened fire on unarmed crowds, arrested thousands, and carried out public executions to instill fear. Young girls, students, and activists were abducted, tortured, and in some cases, poisoned in coordinated attacks on schools. But instead of breaking the movement, each act of brutality fueled more defiance. Though the protests were violently suppressed, the *Woman, Life, Freedom* movement left an unshakable mark. It proved that the fight for justice in Iran is no longer a whisper—but a roar that cannot be silenced.

We don't have one leader. The beauty and strength of our movement is that every single one of us here is a leader.

—Golshan, Women's Rights Activist in Iran[iv]

1

DR. ARMAN PIROUZI peeled off the heavy lead apron for the fourth time that day. The last surgery had taken three hours and every motion strained the dull ache in his back. As he opened the thyroid shield around his neck and felt the skin and bone under his fingertips, it brought to mind the grotesque scene he saw on the internet as he ate a rushed dinner between surgeries: a young Iranian man with a thick, blue noose around his neck, twisting his bound arms so he could wave and smile at the crowd who came to see him die. The condemned man whispered a few words to his executioner before puffing out his chest and shouting, "Woman! Life! Freedom!" Then the executioner kicked the stool out from beneath him.

Arman sighed, rubbing his tired eyes as he lumbered to the parking garage. It was past dinnertime, and the hospital

1

was quieter than usual, a painful reminder that his workday had started at eight in the morning. He couldn't do anything to help that man in Iran, but he *had* saved a patient here, tonight.

Leaving work on time means people can die, he thought, and the brutal realization seemed to make his shoulders ache even worse. The smiling face of the young man—his countryman—haunted Arman as he drove. At a stoplight, he noticed people huddled in an alley, trying to keep warm beneath a tattered blanket. Though America offered many more freedoms than Iran, the country was far from perfect. He turned down Center Boulevard and pulled into the garage beneath his apartment building, waving his parking pass at the young security guard who wore earbuds and barely looked up from his phone. He could probably hold up a napkin and get through, but he hadn't chosen the apartment for the security—that wasn't something he had to worry about here.

Another twinge of pain ran through Arman's back as he got out of his car and shuffled to the elevator, which would deposit him in his penthouse apartment. If he were any other doctor, he'd probably be dreaming of a nice glass of wine and expensive takeout. While takeout was a possibility, the wine was not—for all he knew, his night was far from over. Such was the life of an expert interventionalist[1].

---

[1] Interventional medical practitioners are specialists who do minimally invasive procedures instead of surgery or other treatment. Most often, these procedures utilize various imaging and catheterization techniques in order to diagnose and treat vascular issues in the body. —https://pmc.ncbi.nlm.nih.gov/articles/PMC2745361/

He pushed through the door and sighed as a fluffy ball of cream and black fur scampered from the back room, meowing loudly and rubbing himself against Arman's legs. "Hello there, Anâr," Arman said, picking up the plump Persian cat. "Have you kept the place safe for me?" Anâr responded with a dissatisfied meow, jumping from Arman's arms and racing into the kitchen. He spun twice before sitting beside his bowl. Arman shook his head as he followed. "Get a cat, they said. Cats are independent, they said."

A note from Laura hung on the refrigerator:

I fed the dumb cat but he just looked at me.

Hopefully he ate.

Can't wait to see you tonight!

— Laura

Anâr meowed loudly again, swishing his tail and holding his chin in the air, no doubt in disgust over the now-crusty food in his bowl. Arman picked up the bowl. "This won't do, will it? Laura knows perfectly well that the only person on the planet who can open a can correctly and put it in your bowl is me, right? Silly, silly human."

He cleaned the bowl out, rinsed it, and dumped in a fresh can of food. Anâr pranced over and lapped it up without hesitation. Why the prissy animal thought a can from Arman tasted better than a can from Laura he had no idea.

His pager buzzed at his hip and Arman sighed. *So much for a quiet evening.* He checked the number displayed, then punched it into his phone. "This is Dr. Pirouzi," he said as it connected.

"Dr. Pirouzi! Thank goodness!" a panicked voice answered. "We need you in the maternity floor. A mother just gave birth and they can't stop the bleeding."

Arman rubbed the sting of exhaustion from his eyes. He was sometimes called to assist in delicate procedures even when he wasn't officially on call. His peers trusted him with their patients' lives. That kind of trust didn't come easily, and he was proud he'd earned it, but it could also be exhausting. Sometimes it seemed like exhaustion was the only reward for his years of study and steady pair of hands. Still, he wasn't the only person who could save the woman.

"Where's Stevenson?" he asked.

"Already in the O.R. with another patient."

"Jacobi?"

"Out of town."

It seemed like there was always another emergency—one of the downsides to living in a big city.

Anâr rubbed against Arman's leg, purring his thanks for the delectable meal. He moved the phone from one ear to the other. "I'll be there in fifteen. Get the patient to the angiography room and have everything set up when I get there."

"Will do."

He changed into fresh scrubs and grabbed his keys from the tray on the dresser, taking a moment to look at the picture of him and Laura next to it. Her adorable dimple was in full display, and he smiled, thinking of how much she groaned whenever he brought it up. His dark hair had been much longer back then. They both looked happy. Content. That was before Arman became an interventionalist at Memorial Hospital. He called her as he pulled out of the parking garage.

"Hi, babe!" Laura said as soon as she picked up. "Wait till you see the new dress I picked up. You may want to skip dinner and go right to dessert!" Arman took a deep breath and released it slowly. He wanted nothing more than to see that dress and then remove it. But Fate had other plans for him tonight. "What's wrong?" Laura asked when he didn't respond.

"There's an emergency at the hospital."

"There's always an emergency at the hospital," she said, her voice immediately turning cold. "You're supposed to be off tonight."

"I got called in. Stevenson is already in the O.R. and—"

"You should have told them no!"

"Laura, someone is dying. I can't just—"

"It's not fair. There are other doctors!"

It was true, but chances were, even if Stevenson or anyone else were available, Arman would still be called in. He had made a name for himself, not just because of his skill, but because of his readiness to do whatever it took to save lives. Sadly, not all doctors were as dedicated to their patients.

"I'll try to get out of it next time, but tonight, I need to be there. I'll make it up to…"

The connection was already dead. He could imagine her throwing her phone at the couch and yelling at the blank screen in frustration. Unfortunately, this was not the first time—or probably the last—he would disappoint her.

When they began dating seriously, they had a long talk about the responsibilities of his career and the hours he'd have to work, especially for the first several years. She'd been fine with it; happy he was anything but a military man like her father, who had been gone often and ultimately died in the line of duty.

Arman remembered a similar conversation with his previous girlfriend, Zhina Farzin. They'd planned to marry after medical school, and both worried their demanding schedules would leave little time for each other. Zhina seemed to better understand the expectations of the profession and the pressure of having another person's life literally in your hands. Arman couldn't just turn it off like Laura seemed to think he could. He probably would have married Zhina had family obligations not forced her to return home to Iran.

Maybe things would be different if I had…

He shook off the doubt. Laura would come around—she always did. She was in this for the long haul, just like he was. They were both looking forward to the day when he'd be head interventionalist and be the one calling the shots. Until then, he had to pay his dues, even if it meant missing yet another date night. He flipped on the radio, hoping to take his mind off the inevitable fight waiting when he got home much later.

> *In world news, despite government crackdowns in Iran, thousands of young men and women took to the streets today in protest of the recent arrest of students by the morality police. Five protesters were shot in front of the capitol, three of them under the age of eighteen.*

Arman shivered and turned it off. *What a disaster. They'll bring the entire country down around them.*

He parked in the emergency-doctors' parking and sprinted into the building, flashing his badge at security as he headed for the O.R.

A nurse met him. "Dr. Cruller is still trying to stop the bleeding."

Arman snatched the offered surgical booties and put them over his shoes as he calculated how long the patient had been bleeding; the woman likely had precious little time.

He scrubbed his hands and donned the lead apron as the nurse helped him with the smock, gloves, and bonnet. "Security already phoned in to tell her you're here."

The weight of the apron felt like it had doubled since he'd taken it off barely two hours earlier, but wearing it wasn't an option—X-ray equipment was a necessity for intricate vascular surgeries and bombarding his body with radiation wasn't something he would risk.

Holding his hands in the air, he used his back to push through the doors into the surgical suite. Dr. Cruller's eyes widened over her surgical mask, and her shoulders slumped in relief as she stepped back, quickly rattling off the patient's vitals and what she had done so far. A nurse was holding a blood pack, manually pushing the life-giving fluid into the patient's IV to keep her alive.

Somewhere in the maternity ward, a baby lay in an incubator, waiting to meet their mother for the first time. Arman needed to make sure that happened.

Arman took the ultrasound probe from the instruments the nurses had prepared and placed the device on the patient's groin until he found the right common femoral artery[2]. It was significantly smaller than usual, but that was to be expected since the patient had been bleeding for so long.

---

[2] Your femoral artery and its branches supply your lower body with blood... The common femoral artery is about 4 centimeters long (around an inch and a half). The deep and superficial portions continue down your leg. The diameter of the artery varies widely by sex, weight, height and ethnicity. But it's usually between 7 and 8 millimeters across (about a quarter-inch). The wide diameter of the common femoral artery makes it an ideal access point for endovascular procedures. A surgeon can insert a catheter (thin, flexible tube) into your femoral artery to access other blood vessels in your body, especially those near your heart. — https://my.clevelandclinic.org/health/body/21645-femoral-artery

Arman spared a glance at Dr. Cruller. "She's in hemorrhagic shock."

The OB/GYN's eyes widened. "Can you save her?"

He nodded. "Have as much blood at the ready as you can. Whatever you have here is not enough. We need to prepare for the worst."

A nurse was already heading for the door. "On it."

The blood was only a precaution, but he'd learned that it was best to be prepared for anything. Rolling his shoulders, Arman cleaned the patient's groin and injected lidocaine[3] before making a small incision to access the femoral artery.

The nurse returned with an entire cart of blood. It was more than they'd need unless the patient's uterus ruptured, but he appreciated the nurse following his instructions.

Arman used the ultrasound to monitor as he advanced a small hollow needle into the artery and watched for a few drops of blood dripping from the hub. Next, he slipped a tiny wire into the artery through the needle before pulling the needle out and advancing the vascular sheath over the wire into the artery.

A nurse replaced several instruments on his tray. "Are you okay?" she asked. "You're sweating."

---

[3] Lidocaine belongs to the family of medicines called local anesthetics. This medicine prevents pain by blocking the signals at the nerve endings in the skin. This medicine does not cause unconsciousness as general anesthetics do when used for surgery. —https://www.mayoclinic.org/drugs-supplements/lidocaine-topical-application-route/description/drg-20072776

Arman nodded. "The artery was so spasmed, it barely allowed the sheath to go in, but I got it." He looked at the other nurse. "I need a pressure bag of saline attached to the side arm of the sheath to ensure continuous flow of fluid into the artery and avoid clots."

Dr. Cruller remained glued to the monitor showing the patient's vitals. If there were any problem with clotting, the patient could lose her entire leg.

With the saline set, Arman inserted a catheter through the sheath and into the artery. He watched through the fluoroscopy[4] screen as he carefully advanced the catheter to the uterine arteries on the left and injected contrast to visualize the blood vessels supplying the uterus. No issues appeared on the screen, so he prepared to search the right side of the pelvis.

His catheter had initially entered the right groin, and it would be easy to navigate to the left side of the pelvis by following the normal anatomy; however, to change trajectory while inside the patient, he had to create a loop in the middle of the catheter inside the patient's aorta. By folding the catheter on itself, he could pull the catheter down in the artery on the right side of the pelvis, allowing the catheter tip to engage in the artery that feeds the uterus from the right side of the body. It was tricky work, but his years of study and practice paid off.

---

[4] Fluoroscopy is a type of medical imaging that shows a continuous X-ray image on a monitor, much like an X-ray movie. —https://www.fda.gov/radiation-emitting-products/medical-x-ray-imaging/fluoroscopy

The nurse stared at the fluoroscopy screen in disbelief. "I've never seen that before."

Arman smiled. "All hail to Waltman for inventing the move. He's the epitome of surgical artistry." He pulled the wire back inside the catheter. "This will make the proximal part stiffer than the distal part. This way, I can push the catheter up in the aorta and have a point in the middle of the catheter to serve as the folding zone."

The nurse nodded, never taking his eyes off the screen, and Arman felt a burst of satisfaction. He loved teaching nearly as much as he did saving lives. Maybe the nurse had aspirations of continuing his studies and becoming a surgeon himself.

As Arman continued to pull the wire back into the catheter, he experienced some resistance, and then the movement stopped. He could feel more sweat beading his brow—they were running out of time.

He glanced at the surgical nurse. "The patient's aorta is too small to fit a looped catheter. We need fast replacement of her blood to push it through." He pointed his chin at the blood the nurse was slowly pumping into the patient. "Squeeze harder."

The nurse nodded and grabbed the bag, squeezing with both hands.

"Good. Let's try this again." Arman made the loop and pulled the catheter down again. With the help of the extra blood flow, the catheter shifted into place. "We're in!"

He injected some contrast material and there it was—an artery gushed the now contrast-opacified blood. Now that he'd identified the source of the bleeding, he began injecting small, spring-like coils through the catheter into the damaged uterine artery. The coils blocked the blood flow to the bleeding sites, allowing clots to form.

"How do you know when the bleeding has stopped?" the nurse asked.

"Let Dr. Pirouzi work," Dr. Cruller said.

Arman shook his head. "It's fine." He pointed his chin to the screen as he injected additional contrast. "See? The flow has stopped. No more internal bleeding."

"Fascinating. Thank you."

"Blood pressure?" Arman asked.

Dr. Cruller's eyes crinkled over her surgical mask. "Going up!"

"Good." Arman turned to the nurse. "Increased blood pressure is the first sign of a successful procedure."

He removed the catheter and sheath before using a closure device to seal the incision site and prevent further bleeding from the artery in the right groin. When he was finished, he lifted his bloodstained hands and stepped back.

"Vitals?"

"Stabilizing," Dr. Cruller said with a relieved sigh. "Thank you. I was afraid I was going to have to tell that poor man outside he just became a single father."

"You did good," Arman said. "You kept her alive until I got here. It was a team effort." He turned to the inquisitive nurse. "Are you thinking of becoming a surgeon?"

"I've considered it."

"Feel free to see me during office hours if you have any questions," Arman said. "It's not a profession to go into lightly."

The nurse smiled and nodded. "I might do that, Doctor. Thank you."

As Arman left the O.R., he found Dr. Owen Smith, the Chief of the Department of Surgery, at the monitoring screens. The man ran a hand over his salt-and-pepper beard, his lips pursed.

It seemed Dr. Smith's one job was complaining about how many mistakes doctors made—even if they'd saved a life. After the day he'd had, Arman had no interest in whatever lecture the man had. He kept his head down and tried to pass silently, but Smith turned to him.

"You know, Dr. Pirouzi, I've always believed that foreign doctors would be the ruin of American medicine, but I have to admit, you did a good job on this one... for a foreigner, that is."

Arman smiled through gritted teeth. "I take that as a compliment, Dr. Smith. Now, if you'll excuse me, I need to run."

He walked to the exit door and removed his scrubs before washing his hands and arms, his eyes burning from exhaustion. In some ways, Laura was right—he should take more time off. Performing surgery while tired was a recipe for disaster, but there just weren't enough good interventionalists to go around.

As Arman stepped into the hall, he found Marty sitting at his usual place behind the security desk. "Hey, Doc. You hear about those protests in Iran?"

Arman nodded. It was the last thing he wanted to think about—all he wanted to do was get home and sleep.

"I've been watching the news," Marty continued. "They killed that girl because they didn't like the way she wore her scarf. Those kids are so brave, man. I mean, to stand up to those bastards empty-handed is something else."

Arman lowered his eyes. He made it sound like they were heroes. "I am afraid they are wasting their lives. That country is cursed."

Marty looked surprised. "You think they shouldn't be protesting? I thought you'd be on their side."

Arman stopped and turned back as he walked through the gate. "I am on their side. I'm just not sure if anyone can do anything to save that place."

It was simply more pointless bloodshed. The protestors only wanted basic rights, but they were dealing with men with far too much power, with no hope of being reasoned with.

Whenever there was unrest, Arman hoped things would be different. But each time, the protests just led to more senseless death. As much as he wanted to see his country free, he no longer had the stomach to see young lives cut short. He took a deep breath of the clean night air and checked his watch: *12:30 a.m.*

So much for date night.

2

Queens, New York

ARMAN'S EYES BURNED as he stepped off the elevator to his apartment. Every time he came home, his eyes hurt. Under different circumstances, he would have thought he was allergic to something in the building, but he knew the signs of exhaustion when he felt them.

Anâr immediately weaved in and out of his legs as Arman stepped inside his apartment. "Hungry already? I just fed you." He checked the clock. "Okay, I suppose it was four hours ago. But that doesn't mean I'm going to feed you every time I walk through the door."

After trudging to the kitchen, Arman placed a dollop of food into Anâr's bowl and headed to bed. With each step, his legs felt heavier than the last. He needed some time off—a few days to sit, relax, and think about nothing for a while. Yes, a vacation was definitely in order.

He flicked on the light in the hallway and the soft glow fell over Laura's silhouette in the bedroom. As he undressed, she shifted, turning her back to him. Arman slipped into bed and leaned over to give her a kiss, but she shrugged him off.

His stomach sank. "You're angry."

She said nothing.

"I know tonight was important to you," he continued. "I'm sorry."

She sat up and glared. The light from the hallway illuminated her golden hair like she was a ghostly, vengeful angel. "You always say you're sorry, but you never change."

Arman looked down at the comforter. When they'd first met, she'd been fascinated with his work and thrilled to hear how his knowledge and skills had touched others. Maybe reminding her of that would help.

He looked up. "I saved a life tonight. A young mother who'd just given birth. Ten years ago, she would have died and the baby would never have known its mom."

The glare softened but did not vanish. "Saving a life is always a good thing, and I'm sure that family is grateful. But while you're out there saving lives, I'm back here dying of loneliness."

Anâr jumped onto the bed and kneaded the blanket between them.

Arman smiled, stroking the cat's head. "How can you be lonely where you have such cute, fluffy company?"

Laura rolled her eyes and lay back down with her back to both of them. The conversation was over.

All Arman's friends said the secret to a long, healthy relationship was never going to bed angry. But what was he supposed to do when she was almost always angry and refused to work it out? He wanted to reason with her, but after working the equivalent of two shifts back-to-back, he didn't have the physical or mental energy to do so. Arman rolled onto his back, and Anâr nuzzled up his arm.

It wasn't like he was the manager of a bank. If he didn't go to work, people could die. Why she couldn't understand that was beyond him. His phone buzzed on the nightstand. Laura made a disgusted sound and pulled more of the blankets toward her.

Arman sighed, rubbing his forehead. He couldn't possibly go, even if it was another emergency. There was no way he could keep his eyes open long enough to operate.

He grabbed the phone and stared, bleary-eyed, at the picture of Ârash on the screen. His childhood friend knew full well there was a huge time difference between the United States and Iran. He would never call at such a late hour unless it was an emergency.

Arman slipped out of bed and went to the living room as he answered. "Ârash? Is everything alright?"

"Arman…" His voice sounded tentative. Tired.

"What is it?"

"It's Niki."

Arman's stomach clenched. Niki was Arman's goddaughter, a cherub-cheeked baby girl... who was twenty years old now and an engineering student, a brilliant young mind they were all proud of. He wiped his brow. "What happened?"

"We told her not to go. *Dokhtareye kalle shagh!* You even told her not to go!"

Bile built at the base of Arman's throat. Just last week, Niki had FaceTimed him, telling him about the unrest and how the youth of Iran were protesting...

> *Brown ringlets framed her face within the screen, calling attention to her wide, expectant eyes. It was a shame she needed to hide her beautiful hair whenever she was in public.*
>
> *"Uncle Arman, should I go to the streets and protest?" she asked.*
>
> *The answer would have been simpler if he didn't love her like his own child. "Leave the protesting to others. You need to finish school."*
>
> *"If I don't go, who will do it? How are we going to save this country? We all have responsibilities. We all have dreams. If we all sit in our homes and pretend things are better*

than they really are, we will never live the lives we deserve."

He could feel her enthusiasm even through the phone. It was amazing that so many were risking everything to change their country for the better. The sad truth, though, was that those in power cared little about people's ages. Dissent was still not tolerated within Iran's borders.

"You should avoid any conflicts," he said. "You live only once and yes; you need to look for a change if you can. But in your case, the change will come when you finish your schooling and move to a free country. There is a world of opportunities for you in the United States or even in Europe."

She frowned. She had probably thought that her Uncle Arman—one of the lucky ones who'd actually been able to leave—would understand. Niki lifted her chin. "What about all the other kids, Uncle? Who is going to help them? What if they don't have an uncle like you to help them get out of this horrible place?"

Arman stared at her through the screen, unsure how to respond.

"I don't want to go out and protest for me, Uncle, I want to help those who have no other options."

He wanted to reach out and hug her. How was it that a twenty-year-old kid could be so selfless and wise? He kept his face stern. "It's too risky. Let others protest. You can help in other ways."

She looked down. Arman hated disappointing her, but keeping her safe was more important. He'd rather she hate him and be alive than face a line of men with guns, itchy trigger fingers, and no capability of mercy or remorse.

"Arman?" Ârash asked. "Are you still there?"

Arman gripped the phone tighter. "What's happened?"

"She went to the protest. She didn't march, but she was on the sidelines as a bystander."

The military often used tear gas to scatter people. Had she been hurt, even on the sidelines?

"They arrested her just for being in the area. She's being detained in Ghezel Hesar Prison."

Arman went cold. He didn't know the prison, but any arrest in Iran was dangerous—especially for a woman.

"My brother is lobbying for her release. We have proof that Niki was not part of the protest. He believes he can get her and the three friends she went with freed."

"Good, good."

"Yes, but…" Ârash choked out a sob. "Why didn't she listen? Why did she risk herself?"

Because she believed in a better future for her people. Niki had a good, pure heart. Arman couldn't help but be just as proud as he was horrified.

"It is not illegal to be near a protest," Arman said, as much to reassure himself as his friend. "She'll probably be free by morning."

"We don't know about that. The Islamic Revolutionary Guard Corps (IRGC) is threatening to execute any protestors. They're tired of all the unrest."

Arman started to pace as his friend began to sob. Anâr walked in and out of his legs, keeping time with his stride. That would be very like them—young lives meant nothing to those in power. If this played out like it had so many times before, time was of the essence. There were ways to get her out, but they couldn't waste a moment.

"Don't you dare give up on her," he said. "Find the best lawyer in the country and get ready for the trial. Don't worry about the money, I will send you anything you need. You need to get yourself together, Ârash. She needs you more than ever."

"I'm so afraid." His voice sounded so weak; a shadow of the strong man Arman knew him to be.

"I understand. But control that fear and concentrate on the problem. There are IRGC members who can be bought. Whatever you need, I will do it."

"Thank you, my friend. I'm not sure what I would do without you." He coughed like he was forcing a sob away.

Arman wiped his cheeks. It was rare he ever wished he could be back in Iran, but now was one of those times. "It will take the courts a few months to convict, so we still have time to get good lawyers and pay off whomever we need to in order to make this right. Then as soon as she's out of prison she's coming to live with me."

Thirty years ago, a man named Dr. Rastin had gotten a work visa to get Arman and his mother out of the country. He would do the same for Niki now. Then Arman would find a way to get Ârash and his wife out too.

"You are the best friend I could ever ask for." Ârash sighed again. "It's late there. I should let you go."

"You are like a brother to me, you know this," Arman said. "You call me anytime, no matter what."

"Thank you, my friend."

After he hung up, Arman opened his banking app and sent Ârash ten thousand dollars. *That should be more than enough to get her out quickly.* The funds would transfer first thing in the morning, and then Arman would start working on a visa for her. Now that she'd been arrested, the eyes of the IRGC would never leave her. One loose hijab and she'd be in jail again. Iran needed to be nothing but a bad memory for her long before that became a concern.

Arman crawled back into bed, unable to stop thinking about his niece. It was not uncommon for IRGC to detain spectators to make sure they were not involved or to simply scare people from joining protests in the future. Niki would be kept in a dark cell, deprived of food and water, maybe even be forced to endure a mock execution, and then they'd let her go with a warning. Hopefully, this would be enough of a scare for her to set her sights on school and getting out of that hope-forsaken place.

Unable to sleep, he grabbed his iPad and called up the news. His feed was filled with videos of brutality against peaceful protesters in the streets of Tehran and other Iranian cities. A shiver ran down his spine, despite Anâr's warm body curled up beside him. His former home seemed like a different world now—galaxies away rather than simply on another continent. Yet at the same time, it was still close and horrifyingly familiar, especially knowing Niki was in the thick of it.

He closed his eyes, concentrating on Anâr's and Laura's breathing. The ache in his muscles subsided as he drifted away, weightless, over water and beaches, and finally, over nondescript houses before his feet set down on a dirt road.

He hefted a thick burlap bag over one shoulder and wiped sweat from his forehead with his other hand. Vendors lined the street with carts. They held up fruits, vegetables, and eggs on one side of the street and fabrics and clothing on the other as they shouted to passers-by, hawking their wares.

Dust kicked up around Arman's shoes as the heat of the sun scorched through the wrap around his head. Clouds drifted overhead, giving some respite, but his clothing still clung to him with sweat. He smiled, thinking of the different ways his mother would use the fruits in his bag and how many delicious meals she'd make once he—

A hissing sound filled the air, and people screamed. A smoky white line sliced through the sky before the ground shook. Arman fell to his knees as a boom echoed through the sky and a cloud of fire and debris rained down onto the road. Trembling, he stood staring at the glowing plume of smoke and fire at the end of the street—the direction of his house.

He dropped the bag as flames billowed into the sky. Fruit rolled across the scorched dirt as the blinding plume of fire consumed him. His clothing burst into flames and his skin peeled as he tried to scream through melted lips.

"Arman!"

Laura's concerned face hung over his. Her beautiful brown eyes were narrowed in concern as she tucked a few strands of her long blonde hair behind an ear.

Arman took a deep breath. He wasn't in Iran. He was safe, in bed, at home in the USA. He sat up and realized he was drenched in sweat.

Anâr peeked out from beneath the dresser as Laura rubbed Arman's back. "You were screaming. Bad dreams again?"

He nodded. His throat felt dry, and he could almost taste the dust from his dream.

Laura dragged her fingers through her hair. "Have you been taking your meds? PTSD is no joke."

Arman snorted a mirthless laugh. "Is that your formal opinion, Doctor?"

She slapped his shoulder. "I'm not kidding. You need to take this stuff seriously."

"I am. I'm just tired, it's always worse when I'm tired."

"Well, you're also supposed to be avoiding stressors like not pulling double shifts. I know you want to save everyone and that's admirable, but you need to live your life, too."

"I know, I know." It wasn't just work, though. He rubbed his face. "You know what I've lived through. Some nightmares are a lot worse than others."

"Are you still having dreams about the military dragging you back to Iran?"

He shook his head. "No. I keep dreaming about the day my neighbor's house was bombed."

She moved closer. "Any new memories?"

Arman offered her a weak smile. He'd blocked out a lot of that day, and Laura had been using her psych training to help him work through it. Oddly enough, she'd helped him remember far more than professional regression therapy had ever achieved. Honestly, he didn't want to remember, but if he refused to talk about it, she'd just remind him that unboxing his past was part of the healing process.

Maybe opening up a little will help her forget about missing date night.

"I remember standing in the street carrying groceries for my mother, when a whooshing sound filled the sky, and a white line cut through the air above me. A second later, the ground rumbled. There was a flash and a huge bang." He fiddled with his ear. "A shrill tone filled my ears, blocking out almost everything else as a cloud of smoke and fire filled the air above where my house was."

He looked down. The dust scorching his lungs still seemed fresh, as did the muffled sounds of screams lurking beneath the relentless ringing in his ears.

"I ran home. I was stunned my house was still standing. But everyone was screaming and running, and the heat..."

He held up his hands, protecting his face from the flames, just as he'd done all those years ago. Laura gently took his trembling hands and lowered them to his lap between her own.

Had it really been almost thirty-six years ago? Arman choked out a sob. It was still so fresh... the wounds were open and bleeding like it was just yesterday.

Laura rubbed his back. "Why are you crying?"

"I still feel guilty."

"Did *you* drop the bomb?"

"No."

"Then why do you feel guilty?"

"Because I was relieved. All I could see was my home, and it didn't matter that people were screaming and crying—all I cared about was my mother."

Laura squeezed his hand. "It's natural to feel relief. You were afraid your mother was hurt. You shouldn't blame yourself for loving her."

Laura didn't understand—she couldn't. She hadn't been there, hadn't smelled the smoke or the sickly tang of burning flesh in the air.

"I don't blame myself for worrying about my mother, but there were other people I loved." Arman gulped back the painful knot in his throat. "After I got over the shock, I realized everyone was running across the street." His hands started shaking again. "I turned around, shielding my eyes from the heat and the brightness of the flames." He closed his eyes. "Ârash's house was gone. Pieces of the roof and furniture covered the street. The walls were completely flattened."

Arman played there nearly every day. It was a place of joy and love, and in an instant, it was reduced to a pile of burning debris. The ringing in his ears started to subside, but the screaming only grew louder. It took a woman near the rubble screaming Ârash's mother's name for him to move.

"I ran toward the flames. My head was pounding and my ears were still ringing with this shrill sound." How clearly he remembered that sound. For years, anything high-pitched made him jump. "I started pulling aside the rubble. I knew Ârash's mother was in there. She was always making dinner at that time of day." He wiped his eyes, tears streaming down his cheeks, just as they had that day. "I knew that if she survived, I had precious little time to save her."

Arman looked at his palms which were covered in dirt. He wiped them on the sheets, trying to get them clean.

"Arman?"

He looked up at Laura, then back to his palms, which were clean. He swallowed. "I was too late. She'd been crushed. Maybe she hadn't even survived the bomb. She was gone."

She was a good woman. A kind and generous person. She didn't have anything to do with the war with Iraq. It wasn't fair.

Laura pulled him into a tight hug. "You tried your best. Her death wasn't your fault."

"I know, but…" He closed his eyes again and could hear the faint ring in his ears that had never completely gone away.

"But what?"

"After a man confirmed she was dead, I heard a scream." The sound still haunted him some nights. "I turned to see

Ârash standing at the edge of the street, staring at the rubble. He dropped his bag and ran for the house screaming, 'Maman, Maman!'" Arman looked down. "His mother—she was broken and bleeding. All I could think of was that I'd never want to see my mother like that. So I ran to him."

The dirt was hard beneath his feet, each stomp of his shoes reverberating up his legs and spine and thumping inside his head, and all the while, that incessant ringing filled his ears.

"I grabbed him and held him back while he screamed for his mother. An older woman said prayers while the neighbors made a wall around her, making sure Ârash couldn't see. Finally, my mother came out of my house across the street and pulled us both inside."

Ârash's eyes were hollow, like part of him died in the explosion. In many ways, it was true.

"We formed a brotherhood that day. We decided we could only really count on each other."

They came up with a simple gesture to remind each other they needed to stay strong, and they would be there for each other when the other needed it, no matter what. They would lock their right index fingers. It was simple, but they still greeted each other that way anytime they met, their own personal handshake.

Arman pinched a bit of the sheet between his fingers. "Now the whole country is like Ârash's house, and there are dead bodies being dug out of the rubble every day." He rubbed his nail on the sheet, remembering the dirt and blood caked beneath it that day. "Ârash called me last night."

Laura's eyes widened.

"Niki was at one of the protests in Iran yesterday. She's been arrested."

"Is she going to be okay?"

It was a question not easily answered—nothing was certain in Iran. "Ârash thinks she'll be released sometime today." He met her eyes. "But she is still a woman in a country where women have few rights. He needs to get her out right away."

Laura leaned back. "Wow... I'm so sorry."

"Yeah." He checked the clock and groaned—it was already past six. "I need to get up."

"Are you sure?" Her expression was wry. "You look like hell."

"It's nothing an espresso won't fix."

"Maybe make it two," she said, giving his hair a playful ruffle.

"Gee, thanks."

Laura tossed back the covers and stood, stretching. "I can't believe they're making you work after pulling a double shift yesterday."

He stood and kissed her. "If the doctor with the most face time gets the promotion, then I'm a few steps closer today."

She rolled her eyes. "Yeah, if you live that long."

"Believe me, I have every intention of living through to a calm, comfortable retirement."

"I sure hope so." She pulled him into a hug and held him close. "Sorry I got so mad last night."

Arman closed his eyes and took a deep whiff of her hair. Cantaloupe and cucumber, a smell so distinctly Laura. He wanted to soak in the unexpected affection a little longer—her anger was rarely so easily averted. But once again, his job called.

After a quick breakfast, he got in his car and headed to the hospital, turning on the news as he drove.

In international news, this just in from Tehran. Ambassador Mohammad Hesabi was publicly executed today outside the Parliament building in Tehran. Hesabi was a former IRGC general who, two days ago, was arrested at the airport after being accused of spying for the British government. Demonstrators rallied in the streets, protesting the rushed, biased trial and what they are calling a summary execution. This latest event has created yet another point of contention for protesters in favor of government reform in a nation already riddled with internal turmoil.

Arman wondered if it was that protest that had gotten Niki arrested or one of the dozens of others. It seemed every day it was something new—and rarely good. His mother left Iran in fear for herself and her son. Now, more than ever, he knew she made the right choice. He loved his homeland, but not its callous rulers.

Arman shivered, feeling the heat of the bombs once again as his heart started to flutter. He took a deep breath and released it slowly and then repeated the process, just as his therapist had taught him.

He repeated his therapist's words: "I am no longer in Iran. I live in a free country. I have rights."

The simple affirmation gave him comfort. He switched off the radio and started the exercise anew. Really, what he needed to do was stop listening to news about Iran.

He was never going back there.

———

As Arman walked to his car later that afternoon, after another long shift, two men in dark business suits approached. One was older, with tanned skin, a sparse mustache, and gray hair. The other was younger, in his early thirties, with dark hair and a Middle Eastern complexion.

"Dr. Pirouzi?" the older one asked. Arman glanced at the security booth, where the guard was watching television. Hopefully, he'd step in if these men were up to no good.

"Yes, how may I help you?"

"I'm Agent Barlow from the CIA, this is my colleague Agent Zarabi." He handed Arman a business card. "We need a few minutes of your time."

"Why?" Arman flipped the card over to look at the back. It looked official, but he had no idea what a real CIA business card would look like.

"This is a matter best discussed in private, Dr. Pirouzi. We were hoping you'd come with us."

A shiver ran down Arman's spine. In Iran, being "invited" by government officials to private conversations behind closed doors meant a good chance you'd never be seen again. This was the USA, not Iran, but a fear of government officials was hard to quell. "Is this an order? Do I have to come?"

"No, Doctor, but I can tell you this is a matter of national security, and it relates to your motherland, Iran."

"Iran?" Arman looked over his shoulder. "Do I need to bring my lawyer?"

Both men laughed. "You don't need your lawyer. She wouldn't be able to help in this situation, anyway."

Arman flinched. He'd never said his lawyer was a she. These two had obviously been checking up on him—the only question was why?

Part of him wanted to tell them to leave him alone, but he couldn't deny being intrigued. If he didn't at least find out what they wanted it would haunt him for months. If he wasn't under arrest or in any trouble, there shouldn't be any harm in hearing what they had to say.

He nodded. "All right. Where are we going?"

"We have a secure location downtown. You can follow my car, and Agent Zarabi will follow you to make sure you don't get lost."

Arman's throat went dry. It was clear the escort was to make sure he didn't get cold feet. This wasn't as voluntary as they were saying, which meant no matter what, it would be better for him to comply. If he refused, they'd probably come next with a warrant.

"Alright. I'll follow you."

He shook both of their hands and felt a chill, wondering if he'd just opened a door he'd never be able to close.

3

NONDESCRIPT ART PRINTS of flowers hung at precise intervals on the cream-colored walls as Arman walked through the halls of the CIA field office, following a man in an ill-fitting brown suit who claimed to be taking him to a conference room. The moment they stepped into the building Zarabi and Barlow disappeared through a glass door emblazoned with the CIA logo. The receptionist invited Arman to sit while he filled out paperwork that felt like a job application. After about ten minutes another agent called his name, gave him a badge, and had him check in his phone before asking him to follow.

If this were Iran, he'd be looking for an escape, even though it would have been fruitless. Everyone knew long hallways like this led to torture and, ultimately, death.

His therapist's words inched back into his mind: *You are not in Iran. You have rights now.* Somehow, it did help settle his nerves. He'd learned PTSD was something he may have to deal with for the rest of his life. Arman knew he was no longer under the thumb of the Iranian government and its tyrannical military, yet his body still wanted to flee. Ten years of conditioning—ten years of horror—had a way of sticking with you, even though he'd been in the USA his entire adult life.

The man he was following smiled as he held a door open. Arman held his breath, ready to see a room with a single chair and a table filled with sharp instruments. He peeked inside to find Agent Barlow sitting in a conference room at a circular table, drinking from a steaming mug, relaxed, in fact seeming not even remotely concerned. Of course, the IRGC never looked concerned, either... even when they were executing someone.

Agent Zarabi met Arman at the door and shook his hand again. He had a long scar on the side of his face that looked like an old burn. "Dr. Pirouzi, thank you so much for meeting with us." He motioned to a cushioned leather seat. "May I get you a cup of coffee?"

Arman nodded. "That would be nice, thank you." He tried to control the beating of his heart. If they were going to torture him, they would not be offering him coffee. Probably.

He took a seat opposite Agent Barlow as Agent Zarabi placed a mug into a single-cup coffee maker. The sudden gurgle of the machine made Arman jump. He dabbed the sweat from his brow. *Not Iran. Not Iran. Not Iran...*

Agent Barlow smoothed out his mustache. "Thank you for agreeing to talk with us."

Arman gave a curt nod, fingering the business card he'd tucked into his pocket. Agent Barlow leaned back in his chair and folded his hands. "Do you follow the events in your home country, Dr. Pirouzi?"

"Yes, of course. It's good to keep up with world news."

Agent Barlow nodded. "That's good to hear. The news outlets replay the basics of what's going on, the... ripples on the surface, so to speak."

"What do you mean?"

Agent Zarabi set a mug of coffee on the table in front of Arman. "Things are a lot worse than they seem."

Arman shifted in his seat. How was it possible for things to be worse than children and students being murdered on the streets for wanting better lives? "How so?"

Zarabi sat beside him. "Based on the intelligence we have received, Iran is in the last stages of developing an atomic bomb."

Arman's stomach sank as did the blood from his face. "That would..." Be a nightmare? The end of the world? He couldn't begin to imagine it.

Barlow leaned over. "If these reports are correct, this will change the geopolitics of the Middle East forever—and for the worse."

Arman's mind swam. *Why are they telling me this?*

"Of course, this puts the United States in a very precarious position," Zarabi said. "We're looking at either a full military intervention, strikes on nuclear sites, or increasing international economic pressure on the government and supporting the coalition of internal and external opposition."

Arman looked down. "Is it really that bad that they are considering military intervention?"

"We believe it is," Zarabi said.

Taking a sip of coffee, Barlow settled back in his chair. "Unfortunately, the United Nations disagrees. The European governments are against these options unless information clearly shows Iran is headed towards making a bomb."

"Israel is our only ally in this," Zarabi said. "They're ready for either military option and POTUS has asked the Pentagon to create a war plan."

Of course Israel was ready for military options. It was their first choice rather than a last resort; they'd shown that time and time again over the years. "The people in control of Iran are zealots. People with no regard to the value of human life. Israel is a small country. Their backing may not be enough to get you through this."

"That's very astute of you, Dr. Pirouzi," Barlow said. "You are correct that sanctions only work on a global scale. The United States embargo on Iran has barely affected the government's behavior. If Europe doesn't get on board, any further sanctions the USA or Israel decree will be meaningless."

Zarabi nodded. "The regime barely blinked when the embargo started in 1995, they simply diverted their exports to different countries. The bomb—if there is one—would still be built."

Arman adjusted his weight, trying to hide his concern. "I'm hoping that you have come up with a way to convince Europe to impose the same sanctions?"

He shouldn't have been worried about Iran anymore, but despite cutting political ties, it was still the country of his birth. Ârash was there, along with his family. Niki was still there, at least until she got her degree and Arman could get her a work visa. There were still good people in Iran who deserved so much more than their government allowed. Niki and her friends protested because they wanted better lives— the last thing they deserved was more war.

Barlow rapped a knuckle on the table. "The European Union has agreed that if the United States can provide irrefutable proof that Iran is setting itself up to be a global threat, they will join in sanctions, as well as prepare their militaries as a last resort."

"Of course, the hope is that it won't get to that point." Zarabi held up his palms. "We've gone down that path before and found no nukes. POTUS is very wary of that kind of bad publicity happening on his watch. He's invested in trying sanctions in hopes of stopping this before it becomes a problem."

"So you just need to find the proof," Arman said.

Barlow smiled grimly. "We already did. It's with a covert operative in Iran. We need someone to go in, get the information, and bring it back." Arman's stomach churned. Certainly, they weren't suggesting that *he* be this person! Both agents stared at him, waiting for him to digest everything they'd said.

He'd sworn he'd never go back, and with good reason. Iran would be just as dangerous for him as it would be for an American. Iran watched its borders like a hawk waiting for a clean kill. What they were suggesting was insanity.

Arman shook his head, the act leaving him a little dizzy. "I'm a doctor, not a spy."

Zarabi handed him a bottle of water. "We realize that," he said as Arman fumbled the lid off and took a long drink. "What we need is the help of a skilled surgeon."

"To do what?"

"Remove a pacemaker."

Arman frowned. "There are plenty of surgeons who can remove a pacemaker."

"Not this one." Barlow glanced at Zarabi. "We have a nuclear scientist working for us. They've been on the inside for the past three years. In his last direct communication, he informed us that he now has access to the Iranian nuclear bomb program. This is the irrefutable proof we need that Iran is attempting to strategically entrench themselves as a nuclear power."

Zarabi steepled his fingers. "It's exactly the information we need if we want sanctions and not a war."

Barlow nodded. "Problem is, the documents are stored in a SCIF—that's a *Sensitive Compartmented Information Facility.*"

Zarabi continued. "It's a high-security room with twenty-four-hour guards at the door as well as video monitoring of all entrances and exits. Inside the room is a completely tech-free zone. They don't even have CCTVs inside."

It made sense. The Iranian military was very good at keeping their secrets. He wouldn't be surprised if they still kept records on paper, just to make things even harder. Still… why were they telling him this? Certainly, they didn't want him to break in, *Mission Impossible* style?

"Once documents are deemed classified," Barlow said, "they go into the SCIF, and they don't come out without the permission of Iran's Supreme Leader himself. We've been trying to get in for years."

Arman stared at a single coffee ground stuck to the side of his mug. *What does this have to do with a pacemaker?*

"And I guess you did?"

Barlow smiled. "Our contact is one of the few people with access to this room. However, he still has to leave his wallet and phone in a bin and go through a scanner before he enters the room to make sure he isn't bringing any piece of tech inside."

Arman wouldn't be surprised if they made the man strip naked before entering. The only thing the IRGC was more famous for than keeping control of people was keeping secrets.

"So how did your man get the information out?" Arman asked, fascinated in spite of himself.

"Our engineers came up with the idea of implanting a cardiac pacemaker with undetectable close-range Bluetooth capability into our operative's chest wall. The storage capability is only accessible through a Bluetooth connection to a government-issued micro camera safely concealed within an agate ring."

Arman gaped. It was reckless, but also genius. It was said that the Prophet Muhammad had worn an agate ring to protect himself and many high-ranking officials—or those who could afford it—wore similar rings, the larger the better, as a status symbol. The rings were so common in the aristocracy of Iran that no one would question even an oversized one. More importantly, with the religious significance, most guards would be too afraid to ask someone to remove it.

It was Zarabi's turn to smile. "Clever, right? All he needs to do is spin the ring on his finger and the camera snaps a picture and shoots it into the pacemaker. It's ingenious and completely undetectable."

Arman grimaced. "Still sounds very risky."

"Sure, and it was, but he agreed." Zarabi's smile faded. "Unfortunately, we've encountered some difficulties. Just under a month ago, our spy activated a signal on his pacemaker, telling us that he'd downloaded the necessary information, but when our operatives tried to extract the files remotely, the tech failed."

Arman frowned. Barlow spoke before he could. "The files are still there, so the mission isn't a failure. We simply need to pick up the pacemaker so we can manually extract the data. When Plan B went into effect, the pacemaker sent an emergency code to his doctor, telling him there was a malfunction. Since this is such a critical instrument, I'm sure you can understand that the doctor wants to have it replaced right away."

"As a precaution, we made this a special pacemaker not available anywhere in Iran and Iranian doctors aren't familiar enough with Western technology to try to fix it. So he must travel to Germany to remove the pacemaker and get a new one."

"That's... actually smart," Arman said. "You'll have him out of the country and get all your information and no one will be the wiser. It sounds like you have it all figured out." He sat a little taller. He'd expected that they were going to ask him to do something insane—he'd been to Germany several times. There were great medical conferences there and he might even be able to take in some sights. It would be like a working vacation, and he'd get to do a little good for both their countries at the same time.

Agent Barlow leaned back in his chair. "Unfortunately, for security reasons, the Iranian government has canceled all international travel for the nuclear agency's high-ranking workers until further notice."

Arman's stomach sank. He should have known better than to think he'd get that lucky.

Agent Zarabi handed Arman a brochure. "In forty-three days, there's a cardiology conference in Tehran with a workshop to teach Iranian interventionalists about new pacemakers and other devices."

"You have to be kidding me. That's just a little bit too much of a coincidence."

"Of course, it is," Zarabi said. "It took a lot of work to get it arranged so quickly. We thought we had it solved and had our own CIA-trained surgeons lined up, but we hit a brick wall."

Arman nodded. "The IRGC isn't going to allow a foreign doctor to operate on anyone essential to their nuclear program."

"No, we considered that. All our applicants were former Iranian citizens, both to blend in with the culture and also to avoid any language barriers. The bigger problem is the Iranian government's interest in the conference, since so many important people will be in attendance. They're being quite *helpful* in vetting applications."

Arman took a sip of his coffee, which did little to calm his nerves. "Let me guess. All your applicants were denied."

"Correct." Agent Barlow tapped a finger against the side of his mug. "Correct me if I'm wrong, Dr. Pirouzi, but haven't you written four papers for *The Iranian Journal of Cardiology*?"

"Five, actually," Arman said mechanically.

Zarabi let out a low whistle.

Barlow glanced at a tablet on the table next to him. "You've also turned down two offers by one…" He tapped the screen. "Dr. Hajipour to speak to their interventionalists about modern Western advancements."

Arman wiped his brow. "Yes. So?"

Barlow gave him a lopsided smile. "So, Dr. Hajipour just happens to be running the conference. Someone may have recently mentioned your name to him. I'd expect you'll be getting another pre-approved invitation any day now."

Arman ground his teeth. The lingering question, *why him?* had finally been answered—they couldn't get any of their preferred operatives into the country.

"What we need from you is simple, Dr. Pirouzi," Barlow said. "You'll go to the conference as a speaker. While you're there, someone will come and talk to you about our operative's predicament. You will act like this is the first time you're hearing about it. It will be a stroke of luck as far as they're concerned. All you need to do is agree to replace his pacemaker. They'll look at you as a hero."

"But you're asking me to do a little bit more than replace a pacemaker."

"Once you replace the modified pacemaker with a standard one, you just need to place it in a box and tell them you'll take it to Germany, where they can run a proper diagnostic to see what went wrong. Then you'll get back on a plane for Germany and be home free."

"You can't think it will be that easy," Arman said. "What if they catch me?"

Zarabi glanced at his partner, then at Arman. "I'm sure you know the answer to that question, Doctor. Iran's military does not take kindly to spies." By the time they got around to executing him, it would likely be a mercy. Iranian prisons were infamous for creative torture.

The room started to spin and Arman's stomach twisted. It was ridiculous. He didn't know what kind of facilities they'd be asking him to work in. For all he knew, the military would send in an agent under the guise of being a nurse for the sole purpose of watching the procedure, making sure the operative was not using this as a means of escape. And if the IRGC was there, what would stop them from asking for the pacemaker as soon as it was removed? If they suspected Arman for even a *moment*, they would arrest him.

There were simply too many ways this could all go horribly wrong. If he was arrested, there would be no way for the CIA to get him out of the country. Even if they tried—which they had no reason to do—he would be long dead. If the slightest thing went wrong, it would be a suicide mission.

"What do you say, Dr. Pirouzi?" Barlow asked. "Are you ready to serve your country and save your motherland?"

Arman gulped as the two men looked at him expectantly. This sort of meeting was probably an everyday occurrence for them. How many people had these two men talked into serving their country… and how many had never come home?

He had a life here in the USA—one he'd fought hard for. He had a girlfriend and, most importantly, a mother who'd sacrificed much to give Arman chances she never had. She was most likely living her last days. If he asked her, he was sure she'd want to spend those days with her son. He owed her that much… giving her comfort in her last days. It wasn't much to ask of a son, and he needed to step up to his familial obligations before helping people, and a country, out of his control.

He pushed his chair back and stood. "This plan is insane. Too much can go wrong."

"We assure you," Barlow said, "you'll go in with the most updated technology. You'll be as safe as possible. We have reason to believe—"

"Reason to believe?" Arman snapped. "Are you insane? You have obviously never been to Iran, or you would not be making these statements so rashly. The IRGC takes what it wants from whom it wants to take it from. Those who speak up are executed. Spies are not tolerated. Haven't you been listening to the news?"

"We have," Zarabi said. "And that's why we're coming to you. You are exactly the kind of Western success story they'd love to show off as one of their own. We believe you have the best chance at getting in and out of Iran alive."

Arman scoffed. "Chance?"

Barlow spread his hands. "We aren't going to sugar coat it, there's risks. But not going has risks too. The last invasion of Iran cost a lot of lives. We're trying to avoid that."

"You have soldiers and trained personnel for this." Arman pointed at himself. "I have seen war close up. I have helped dig the bodies of people I love from the rubble with my bare hands." He shook his head. "I left Iran to get away from all the heartache and fear and make a life for myself. I've done that and I'm not going to throw it all away to make your jobs easier. You can figure out some other way."

He turned and walked through the door, slamming it behind him.

The man in the brown suit who'd escorted him in was waiting outside. "Would you like me to show you out?"

Arman spoke through gritted teeth. "Yes."

The younger man had to jog to keep up as Arman stormed down the hall. How could they even ask this of him? The last time the USA believed there were weapons of mass destruction in the Middle East, they used their military to intervene and found nothing. How were they sure this time would be different? He could be walking into the sights of a firing squad for nothing.

After retrieving his phone, Arman pushed through the front door and took a deep whiff of the crisp, clean air outside. It had been many years since he felt as stifled as he just did in that building.

A bus passed the rows of cars stacked bumper-to-bumper along the curb. Past the traffic light, a man holding a large *Sale* sign tried to coax people into a corner shop. It was all familiar and right, even the trash blowing across the sidewalk and hitting the edge of his polished Italian loafers. This was what life should be. No one here needed to worry about the government coming for them in the middle of the night. He closed his eyes and let the sun warm his face. Each breath came easier than the last as he let the memories of their ridiculous request fade away.

His phone buzzed with a message from Laura, the third since he'd handed his phone over to the CIA. She cared, unlike the men in that building asking Arman to risk his life.

I'm coming home, he texted her, then slipped his phone into his pocket.

He'd worked too hard to gain his freedom. He'd paid his dues. He'd known loss most people couldn't even fathom. It was someone else's turn to risk everything. The CIA would have to find another puppet.

4

WHEN ARMAN ENTERED his apartment, he found Laura sitting on the couch with her arms folded. "Have you been sitting here all day?"

"No. I've been sitting here since Dr. Smith called me and said you'd met two men in suits outside the hospital and left with them, and then you refused to answer your phone. What's going on?"

Arman sighed. *Smith.* The man thrived on knowing everyone else's business. Arman had hoped he could forget this afternoon ever happened, but apparently that was too much to ask. "It was the CIA."

Her eyes widened. "Are you kidding me?"

He rubbed his face as he sat beside her on the couch. "I wish."

"What did they want?" she asked, resting a hand on his shoulder.

"They wanted me to spy for them." He shouldn't have just blurted it out like that, but there was no way to make it sound better than it was.

She gripped the edge of the couch. *"What?"*

"They need someone to enter Iran and smuggle out information."

"That's—that's insane! Why you?"

That was the million-dollar question. "There's a medical conference in Iran that requires speakers of Persian descent."

"Bullshit. The CIA has to have Iranian doctors on their payroll."

Arman nodded. "They do but they seemed to think my connections and work in Iranian medical journals gave me an edge their people don't have."

"And you told them to screw off, right?"

Arman opened and closed his hands, staring at his palms... the same palms that dragged his best friend's lifeless mother from the rubble when the bombs fell in his village. He'd thought he'd left that world behind him. In many ways, he had, but Niki looked so disappointed in him when he didn't support her desire to protest. She did the right thing, going out there to speak for the people, even if those in power called them "criminals."

Playing spy was a different matter entirely. If he were caught, there would be no twenty-four-hour hold and release. He would be risking his life.

Laura frowned at him. "You better not be considering this. One of the reasons I put up with you and your insane schedule is because no matter how late you come home, at least I know you're not going to do it in a box."

He held up his hands. "Of course not. I told them they were crazy." The last time he was in Iran was for Niki's birth, and he'd sworn never again. It was simply too dangerous.

"Why do I feel like you're not telling me the truth?"

Arman shrugged. "I *did* say no, but to be honest, I feel a little guilty about it. There are kids over there risking their lives to speak out and here I am safe in this beautiful home with you and my new life. It feels like I've betrayed them."

"You did what was right for *you*. You can't save everyone, Arman. It's impossible."

"Yeah, I know."

"If you did something like this, that would be the end of us, you understand?" Her eyes were wet. "I'm not going to go through that again."

Laura's father had died in Afghanistan when she was only a teenager.

He wrapped his arms around her. "I understand. I told them no."

She hugged him back, wiping at her eyes. Anâr scurried out from under the chair and trotted to the kitchen meowing loudly.

Laura laughed and untangled herself from the hug. "You better go feed him."

"Oh, you don't want to?"

She rolled her eyes and shoved him away. "I did an hour ago and he ate exactly zero of it."

Arman walked over to the kitchen and cleaned out the bowl before pouring fresh food inside. He stroked Anâr's back as the cat began eating happily.

"It's really the same food. You can eat it when Laura gives it to you. I swear. It will taste the same."

"He's a dummy but I still love him," Laura called from the living room. "Remind you of anyone?"

Arman smiled.

5

Queens, New York

ARMAN SAT ON the balcony of his mother's apartment, looking out over the peaceful, grassy courtyard below. He was glad she found a home where she could enjoy some of the lovely scenery this country offered. The door opened, and his mother came out carrying a small tray of tea and Persian cookies.

He stood. "Let me help you."

She adjusted the scarf on her head. "Such a sweet boy."

Arman tried to look like he hadn't noticed. Just a year ago, her long, peppery-white hair was styled to perfection. She'd taken pride in her hair ever since she could walk around in public without a hijab. The morning after her third chemo treatment, she called crying after finding a clump of hair on her pillow. It broke his heart. He wondered if she'd start wearing the hijab again to hide her hair loss, but she'd adapted in a more American way.

"Are you still happy here?" he asked. "Are you glad you decided to immigrate to the USA?"

"Oh my, yes. There really wasn't a choice for me."

"What do you mean?"

She sat and took a sip of her tea. "When your father came back from the front lines in a casket, my whole life changed. I was a young widow, alone with a ten-year-old son."

In Iran, if his grandfather had wanted to take Arman from her, he legally could have. Luckily, for them both, his grandfather was an amazing man, and he treated her like his own daughter.

His mother placed her cup down. "I wanted to be independent. I didn't want to live under someone else's wings." She watched a squirrel jump to another branch. "After your father died, I went back to work, but everyone treated me differently. It was hell. Many were trying to be nice to me, but at the same time pitying me. I hated that they saw me as a victim, but I couldn't escape it."

Arman took her hand. Part of that victimization, he knew, had come about when the bomb had dropped on Ârash's house across the street. She didn't like to speak about that and he wasn't about to bring it up—Ârash's mother had been a good friend of his mother's too. "You did great. We lived a good life."

"I know. I never told you how close we came to the worst of possibilities."

"What do you mean?" Arman asked, surprised.

"One day, I went to work, and my employer offered for me to be his second wife." She grimaced. "That would have removed any choices I had, and also you would have belonged to him." She caressed his cheek. "You were such a beautiful little boy. I couldn't put you through that."

Arman shuddered. Women had no rights in Iran, but children had very few rights as well. A *beautiful* ten-year-old boy moving into the household of an aristocratic father was far from ideal. Arman had trauma from war, but knew well there were other horrors he had escaped.

"I had no idea."

"Because I didn't tell you. I quit my job that day and called your father's friend Dr. Rastin in the United States. Luckily for us, he was able to arrange a work visa." Her eyes searched his. "I left for myself, but even more so, I left for you. I wanted you to have the life you deserved... the life the military took from you the day they forced your father to go to the front lines to help treat the wounded."

Arman watched the wind shake the leaves in the trees. He had no idea how close he'd come to living a very different life.

"Don't look so distraught," his mother said. "I didn't only leave to keep you safe. I left for me. There I was, a widow, someone to be used. Here, I had a chance. I worked hard, and I made it. We both did."

Arman nodded, his thoughts on a day thirty years ago when his mom worked for Dr. Rastin. She came home and Arman went to hug her, but she backed away…

"I need to shower and change first," she said.

Arman was confused, and when she returned and gave him a tight hug, he asked why she wouldn't let him hug her before.

She sighed. "Well, I'm now in charge of cleaning the scopes."

"What does that mean?" Arman asked.

She lowered her eyes and frowned. "Dr. Rastin uses scopes when he does colonoscopies. They need to be cleaned and sanitized after each patient."

"What's a colonoscopy?"

She smiled, tapped his knee, and stood. "How about you help me make dinner tonight?"

Arman always loved helping the cook, and the distraction worked. But when he found out what a colonoscopy was, he cried the whole night.

Arman looked from the trees back to his mother. "You sacrificed a lot for us, Mom. Thank you."

She waved her hand dismissively. "I would do it again in a heartbeat! I am so proud of my life and my decisions. For one, I have a brilliant son like you." She grabbed a cookie and dipped it into her tea, an interesting habit she'd picked up since moving to America. "I feel sad when I see the young people in Iran these days. They look just like me thirty years ago. All they want is to be free and independent. That country needs someone to sacrifice for those kids."

Her words brought his pang of guilt back to the surface. "Would you help them if you knew you might die for it?" he asked quietly.

She placed the wet cookie on the edge of her plate. "I did it before for *us*, and if I knew there was a chance to make a difference, I would definitely do it for *them*."

He looked back inside at a picture of Niki on the wall. Her eyes smiled back at him, so full of hope. So full of dreams.

People walked by on the street chatting, laughing. They had no idea how good they had it; how lucky they really were.

Maybe nobody realized how good their life was until bombs started dropping on their street.

6

Queens, New York

NIKI'S PIERCING EYES haunted Arman as he slipped behind the driver's seat and pulled out of the parking lot in front of his mother's home. An ambulance passed, and he resisted the urge to follow it to make it to the hospital faster. Today, he looked forward to a longer drive to work. He had too much to think about and, at the same time didn't want to think about any of it. Iran was in his past, but in many ways it was still so much a part of who he was. The dichotomy was maddening. He flipped on the radio, but it failed to distract him.

When the CIA mentioned Germany, he thought they had a good plan. Germany was a country where people could feel safe. It wasn't safe in Iran for the people who lived there, let alone anyone wanting to help bring down their tyrannical government.

So much propaganda proudly proclaimed that *one man can make a difference.* In some cases, that might have been true, but not in Iran. One man would be executed—silenced forever. The only chance the people of Iran had would be thousands of voices screaming at once. Even then, a good portion of them would be killed in an attempt to silence the others. That was why the mass protests were being organized. All those kids knew there was a chance they wouldn't come home, but they were willing to risk their lives for a better future, even if they weren't there to see it.

A shiver ran through him. Too bad all their efforts were probably useless. The military was too entrenched and too in control. This situation was bigger than the protesters, or maybe even bigger than the CIA could fathom.

Arman was relieved when he stepped out of the unmarked CIA building, finally free after deciding to stay as far away from his homeland as possible. Now he felt guilty again—which was ridiculous! He needed to get over the remaining *survivor's guilt* plaguing him so he could live in the real world. There were people trained to do the kind of job the CIA was asking him to do. He was a doctor, not a spy. He made the right decision.

> *In international news: Three students who were arrested at the protests in Tehran this week were executed this morning after an expedited trial in Iran's Supreme Court as Tehran continues its attempt to quiet the voices of the country's outraged youth.*

Arman's stomach plummeted. Executions never happened that quickly. They had to be wrong—it was probably protesters who were arrested a month before. Niki was not involved in that last protest. Her stay in prison would be hard and uncomfortable. They might even torture her until she confessed to a crime she didn't commit. But Ârash said they had *proof* she wasn't involved. He would find a way to bribe the right people to set her free.

Using emergency-doctor parking, Arman jumped from his car and ran to his office, ignoring Dr. Smith as he called his name from down the hall. Arman pushed past two nurses talking and laughing. One greeted him but he didn't turn back or respond.

When he got to his office, Arman closed the door and pulled down the shade. He didn't want to be disturbed before he could confirm that everything was all right. He reached into his pocket and grabbed his phone. Agent Barlow's business card came out along with it. He tossed it away. The last thing he needed was to be reminded of the CIA.

Heart pounding, he dialed Ârash. The phone rang for a long time before someone picked up, but they didn't speak.

"Ârash? Are you there? It's Arman."

The silence was deafening. "Arman... They c-called us last night to tell us... w-we begged them. W-we tried everything."

Ice flooded Arman's veins. "Where is Niki?"

Ârash broke out in a sob. "S-she's gone, Arman. The IRGC… They… they executed her this morning."

Arman clutched the phone so he didn't drop it. The room spun, then the walls seemed to close in. Arman couldn't breathe. He wasn't sure he even remembered how. A dull pounding drummed between his ears, blocking out the laughter in the hallway.

This couldn't be real. It wasn't possible.

They were getting her out—they had a plan.

But none of it mattered.

The IRGC probably tortured Niki and her friends to extract confessions before slaughtering her for the simple crime of wanting a better life for herself and others. And the worst part was, they would get away with it because there was no one the people could turn to. The government that was supposed to protect them was the very monster lurking under the bed of every innocent person in that country. Tears burned Arman's eyes. It wasn't right. Niki was meant for better. She was finishing college to become a mechanical engineer at one of the best universities in Iran. She was brilliant… a star just preparing to shine. Now that star had been snuffed out. And for what?

Arman's hand trembled as he dragged his fingers through his hair. The last time he'd gone to Iran was for Niki's birth. He was nervous about going, but Ârash and his wife, Marjan, insisted he needed to be there. The truth was, Arman *wanted* to be there. Ârash was like a brother to him, and he wanted to stay a part of his life.

Arman remembered the moment that adorable baby with chubby cheeks and soft feet was placed into his arms. It was instant love. From that moment on, every year or so, he'd take a vacation with Ârash and his family. Niki started to call him *Amoo*, which meant *uncle* in Farsi. Technology and less restrictive travel allowed them to see each other for special occasions, keeping Niki in Arman's life.

She grew up so fast, with dark, curly hair and big, expressive eyes and such a love for life. Every day, she started looking more and more like Ârash's mother. Just looking into Niki's eyes reminded Arman of the woman's kind, gentle soul. Ârash noticed it, too, saying he felt like his mother had sent him a gift from heaven so he could remember the better days they'd had when he was younger. Ârash's mother was the type of person who would have given him a gift like that had she been able. Yet another life snuffed out too soon for no other reason than a petty war between nations.

Ârash continued to sob on the other end of the phone line.

He didn't know what to say—there simply were no words. This defied logic. It couldn't possibly have been real. He tried to calm himself, but his chest only tightened. If he couldn't deal with this, what was Ârash going through? How would he and Marjan possibly cope?

Arman started to pace around the room. *I should have wired more money. I should have made the phone calls myself.* He put a hand to his head, struck by a wave of dizziness.

"This-this wasn't supposed to happen." It was a ridiculous thing to say. Of course it wasn't supposed to happen. He just couldn't find a way to put words to his jumbled thoughts. "I…" He what? His mind whirled, completely at a loss.

"I don't know what I'm going to do," Ârash sobbed. "She-she was our world."

"As she was mine," Arman whispered.

It was too much death… too much heartache. It was like they had been placed on this earth for the sole purpose of suffering.

The line crackled as Ârash switched ears. "I need to go. I have to find a way to collect her body."

Arman nodded. "I understand, and Ârash…" There were so many things he wanted to say, but none of them were right.

"I know, my friend," Ârash said. "I wish you were here, too."

Arman set the phone down. The air seemed too thick to breathe. How could Niki have been alive one moment and then simply gone the next? He sat at his computer and looked for Iranian news. Part of him hoped to see Niki being released, to see her smiling face, to find out it had all been a mistake. It was a nice dream.

One that he knew wouldn't come true.

Instead, the face of General Moradi of the IRGC appeared as he gave testimony in front of the Supreme Leader. His gray beard and white hair glowed in the lighting, making him look larger than life. This was probably not by accident.

Moradi's eyes narrowed at the camera. "I know the meaning of giving myself up for God, for Iran, and for our Supreme Leader. I have stood on the front lines with my brothers and have made sacrifices."

Arman sneered in disgust. What kind of sacrifice could that monster possibly have made? Moradi was alive. So many of his soldiers were dead. Even worse, the innocents... like Niki.

People like Moradi were to blame, not only for the deaths of innocent protestors, but for encouraging the already-brainwashed men carrying guns to enforce archaic laws. For insisting that things remain as they always were despite people rallying to try to better their country.

Moradi raised his hands and shouted in Farsi, accusing the US government of causing unrest and supplying the protesters with guns and other weapons. He continued, saying that the protesters were killing each other and blaming the IRGC and Iranian police for these crimes.

Arman shook his head. Was the man so delusional that he thought anyone in their right mind would believe a word he was saying?

General Moradi lifted his chin high, his eyes dark and filled with vengeful hate. "There are spies among us, stirring up and enabling the protestors. I will find and deliver the American spies orchestrating these plots. Their blood will cleanse us of this foreign curse."

Arman glared into the man's eyes. General Moradi was known to manipulate inmates' sentences in IRGC prisons and even watch over tortures and executions as they were carried out. It was quite possible that this man's stern, heartless face had been the last thing sweet, loving Niki had seen in this life. It was unfair and incredibly cruel.

This regime had simply gained too much power. They were too entrenched, and they needed to be taken down. War would mean more children being forced to dig the bodies of their mothers from the rubble of their homes. There had to be another way. Someone needed to stand up and help make a difference.

He stared at Agent Barlow's business card sitting on the desk. Arman had already told them no. Staying here, safe, in the United States was the sensible thing to do. His mother needed him, Laura needed him, the cat needed him—not to mention his patients.

What would happen if he took an extended leave? Would Dr. Smith start spreading rumors? Would another doctor take Arman's place, erasing years of his work towards a promotion?

Niki's eyes were wide and sincere when she asked him, "What about all the other kids, Uncle? Who is going to help them? What if they don't have an uncle like you to help them get out of this horrible place?"

Arman felt he was going to be sick. She'd had such faith he would get her out. He screwed his eyes shut. She only had one more year of school! Then she would have been free. Safe. Why did she have to protest now?

Her sweet, beautiful eyes pierced his mind. *I didn't go out there for me, Uncle. I went to help those who have no other options.*

And that was the horrible truth. For *so* many in Iran, there were no options.

The IRGC was in power because people were afraid. They counted on the basic human instinct for survival—that most people would rather simply obey than risk injury or death. Those who didn't obey could be silenced. All the IRGC needed to do was fill the prisons and military with men who didn't mind killing.

Arman pressed his palms against his temples. Niki died for what she believed in. She was a hero. Yes, she deserved better, but the only way for her death to have meaning was if others took up the mantle and added their voices to the cause. Iran needed more than just voices, though. It needed the silent few who could help take down the IRGC from the inside. That was why the agents came for Arman. Not to ask him to senselessly endanger his life, but to take a chance for the greater good—just like Niki.

Yes, the timing was bad. He had other obligations. But there would always be obligations. There was never a good time to risk your life, but it was always a good time to do whatever you could to thwart tyranny.

He picked up the business card, flipping it between his fingers. His mother said she'd sacrifice to save others; she would understand. Laura may not, but hopefully, she'd come around. And the cat? Well, Anâr would have to learn to take his food from someone else for a little while.

Arman grabbed the phone and dialed the number before he had a chance to talk himself out of it.

"Agent Barlow speaking."

"Hello, Agent. This is Arman Pirouzi."

"Dr. Pirouzi? I didn't expect to hear back from you so soon. Or at all, if I'm being honest."

"Did you hear about the three protestors who were executed in Iran?"

"Of course."

He gripped the phone tighter. "One of them was my goddaughter."

There was a long pause. "I'm sorry to hear that."

Arman stared at Niki's picture on the wall. Her beautiful face seemed to stare back at him. He'd never see those eyes again. So filled with hope. So filled with dreams.

"I believe I refused prematurely." He gritted his teeth. "I'd like to meet with you tomorrow."

Barlow let out a breath. "Name the time."

"I have one demand."

"I'm listening."

"I hate the IRGC, but I still love the people of Iran. If I do this, if I get you the information you need, I want confirmation from the United States government that we will not go to war with Iran. I want a promise that the people will not see foreign bombs dropping on their houses."

"That's... a little above my pay grade."

"Then it sounds like you need to make some calls."

Barlow took another long, slow breath. "I'll see what I can do. Come in tomorrow, and if we're able to make the right connections, I'll have an answer for you."

7

Queens, New York

ARMAN STEPPED UP to the door of his penthouse, holding a small bouquet for Laura. With any luck, he'd make her understand why he chose to risk himself for something so far removed from their lives here. He hesitated as he reached for the doorknob.

Laura made it clear from their first date she didn't want to become her mother, that she wanted nothing to do with a man willing to risk his life for others. Arman could understand that. The last time Laura celebrated her birthday was the day of her father's funeral. Arman tried to celebrate Laura's birthday ever since they were together, but she always shut down the idea. It reminded her too much of Dad. Now, she wanted someone safe in her life and, even with his faults, Arman had been safe for her—until now.

He pushed the door open. "I'm home."

Laura smiled at him from the stationary bike in the living room. "You're early!"

He held up the flowers. "I thought we could have a quiet dinner together."

She grabbed a towel and hopped off the bike, dabbing sweat from her forehead as she walked over. "That sounds nice." She gave him a kiss and looked at the bouquet. "And I can't remember the last time you got me flowers."

"Oh, this? They're not for you. They're for Anâr."

She slapped his shoulder playfully and rolled her eyes. "I'm going to go take a shower."

"I'll get dinner ready."

Arman pulled two microwave meals out of the freezer and got them cooking. He probably should have picked up some takeout along with the flowers, but he'd been too preoccupied. After setting the table, he put the flowers in a vase in the center. It wasn't much, but at least he'd made an effort to make things special.

Arman pulled out Laura's chair and joined her at the table. Anâr wove in and out of Arman's ankles, trying to get his attention, but Arman kept his focus on Laura. As she dug into her food, Arman pushed his mashed potatoes around the edge of his plate. It had been a long time since he'd been alone. If she really left, how would he cope? Yes, they had their problems, but Laura was still someone to come home to at night. At least he wasn't lonely.

She set her fork down. "Okay. What's going on?"

"What makes you think something is going on?"

"The flowers, the dinner, and for once, you didn't feed the cat first."

Arman snorted out a laugh.

She folded her hands on the edge of the table and frowned. "Let me guess—your boss asked you to cancel our trip to Jamaica next month so you can work double shifts for him again?"

Arman shook his head. "No. Not yet at least." Hopefully, his new unplanned side trip didn't use up so much vacation time that he'd have to cancel his real vacation.

"Okay, did that old bigot Smith tell you something new he hates about foreign doctors?"

"No. He called my name and I just ignored him."

"Good for you! You should do that more often." She rested her chin in her palm. "So, what's wrong, then? How many times have we had this discussion, Arman? You need to talk when there is something on your mind."

"I know. I just don't want to make you mad."

"You trying to butter me up with roses and microwave dinners without telling me what's going on is making me mad."

Arman looked down at his plate and took a deep breath before meeting her gaze. "My godchild, Niki, is dead."

Laura's eyes went wide.

Arman gripped his knees under the table. "They sentenced her and carried out her execution the same day. She never got out of prison."

Laura covered her mouth as tears pooled in her eyes. She reached across the table and he put his hand in hers. "Oh my god! I'm so sorry, Arman!"

He nodded slowly. "I have to go to Iran."

"For the funeral?"

"No."

She frowned. "Just… to be with Ârash and her mother for a little bit?"

Arman took a sip of his wine and steeled himself. "I called the CIA back."

She pulled her hand from his like he'd burned her. "Are you joking?"

"I can't sit idly by anymore. They told me that I can help expose a real threat to the free world and ultimately help break the IRGC's control so the people can take back the government of Iran."

"What are you—are you insane? You're going to *spy* for the CIA?"

He held up his hands. "I know, I know. I'm not going to try to sugarcoat this, it will be dangerous—"

"No *shit!* You aren't a spy, you're a doctor and even going to Iran as a foreigner is dangerous enough!"

"I have to go. It's going to be hard but I want justice for Niki."

She looked at him with disgust. "You can't even stand up for yourself here, in this country, where you're safe. Your boss has made you cover all his weekend calls for the last two years and you didn't stand up for yourself. Now you want to stand up to a totalitarian regime that kills anybody they want? This is ridiculous. Stop trying to be someone you're not."

Was that what he was doing?

Was *anyone* the type to put their life on the line? Maybe people in the military. They'd been trained for it. People spent years preparing for covert operations. She was right that there were better candidates, but none with his medical credentials and none who could go on *this* mission.

Arman lifted his chin. "Well maybe it's time I stood up for myself. If I want a different life, then I need to try different things. I can't keep doing what I've been doing and expect things to be better."

"*Now* you decide to be ambitious when taking a stand means risking your life?" Laura stood abruptly, her chair bouncing back. "Well, you'll be doing it alone." She stormed into the bedroom and yanked her suitcase from the shelf, spilling boxes of shoes on the floor in her hurry.

Anâr darted from the room and scooted under a chair as Arman stood in the doorway. "What are you doing?"

75

Laura was already shoving clothes into the suitcase. "Isn't it obvious? I'm leaving you."

His chest tightened. "Laura, please don't do this. I respect your opinion. That's why I'm talking to you. I want you to stay."

She wiped her eyes and continued packing. "I have seen what my mom went through after my dad's death. I love you, Arman, but I can't go through that again. I earned a master's degree in Middle Eastern Studies so I could understand the people who killed my father. I know more than most people about that part of the world. Let me be clear: I don't think anyone can do much for the Middle East. We invaded them twenty years ago, we tried to give them democracy, we educated them, we tried to teach them about human rights, and guess what happened? We pulled out and in a blink of an eye, they went back twenty years."

Arman said nothing as she shoved a pair of sneakers into her already stuffed suitcase. "Everyone needs to realize that the whole area is just a lost cause." She turned and stared. "What are you going to do with your mom? She's dying. Are you going to make her suffer even more? I have never seen you be so selfish." She attempted to close the suitcase and threw up her hands. "You know what? Just forget about it. I'll have my brother come back for the rest of my things."

She pushed past him as he tried to speak and he heard the door slam as she left the penthouse. Arman sat down heavily on the edge of their bed. His hands felt numb and the apartment already felt colder without her.

The world he'd built piece by piece was falling apart around him. Maybe it had been inevitable. He'd grown up in fear of war and the government in Iran, and his fear barely abated in the USA. Laura was right—he never stood up for himself, he always worried about what others might think or what might happen to him. He lived his life just as the IRGC wanted: with complicity.

Anâr trotted over and Arman scooped the cat into his arms. "She's gone, my friend. And this time, I don't think she's coming back."

A deep, hollow sensation formed in his chest. He felt broken, alone. He only had Anâr and one other person to turn to in the world.

He picked up the phone. "Mom, I need to see you. Can I come over?"

8

Queens, New York

ARMAN EMBRACED HIS mother just inside the door of her apartment. She smelled like a hospital, but she also smelled like Arman's best memories.

"Laura left me," he said into her shoulder. "For good, this time."

Her face fell and she held him at arm's length. "What happened?"

"The CIA wants me to go to Iran, and I may never come back."

The frown deepened. "What does that mean? Why would you not come back?"

He hesitated and decided not to mention Niki. It was bad enough that he was putting himself in danger. There was no need for her to find out that a girl she thought of as a granddaughter had been murdered.

"There's a way that I might be able to help the protesters. I can't share much, but it involves me going against the Iranian government."

Her eyes widened and she let go of him, taking a step back. "What is this for?"

"If I succeed, it could finally force the countries of the world to take sanctions against the IRGC. They can maybe force them to start giving people rights."

"And if you don't go?"

"Then the United States and Israel will wage war on Iran. This time, they will destroy the whole country."

She sighed, walking over and sitting on the sofa. "That would push the country back a thousand years. They are already in such dire straits." She looked up. "This is why Laura broke up with you?"

Arman nodded as he sat beside her. There were so many odd feelings swirling around in his head. Part of him wanted to be a hero, but another part—the bigger part—was terrified beyond measure. He placed his head on her shoulder like he used to as a child.

She patted him gently. "Do you want to go, or are they forcing you to do it?"

"No one is forcing me, Mom. I can call them today and say no and everything goes away."

"Is that what you want to do?"

"No. Yes." He closed his eyes. "I don't know."

"What matters more? Iran or your life? Iran or Laura?"

Arman thought it over. His relationship with Laura had never been perfect, but she was someone he could rely on. However, they had been arguing a lot. She seemed more and more short-tempered every day. What that meant, though, he wasn't sure.

"I think she felt trapped, Mom. I know she loved me, and I loved her, too, but she wasn't happy. To be honest, if she hadn't left me for this, she probably would have left me for another reason. I think we were destined to fail. I'm not sure she was as dedicated to our relationship as I was."

"Don't blame this on her, Arman. It sounds like she communicated what she wanted, but you weren't able to give that to her. That's not your fault, it's not her fault. It's not anyone's fault."

Arman nodded, staring off into space. His mother's words were always wise, but sometimes, he had trouble figuring out how to apply them to his own life.

"You survived Zhina, you'll survive this too."

"Thanks, Mom."

"Now that was a smart girl. Beautiful, too."

He gave her a wry look. "Is this supposed to help?"

She prodded him with a finger. "My point is, is that there are plenty of smart, beautiful women out there. The perfect one is waiting, you just need to keep your eyes open. And maybe your mouth shut sometimes."

He nodded. "But what do I do about the CIA?"

"What does your heart say to do?"

"It's telling me to help. But…"

"But what?" She tousled his hair. "What are you worried about? Are you scared?"

"Obviously, I'm scared. I'm terrified! But I'm not worried about myself. I'm worried about you. What if something happens to me? What if I can't see you again? Who is going to take care of you?"

She raised a brow and cocked her head. "Let's not kid around, Arman. You and I both know that I have very little time left in this world, and there is nothing anyone can do."

He grabbed her hands. "That's what I'm worried about. I want to be here with you."

"If you think this will help save our old country, I want you to do it wholeheartedly. There is going to be a last time we see each other, no matter what. We need to say goodbye one day. I hope I can stay alive until you come back, and we can see each other one more time—but remember, the concept of time doesn't exist for our subconscious. I will always love you as long as I exist, and I know you will do the same. The past, present, and future are just constraints for our physical existence."

He kissed her cheeks. "I want to spend every single minute with you, though. You've always been there for me, and I want to be there for you."

"Oh, please. It's not like I'm going to be gone next week. I have to live six more months."

Arman narrowed his eyes. "Six months?"

"Yes," she said firmly. "I will live at least until my seventy-fifth birthday. That will make me the oldest in my family."

Arman laughed. "I forgot about that."

"As my friends like to point out, I'm a crotchety old gal. Cancer may get me someday, but not until after my birthday." She lifted her chin. "I don't give it permission to take me before."

She placed her palms on his cheeks. "So, you have six months to save the world. Go… do something that may change your life and the lives of millions of others."

Arman nodded. He knew the doctors told her she had weeks to live, not months. Cancer didn't care about the lives it destroyed, it simply killed what it wanted—much like the IRGC. It was very possible this was the last time he'd see her alive.

"I love you, Mom. I will always love you."

"Stop!" She placed her fingers over his lips. "Don't you dare say goodbye. Not yet. I want you to make me a promise."

Arman blinked back tears. "Anything, Mom."

"You know how I feel about tradition."

"Of course."

"You go on your adventure. You save the world and stop the war. Then you come back and bring me a Persian roulette cake for my birthday."

Arman smiled. He'd been giving her the same cake for as long as he was able to pay for gifts on his own. At first, he'd save up for weeks. Now, he could buy her a cake every day if he wanted, but it remained a special birthday tradition he'd never miss.

"How about I bring you a cake tomorrow?" he asked.

She shook her head. "For my birthday. Promise me."

He realized what she was trying to do. This promise had nothing to do with her getting cake, and it had everything to do with making sure that he came home alive.

He grabbed her hand and kissed the back of it. "I promise, Mom. I'll bring you cake."

She smiled. "And it will be all that much sweeter. It will be a victory for us both."

Arman nodded. He was going to do everything in his power to make sure he kept that promise. His mother was sweet, but just as crotchety as her friends said she was. If anyone could defy the odds and live another six months, it was her.

9

A YOUNG CIA agent escorted Arman to the same room where he'd met Barlow and Zarabi before. Today, though, he sat alone. Sweat beaded his brow and the stark walls felt like they were closing in.

What was he doing here? It might have been the single most ridiculous decision of his life. Yes, it was a good cause, but he wasn't a spy. This was foolish—he should run. He should go find Laura and tell her he'd been wrong and she'd been right, and they could still live their lives together, just like they'd planned.

Arman rubbed his face. If he stayed here, if he went through with this, he might as well kill himself. There were far less painful ways to take the high road and do the right thing than walking right up to the IRGC and basically saying,

"Hi, I'm a spy. Go ahead and torture me for days and then shoot me!"

He shivered as the reality of the situation set in. He wasn't trained in stealth. The IRGC would see the guilt in his eyes and he'd be arrested before he even picked up a scalpel.

He gulped down the lump building in his throat. He should probably just get up and leave before…

The junior agent finally came back and turned on a TV. The CIA emblem displayed on the screen as he adjusted the volume.

"Your meeting will start in two minutes," he said before leaving the room and closing the door behind him.

The walls in the room were a disquieting off-white. Could it double as an interrogation room? Were these walls made to absorb screams?

He closed his eyes. That line of thinking wasn't going to help. He needed to stay focused—for Niki, if not himself.

The screen flickered and a clean-shaven man in his fifties in a blue suit and tie appeared. "Hello, Dr. Pirouzi. I am James Warren, the Director of the CIA. I am talking to you on behalf of the President. Your demands have been considered, and we can promise you that if you can bring us the information we need, we believe that the countries of the world will unite, and we will not be forced into any full-blown military action against Iran in the immediate future."

Arman sighed and nodded once. The "promise" was filled with loopholes. "We believe" was not a promise. He'd also left the caveat of "in the immediate future." Which basically meant that they promised nothing. But it was probably the best they could do.

After the screen went blank, Agent Barlow walked in and put a folder in front of Arman. "We are going to work together for the next forty days, Doc. I want you to feel at home. I'm sorry Laura is gone, but I'm sure our hospitality will compensate for part of that loss. In some ways, it'll be easier for you to not have to lie."

Arman shook his head, partly to agree and partly out of shock. Laura had only left him yesterday. Was there anything they didn't know about his life? He opened the folder. The first page had a room number, as well as directions on how to get his clothing laundered and cafeteria schedules. "You want me to stay here? What about my apartment?"

"The CIA will pay your bills while you're under our employ. It will still be there when you return."

"I have a cat."

"Anâr is already with your mother—crawled right up on her lap, according to his handler."

They'd gone into his penthouse? He supposed he shouldn't be surprised. "My mother is sick. If anything happens to her while I'm gone…"

"The CIA will step in and help with any arrangements your mother needs, medical or end of life." Barlow glanced at Zarabi. "And my partner has volunteered to take care of your cat if your mother is unable to for any reason."

Obviously, neither had dealt with a Persian cat before or they wouldn't be so quick to volunteer.

"Anâr only takes food from me," Arman mumbled.

Zarabi smiled. "I have a way with animals. He'll be fine."

Arman rubbed his face. "What about my job?"

"You are going to a very prestigious conference. The Iranian Society of Cardiology made a significant donation to your hospital as a thank you for allowing you immediate time off to prepare your presentation. Someone named…" Agent Barlow looked inside a folder. "Dr. Nathaniel Smith was apparently beside himself and couldn't sign your leave fast enough." He smiled. "Believe me, they'll treat you like a rock star when you get back. You may even get a wing named after you."

Arman frowned. "I can't believe The Iranian Society of Cardiology has that kind of funding."

"They don't. We just made it look like they did." Agent Barlow closed the folder. "Do you have any other concerns?"

Arman nearly laughed. *Concerns? Plenty!* but it seemed like they'd take care of his life here while he was risking his actual life in Iran. At least he didn't have to concern himself with not having a home to come back to, so he could concentrate on the mission. And maybe when he got back Dr. Smith would finally let Arman do his job without the insults. It was unlikely, but a man could dream.

He leaned back in his chair. "Okay, I'm ready. Let's do this."

After an hour of settling into his small but comfortable room, Arman was called down to the medical wing and placed on a treadmill. They increased the speed until he was running at a full sprint. Luckily, he always tried to squeeze in at least twenty minutes of running a day to stay in shape, so he was able to keep up until the machine slowed and finally stopped.

After a quick shower, he was back in the meeting room, where they showed him pictures of their covert operative and his specialized pacemaker. They explained the numerous ways the device had been engineered to make it appear more complicated than it actually was in an effort to make sure no doctor other than someone in the CIA attempted its extraction.

"Once you extract the device," Barlow explained, "you'll need to transfer the data from the pacemaker to a specialized data transfer device."

Arman gaped. "I thought you wanted me to just take the pacemaker back to Germany?"

Barlow shrugged. "Further investigation and analysis required a change of plan. There is a high possibility that they will not allow you to take the device from Iran or that they'd simply confiscate it at customs before leaving the country."

"If that's true, they can confiscate a flash drive, too."

"That's why we have you scheduled with Hal."

Arman frowned. He'd said the name *Hal* like it was supposed to mean something to him. "Who's that?"

"He'll be your new best friend. You'll get to know him very, very well."

Arman did not like the sound of that.

The next day, he worked with Agent Zarabi on the procedure to remove the pacemaker, which wasn't really any different from removing a normal pacemaker.

Zarabi held up a small, black object that looked like a tooth. "This is a prototype of the actual device Hal will give you. We'll train with this until you're ready and then Hal will train you with the real thing."

"When do I get to meet this elusive Hal?"

"Hal is the man who you might be owing your life to, so it's best to leave him to customize his plans for you and your mission and not rush him. He'll show up when he's ready."

Arman nodded, but the explanation only made him more nervous. He imagined a mad scientist working on inventions alone in a dark basement. He might even be a captured spy, working for the CIA rather than going to jail for the rest of his life.

Would this *Hal* person be sane, or was Arman putting his life in the hands of someone who held a grudge against the

CIA? The thought was mind numbing, and he pushed it aside. There were a million things he couldn't do anything about, and worrying about them wasn't going to help.

For the rest of the day, Zarabi drilled him on opening the tiny compartment in the pacemaker and transferring mock data from the device to the small, easily concealed chip. It was so small Arman was worried he might lose it, but he didn't bring it up. After a full nine hours of practice, Arman could transfer the data so fast that the untrained eye wouldn't have any idea he was doing something out of the ordinary.

On the following day, Zarabi and Barlow met him back in the original meeting room. "You already know how dangerous this mission is, but we want to be honest with you about what you may be facing and give you the tools to cope if things should go south."

Arman's heart skipped a beat; he'd heard the stories. He'd even lived some of the horrors himself, so he knew what he'd be facing better than most, but he appreciated the CIA wasn't trying to hide how much danger he would be in. They showed him pictures of the most common torture techniques in Iranian prisons. This was based on reports from prisoners who'd survived. They showed him finger and nail extraction, waterboarding, and whipping the bottom of a prisoner's feet.

Arman's stomach roiled as he imagined Niki tied down to a table as they tore out her fingernails one by one. Or maybe they'd cut off one of her toes and laughed, waving it in front of her face and promising her they'd take another unless she'd confessed. His insides clenched, and he leaned over the side of his chair and heaved until he had nothing left.

A custodian came in and cleaned up while the agents brought Arman water. They probably thought he was worried about himself and it was partly true. *Niki was innocent and pure. She was the epitome of everything good in the world. She deserved better.*

Arman accepted the water, drinking slowly as he sat back in his chair. "I wish you'd shown me this before I agreed."

"The CIA's stance in the past has been to not warn people at all," Barlow said, "but I believe in preparing operatives in every way, shape, and form so they are ready for the worst and don't break under shock if things go awry."

The door opened and an older man with wily white hair and an ancient-looking tweed suit entered with a bag and an easel. "As you were, gentlemen. Just pretend I'm not here." He placed his bag on the table with the coffeemaker and put the easel on the floor by the wall.

Agent Barlow pointed back to the screen that was now blank, but the memories of the tortures hung within Arman's psyche—maybe to never be erased.

"You need to understand, Dr. Pirouzi, this is just a sampling of techniques we know about," Barlow said. "There's a good chance those who never left those facilities endured far worse tortures."

Arman fought the urge to puke again as he thought of Niki. "This certainly isn't comforting."

Barlow pointed to the man in the tweed suit. "That's why Hal is here."

Arman turned, surprised. So this was the infamous Hal?

The tweed suit made him look like he frequented thrift shops in his spare time, and his hair stuck out like it hadn't been combed in days. *This* was the man whose skills were so touted by his peers?

Barlow continued. "His job is to prepare you and help you get through anything the IRGC can throw at you."

Arman shivered. "You're thinking I'm going to be caught?"

"No. But we like to be proactive. I've found it's best to be prepared for the worst, and then never have to use that plan, than not preparing at all."

It made sense. Arman looked at the older man. "They've been talking a lot about you. I guess we're going to get to know each other pretty well."

The old man smoothed back his wild mane of hair. "Yes, yes, quite right. Looking forward to working with you, yes, I am. Always excited to prepare a new recruit."

The way he said it sounded far too much like a chef talking about preparing a cut of meat.

Arman shifted in his chair. "What, exactly, do you do to prepare me?"

A wide smile appeared on Hal's face. "Oh, so many exciting things! This is where my job gets really fun. You're going to be glad you asked."

Arman wasn't sure what he meant by that, but over the next week he came to understand as Hal slowly but surely turned him into a bionic man.

"My research shows you have a dental implant," Hal said. "We are going to use that to our advantage."

"How did you get my dental records?" Arman asked, and Hal just laughed. "Right… the CIA knows everything."

After instructing him to recline in the chair, Hal adjusted the overhead light to shine directly into Arman's mouth. A nurse handed over a tray of sterilized instruments while Hal donned gloves and a mask. Over the next two hours, Arman found out why the transfer device he'd been practicing with looked so much like a tooth. Hal explained he was both a certified oral surgeon and general surgeon as he replaced the stem and Arman's crown with a perfectly realistic version of the device Arman had been practicing with.

Hal held up the tooth. "The dental implant is actually a specially modified memory stick with a connection port that will fit into the small opening of the pacemaker." He showed Arman the inside and then closed the lid, turning it into a tooth again. "All the electronics hide under the porcelain crown, indiscernible to the eye or to X-ray." Hal smiled. "Ingenious, if I do say so myself."

Once they were done, Hal handed him a mirror. Arman couldn't tell the difference from his original crown. He set the mirror down, impressed. "This is amazing. Are you sure your name isn't Q?"

Hal snorted. "Hilarious. That's the most original thing I've heard in my entire life." He rolled his eyes. "But we're not done yet. The next time we talk, you won't feel so comical."

It was quite the understatement.

Over the next several days, Arman was fitted with an internal epidural pump, which could release a long-acting local anesthetic into his spine that would numb his legs in case of torture below the belt. It was activated by a small button, implanted in his shoulder—odd, but they assured him it was the best place to avoid detection. Hal also implanted a touch-activated narcotic pump under the skin in Arman's abdomen, which had enough painkiller for a hundred days.

Throughout that explanation, Arman took long, steady breaths to keep calm. The thought of a hundred days of torture would be enough to make the bravest of men run home screaming to their mothers. But again Barlow assured him they were just preparing for the worst.

The next procedure was the most uncomfortable one. Hal performed a sinus surgery, placing two electrodes at the base of Arman's nose near the opening of the sinuses. These electrodes were connected to a small array of batteries implanted under Arman's scalp. In the case of waterboarding, these highly efficient electrodes would catalyze water into oxygen and hydrogen. The oxygen would be released into his nasal cavity so he could breathe underwater.

"Is that safe?" Arman asked.

"It's worked so far," Hal explained. "And believe it or not, we've discovered breathing hydrogen has antioxidizing properties for the human body and prevents brain injury. It's amazing what we discover while testing things out of necessity."

The next day, Hal extracted a tooth on the opposite side of the new crown and replaced the tooth with a flip-top chamber that housed a small pill. "Take this as a last resort if your other implants fail or if you can't take it anymore. You'll fall asleep within moments and never wake up." He grimaced. "I hope you never have to use it."

Arman blew the air out of both his cheeks. "Me, too, my friend. Me, too."

Somehow, the suicide pill made things more real than everything else he'd been through up to that point. Could it really get so bad that he'd be willing to give up everything? His mother, his job, his very life?

Arman gulped, closing his eyes. These were just precautions. Murphy's Law said that if you overprepared, you'd never need your preparations. He had to hope it was true, because the alternative was unthinkable.

10

Somewhere Over the Atlantic Ocean

ARMAN TOOK A sleeping pill the moment he got onto the plane. Without it, he never would have been able to sleep, and he might have even had a panic attack flying overseas with nothing to do but think about what a bad idea all of this was. Thirteen hours later, he disembarked at Dubai International for a short layover before boarding a final plane to Iran.

Full from a surprisingly good meal at the airport—at the CIA's expense—Arman slumped into his seat for the final leg of his voyage. Despite sleeping most of the previous trip, he fell asleep moments after takeoff.

When he woke, refreshed, in his wide first-class recliner, the man seated next to him raised a wineglass. "Cheers, my very sleepy friend."

Arman wiped his eyes. "How long was I asleep?"

"Nearly ninety minutes. Quite a feat, if I'm being honest. I'm jealous." He offered Arman a hand, and he shook it. "My name is Paolo."

"Arman. What brings you to Iran? That's an Italian accent, if I'm not mistaken?"

"You have a good ear, my friend. I'm on a business trip, I run a chain of luxury goods stores."

Arman lifted an eyebrow. "Luxury goods? In Iran?"

Paolo laughed, nearly spilling his drink. "Everyone says that! And it is even funnier coming from you since I hear your native accent, my friend." He took a sip of wine. "I've made a fortune opening stores that sell luxury Italian furniture, tiles, clothes, and shoes. There is more of a market for it in Iran than anywhere else I sell."

"How?"

"Maybe you've been away from home too long. There is a huge gap between rich and poor in every country, but especially in Iran. While normal people struggle to make a living, the upper echelon of government officials are in my shops, deciding what kind of marble they want in their summer mansions."

Arman had been that poor person growing up, and everyone around him lived the same way. It made sense that there was an upper class, he just never really interacted with them and left Iran before doing so.

When the plane finally landed, the door opened and an Iranian Revolutionary Guard officer walked into the compartment. Arman gripped the arms of his seat.

"Welcome to Iran," the officer said. "You are special guests, and the airline has requested that all their first-class passengers get special treatment."

Arman's knuckles whitened. How much had the airline paid for this *special treatment*? And that was assuming the officer was even telling the truth.

The officer held out his hands to each of them. "Please present your passports, and we will expedite your visas and then you are free to go."

Arman's hands started to shake, and he concentrated on calming himself, just like the CIA had trained him. This was unusual, but it was possible this truly was a special service—he'd never flown first class to Iran before.

As the officer collected their passports, the rest of the passengers filed off the plane, leaving the first-class cabin restless and uneasy.

After about an hour of checking his very expensive-looking watch, Paolo leaned closer to Arman. "Keep calm and quiet, no matter what happens, Dr. Pirouzi. Do not call attention to yourself."

"What?"

Paolo glanced at him. All signs of the happy-go-lucky salesman, gone.

Is Paolo CIA?

A balding man in a blue business suit snapped his fingers at the flight attendant. "This is ridiculous. I have important meetings to get to. I need to get off this plane at once."

The flight attendant smiled. "As the officer said, you are our special guests, and—"

"I don't want to be anyone's special guest. I've been stuck in metal tubes for twenty hours. I want to get off this plane like the rest of the passengers."

The man sitting across from him held up his palms. "Sir, there is no reasoning with officers in Iran. You need to follow the laws or they will take action against you."

"They can take all the action they want as long as it gets me off this plane."

When it became apparent the man wouldn't relent, the flight attendant made a call, and the officer came back.

The businessman stood defiantly. "Why are you making all of us wait?"

The officer's face remained placid. "Sir, this is for your own comfort. The other passengers are in a very long line to get their visas."

The man folded his arms. "I know you background check every single foreigner who enters this country. If I had anything to hide, I wouldn't be dumb enough to step onto this plane."

"You need to respect our process, sir. Every country has its own regulations and laws."

The man's face turned red. "Well, as far as I know, the only *regulation* that talks in this country is money. Now, how much do I need to pay to get out of this damn plane?"

The officer's eyes narrowed. "Sir, please sit down and don't start a situation that will not end well for you."

"Oh, please. What are you going to do, arrest me for wanting to get off a plane? You're wasting my time." He drew his wallet out of his jacket and pulled out several large bills. "How much do you want?" He shoved the cash at the officer. "Here. This is probably more than you make in a week in this God-forsaken hell hole."

The officer's expression darkened. He pulled handcuffs out of his pocket and let one dangle from his finger. "I do not know where you come from, but bribing an officer is illegal in Iran."

The businessman scoffed. "Oh, please. We all know money is what this is about. Just let me the hell off this plane and we can all get on with our lives."

"Fine." The officer took the money with one hand and snapped handcuffs on the man's wrist with his other hand. He shoved the money into his pocket as he dragged the man into the aisle.

The businessman's eyes widened. "Wait. No!" He tried to back away, but the officer snapped the cuff on his other wrist.

"This is ludicrous! I bring business to this country. You need men like me to—"

The officer drove his knee into the man's gut. He leaned over, gasping for breath as another soldier ran onto the plane and helped haul him out, his heels dragging on the ground even as another officer entered, holding a handful of passports. If the man had only been patient a few more minutes, he would have walked off the plane himself.

Arman shivered. The businessman probably took for granted that his foreign citizenship meant something to these people—it didn't. The IRGC had far too much control over civilian lives. This was the very terror from which Arman and his mother had fled. *I knew what I was getting into, but still...*

The officer holding the passports walked down the aisle. "Dr. Arman Pirouzi?"

Ice flooded Arman's veins as he raised his hand. The officer stared at his passport, then at him, before handing it over and calling another name.

Sweat drenched Arman's shirt as he nodded at Paolo and headed down the gangway. Each footstep on the metal floor echoed loudly in the sweltering tube. He wiped his brow; thankful he could blame the perspiration on the climate instead of his nerves—nobody would be surprised at the sight of a sweating foreigner.

At the bottom of the gangway, Dr. Hajipour, the President of the Iranian Society of Cardiology, smiled and walked toward Arman, holding a large flower basket. He was a stout man in neatly pressed pants and a white shirt. "Welcome back to Iran, Dr. Pirouzi. How was your flight?"

Arman shook his hand. "Long, but it's nice to be here now. Thank you for coming to the airport to meet me. I really appreciate it."

"You are most welcome. This is the least I could do. It is an honor to have you help with our conference." They started walking toward baggage claim. "It is a miracle that we could coordinate this. To be honest, I don't even know how it happened, but I am so happy you could come."

Arman was happy to be speaking to a professional who wasn't a CIA agent. All the suits and bureaucracy had become stifling. His smile was genuine as he began his rehearsed speech. "I have to admit, when I received the invitation, I almost didn't look at it. As you know, back in the US, we usually plan for conferences a year ahead of time. It turned out I had a week of vacation that I needed to use or I'd lose it and I was just going to sit at home."

"What a coincidence! It is amazing." He helped Arman grab his luggage. "I'll take you to your hotel now, and I hope you are not too jetlagged, as we have a full day of patients in the workshop for you tomorrow."

Arman nodded, sweat dripping down his temple. He had a feeling he wouldn't stop sweating until he was safely tucked into his bed back in his penthouse with Anâr sleeping on his chest.

11

Tehran, Iran

AFTER A FITFUL night's sleep, Arman prepared himself for the conference and headed downstairs to the car waiting to bring him to the hospital. The driver took him past high-end shops and expensive cars. The men Arman saw on the street were dressed not unlike those in the United States, except they wore long pants despite the heat. Most of the women wore hats rather than hijabs—a far cry from the strict laws of the past, although many still chose to cover all their hair.

"You look surprised, doctor," the driver said, looking at Arman in the rearview mirror.

"A little." Arman pointed at a group of women who wore no head coverings at all; they looked European. "Things have come a long way since I was last here."

"Oh, it certainly has. It's not this way in the smaller villages, though. Local factions of the *Gasht-e-Ershad* morality police have managed to keep a tight rein on any of these *Eastern* fashions for women."

Arman nodded. The man's inflection on the word made it sound like a slur. No doubt he leaned toward the older way of thinking. Still, Arman's heart lightened a little. Seeing women take even a small step toward equal rights in the larger cities gave him some hope for his country. Hopefully, the current regime wouldn't squash them for their efforts.

Massive luxury high rises lifted into the skies on either side of the street. The city was a futuristic metropolis compared to the dirt roads of his youth. If Ârash didn't still live close to the town where they'd both been born, Arman would be questioning his memory.

As they stopped at a traffic light, Arman noticed water cascading through the open sewers on either side of the road. Massive trees grew out of these deep, four-foot-wide crevices, providing shade and a calming aesthetic for all the bustling shoppers scampering past on the narrow sidewalks. With the desert outside, and the streets and sidewalks paved, the sewers were the only water available to foster plant life. The more he thought about it, the more he liked it—he wished there were more trees lining the streets in New York.

The entire aesthetic was a stark contrast to the Iran shown in Western media. People in the United States envisioned the country as a giant desert, which was true in many cases. But Tehran—especially this part of Tehran—was a haven for the rich. If they drove even a few miles outside the city, things would look very different.

At the hospital, he was escorted to the meeting center. He hesitated outside the doors, staring at ornate carvings meant to impress visiting dignitaries. Somewhere inside was the CIA's covert operative and the pacemaker that Arman would need to remove. All his training and drills, all his surgeries, were to prepare him for this day.

His thoughts went back to the airport and the businessman being dragged from the plane by the IRGC, maybe never to be seen again. Everyone here was one mistake from being dragged away. For all he knew, there were officers waiting for him on the other side of the door. If the CIA informant had been discovered, he may have been tortured and already informed them of the CIA's plan.

Arman's heartbeat began to thump in his ears. He gulped, trying to control his breathing.

"Stage fright?" Dr. Hajipour asked.

He forced a laugh. "Maybe just a little." He did tend to have shaky hands whenever he was asked to speak in public, but he had far worse things to worry about this time.

The doctor patted him on the back. "I'm sure you'll do fine."

Arman opened the door, and hundreds of mostly young faces turned toward him. Those who were seated stood and applauded. Arman gaped.

"Your reputation precedes you, Dr. Pirouzi. It's been some time since we've had the opportunity to learn from someone as highly regarded as you."

Arman smiled weakly, shaking hands as he walked in, trying his best to duplicate the way visiting presenters acted when he was in school. He concentrated on making eye contact and saying hello to as many of the young doctors as possible, remembering how that kind of attention had stuck with him for years, even after graduating.

After an Iranian breakfast of fresh *sangak* bread, honey, local butter, Iranian omelets, and sweets, Arman stood and made a short presentation on Western medicine, focusing on progress relating to surgical procedures and interventionalists.

He looked out over the crowd. "One of the most feared complications of any venous procedure is the possibility of an air embolism." A few people shifted uncomfortably and with good reason—it wasn't long ago that an air embolism was practically a death sentence. "Although it is a rare complication, it can be life-threatening. An air embolism occurs when some amount of air inadvertently enters the patient's blood vessel." Arman aimed a laser pointer at the screen behind him, showing an illustration of the veins, heart, and lungs. "If the air enters a vein, it will travel to the heart, and from there it will be pumped into the lungs." He moved the pointer to the lungs. "Here, the air can block the small arteries and prevent the exchange of oxygen in the lungs. In simple terms, the patient will suffocate, as if someone were strangling them from inside."

Anyone who didn't look concerned before glanced around the room, pale. Could it be that some of them hadn't even learned of the possibility?

Arman continued. "Amounts as small as twenty cc of air can be lethal. This is one of the scariest types of death, as you can imagine. It is described as drowning, but even worse, as the patient is awake and can breathe, but their body can't get enough oxygen to stay alive."

The mood in the room grew grim until Arman explained what he did as an interventionalist and how modern medicine could perform what had been considered a miracle only ten years ago.

As he moved on to less dramatic topics, he smiled, warming inside as the young doctors nodded, many taking notes. He'd done presentations in the USA, but many times, the audience only partly paid attention, distracted by their phones. Getting the chance to hear a Western doctor speak—especially one born in their country—was quite a treat for these people, and he was proud to serve them.

As Arman stepped off the platform, Dr. Hajipour shook his hand. "Excellent presentation. First rate."

"Thank you."

Dr. Hajipour motioned for another man to join them. "This is my childhood friend, Dr. Akbari. He has a question for you."

The man stepped over and with a chill, Arman recognized him from the pictures the CIA had drilled into his memory.

Arman forced a smile and shook the man's hand. "Of course. What can I do for you?"

"I am in a bit of a predicament," Dr. Akbari explained. "It is my understanding that you assisted in the development of the surgical training modules for the Medelevan pacemaker?"

Arman widened his eyes, hopefully not too theatrically. "Of course! The technology is extraordinary. But unfortunately, we found that the mechanisms are too complicated for most surgeons. There is fear that the technology will have to be abandoned until more doctors can be trained."

Dr. Akbari nodded. "That's my problem. I was lucky enough to get one when I was in Germany, but I was also unlucky in that mine is malfunctioning."

"Very unlucky. Have you made an appointment to get it replaced?"

"Unfortunately, the closest doctor who can perform the extraction is in Germany, and there is no foreign travel allowed for government officials at the moment."

Arman put on his best frown. "Certainly, they would give you a medical waiver? A pacemaker can mean life or death."

"I'm aware of that, but there is a considerable amount of red tape involved when leaving the country on a normal day, let alone when there is a travel ban." He looked at Dr. Hajipour before turning back to Arman. "I was hoping that you would be willing to extract the device and insert a new one. I know I can't get the same model, but whatever it is, it will be a working device, whereas now I have none."

Arman looked down and gulped. He was supposed to act surprised, but the fear suddenly shooting through every cell of his body was hard to hide.

"I know it's a lot to ask, but when my friend told me you had accepted their invitation, I looked at it as a gift from God." Dr. Akbari held up his hands. "My other choice is to place my life in the less practiced hands of another, who wouldn't be able to help if I start to bleed out."

Dr. Hajipour wrung his hands. "I've read about the Medelevan pacemakers. The one drawback is the number of micro-wires. That's why they are so much more efficient, but also why they are so difficult to implant and extract." He looked at Arman. "Dr. Pirouzi, Dr. Akbari is a good friend of mine. We would both be in your debt if you'd provide your assistance." A smile appeared on his face. "Not to mention the excitement of the students being able to observe extraction of what seems like a space-aged device to many of us!"

Arman's breath caught—the CIA either hadn't considered the possibility of students watching or worse, hadn't told him about it. Maybe that was why they'd drilled him so many times. It was entirely possible that he could extract the information from the pacemaker out in the open and no one would notice—*if* they didn't know what to look for, that was.

Arman pasted on a smile. "I'd be happy to help." He looked at Dr. Akbari. "Do you have a suitable replacement pacemaker lined up?"

Dr. Akbari nodded. "As a matter of fact, I do. I'm so relieved you said yes! I even fasted all day just in case you agreed."

Dr. Hajipour placed his arm around the covert operative's shoulder. "Come, my friend. We can get you prepped for the procedure while Dr. Pirouzi is showing off some other techniques."

Arman changed into scrubs and entered the observation surgical room. Above him, windows lined the walls on four sides so students could watch, looking over his shoulders or on close-up screens near their seats.

Fortunately, the field of view of the camera was narrow. He could easily shift his weight or lean in and block it. He'd need less than ten seconds to extract the information. *I can do this.* He just had to remain calm.

The doctors flowed in, taking their places behind the glass with excited expressions. All the planned surgeries on the docket went smoothly. Questions came over the speakers, and Arman answered when he could without placing the patient in jeopardy. Thankfully, there were no bleeding incidents, although it would have been beneficial for the students to show off his skills as an interventionalist.

They gave him a glass of water and allowed him to sit down and stretch his back before they wheeled Dr. Akbari in on a gurney. Their eyes met over their surgical masks.

"We'll get this taken care of for you in no time," Arman said, hoping the smile showed in his eyes.

Dr. Akbari nodded, but the fear in his expression matched the fear Arman felt in his heart. This was when his weeks of training—and quite possibly years of work on Dr. Akbari's part—could all go to waste.

They put Dr. Akbari under anesthesia and Arman started by injecting local anesthetic. He then made an incision over the implant. Using a small camera, Arman searched for the micro-wires (which did nothing but make the device look complex) and slowly eased them out of the surrounding tissue. When the pacemaker was partially free, Arman maneuvered himself to block the camera and pushed on the small drawer that revealed the memory chip. Grabbing it with a tweezer, he shoved the chip into his glove just as the students started complaining that they couldn't see.

"Sorry," Arman said, shifting so the camera showed the surgical site again. In another moment, the CIA pacemaker was removed and placed on the sterile tray. "Please clean and wrap that for transport to Germany."

"Why?" the nurse asked.

"Because this is the first registered malfunction of this model. The manufacturer will want to do a full diagnostic." And the CIA was also worried that if anyone looked at it *too* closely, they would discover that there was more to the pacemaker than met the untrained eye.

The nurse looked at Dr. Hajipour, who nodded, and she set the device aside to clean. Arman grimaced beneath his mask; hopefully, she wasn't too thorough.

After implanting the new device and closing the surgical site, Arman left the operating room and stripped off his gloves, taking care to slip the memory chip into his pocket. As he left, Dr. Hajipour gestured towards the nurse, who was walking out with the device.

"She will bring back the pacemaker as soon as they sterilize it. That is a wonderful technology. I hope they can find out what's wrong."

Arman nodded. "I'm sure they will."

"I have exciting news," Dr. Hajipour said. "We are having a special dinner in your honor, and a state representative from the Ministry of Health will be there to thank you for taking the time to come and help train our future doctors."

Arman sighed. All he really wanted to do was go back to his room, pack, and sit there away from any prying eyes, until it was time to get on his plane. Less interaction meant fewer chances of discovery, but it would be hard to say no to such an honor, and worse, might raise suspicions.

He nodded. "That sounds wonderful. If you don't mind, I just need a trip to the restroom."

Dr. Hajipour quirked a brow. "Rest-room? Are you tired?"

Arman laughed. "No! My apologies. I meant the toilet."

The doctor chuckled. "Western vernacular. Very funny. The toilet is right this way!"

Inside, Arman stopped at the mirror and considered the dark circles under his eyes. Thankfully, no one here knew him well enough to know this was not his normal appearance, although these past few months, perhaps it was.

He splashed cold water on his face and washed his hands before entering the stall. First, he pulled his crown off, took the device out of his pocket, and placed the small pin into his tooth. Once the data transfer was complete and the light flashed green, he flushed the chip down the toilet and replaced the tooth.

It was done. According to Hal, no X-ray equipment would be able to tell the implant wasn't a real crown, so the hard part was over. He gulped, staring at his quivering lip in the mirror before straightening up and walking outside.

Dr. Hajipour led him to a banquet room filled with tables stacked high with traditional Persian delights. The doctor held out his hands. "All the tastes of home, Dr. Pirouzi!"

Arman grabbed a plate. "It all looks delicious, thank you."

From the appetizer table, Arman took a serving of *kashke bademjan*. The mashed fried eggplant mixed with a special garlic, onion, and mint dairy blend was pure heaven. He also grabbed a dollop of his childhood favorite, *mastomusir*. Technically, he could have made *mastomusir* in America, but the yogurt in the United States never tasted as fresh, and Laura always cringed at the idea of adding shallots to anything, especially yogurt. Both dishes warmed his soul, reminding him of simpler times.

"Our chefs are good, no?" Dr. Hajipour asked.

"Phenomenal." Arman dabbed his lips with a napkin. "I'm looking forward to trying the main courses."

"I had the chef's *chelo* kebab last week," Dr. Hajipour said. "Today, I'm looking forward to the *joojeh* kebab."

Arman nodded. The Saffron rice looked amazing, but he wasn't in the mood for a beef or a chicken kabob. He pointed at the stew with herbs, red beans, and beef. "Is that *ghormeh sabzi*?"

Dr. Hajipour clapped his hands. "It is! I remembered an interview I read with you where you said you missed the dish."

"That's very thoughtful!" Arman took a large bowl and an additional plate for *baklava* and *sholezard*. The rice pudding in the *sholezard* looked a little looser than his mother used to make it, but the smell of saffron filled the air.

Arman sat back in his chair and licked his lips. It was a meal he wouldn't soon forget. Some of the dishes were new to him, having grown up in poverty, but the spices he remembered all too well. Each taste reminded him of happier times before the bombs started dropping and his best friend lost his mother.

After a server took Arman's empty plate, an official from the Ministry of Health approached. His looked Arman over, his eyes twisting in disgust at some part of his outfit. Arman quickly scanned the room, realizing he was the only one wearing a tie. The official wore a neatly tailored white shirt and clean, freshly pressed pants.

Arman had heard that a tie was considered a sign of Western culture and was forbidden in Iran. With the tie being more a symbol of power and success in the USA, he'd thought that had to be an exaggeration, but apparently not.

Arman tugged at the tie. "These things are like torture. It's such a waste of time and effort to put them on. Not to mention making it hard to breathe." That, at least, was true—especially at that moment.

The minister gave a half-hearted smile, but it was clear he didn't give a shit about Arman's discomfort. "The students like to hear an accomplished doctor speak, but why do you waste your talents in the West? Why not stay here and help the people of your own country?"

This—and many other scenarios—had been drilled into Arman's head by the CIA. Anything you said in Iran could be used against you. The rule was to just *say yes and smile*.

He gave the best grin he could under the circumstances. "That's a great idea. I will investigate the options with Dr. Hajipour and let him know as soon as I am ready."

The minister's smile seemed genuine this time, no doubt feeling victorious at stealing back a doctor from the West. Arman had played right into his ego, which was easier than he would have expected. Then again, he'd been catering to his boss's ego in the USA for years.

As the night drew on, Arman started getting uncomfortable being the center of attention. The information hidden safely in his tooth seemed to feel heavier by the minute. All he wanted to do was return to his room and sleep—and not leave that room until he boarded the plane.

Another representative approached Arman and shook his hand, asking, "Did you know Dr. Akbari before the surgery today? I saw you spoke with him earlier."

Do they know? Why is he asking this?

The tag on the lapel of his crisp black shirt read *Dr. Borna*, of the advanced studies department. He should not have been a threat—then again, nothing was as it seemed in Iran.

Arman paused, keeping his voice steady. "I have not been here for the past twenty years, Dr. Borna. Except for my childhood friends and a few remaining relatives, I don't know anyone else."

The man narrowed his eyes. "Interesting. In the United States, they call Dr. Akbari the Iranian version of Abdul Qadeer Khan!"

Arman tilted his head. "Who's that?"

He lifted his chin. "You are telling me you don't know the person who made an atomic bomb for Pakistan?"

Arman raised a brow. "Oh, that guy! Now I remember. The doctor did ask for my assistance with his pacemaker. That's why he was added to the surgery docket. I had no idea who he was before today, though." He leaned closer. "Maybe I should have asked him for some tips, aye?"

Borna sniffed before turning to Dr. Hajipour. "Our good Dr. Pirouzi needs some lessons about our scientific progress. Why don't you bring him to my office for a visit and I can show him things?"

Arman coughed before recovering. "I appreciate your invitation, Dr. Borna. But I'm on a tight schedule. I'm flying out tomorrow morning."

"I was just kidding, Doctor. It looks like you have lost your sense of humor after spending so much time outside of Iran. I am a very busy man, after all. I barely made it here tonight." He laughed, patting Arman on the back. "But maybe the IRGC can talk to you about protecting our nuclear scientists!"

Arman froze. Borna knew something for sure. No words came to mind to stave off the man's implication and Arman just sputtered, looking even guiltier.

Borna laughed harder. "I got you, Dr. Pirouzi! Now you really are scared."

The adrenaline rushed from Arman's veins and his temples started to throb.

What a moron!

He needed to remain as cool as possible. Arman smiled weakly. "You definitely got me."

Dr. Hajipour placed a hand on Arman's shoulder. "I regret that I need to show our distinguished guest to his car. His driver is waiting."

Arman released a breath as if he'd been holding it for hours. Then he remembered he was still missing a piece of the whole plan. "Would you happen to have the pacemaker for me?" he asked Dr. Hajipour, unenthusiastically.

"About that!" Dr. Hajipour responded. "There seems to be some kind of mix-up in the sterilization room. Unfortunately, they can't locate the pacemaker."

"Did someone steal it?" Arman said and immediately regreted it.

Dr. Hajipour's eyes widened. "Who would do that?"

"I have no idea." Unfortunately, that was a lie—if the IRGC was in possession of the pacemaker, they would surely learn its secrets eventually. He needed to get on a plane as soon as possible.

"I will personally make sure that we find the pacemaker and deliver it to your hotel room before your departure," Dr. Hajipour promised.

Arman leaned back slightly, doing his best to project a calm confidence. "Don't even worry about it," he said, his tone calm and collected. "Just let me know whenever you locate it, and I'll send you the manufacturer's address. You can send it to them directly."

"Have a *nice* trip," Dr. Borna said.

The way he said it grated on Arman's resolve. Was he joking again or did he actually know something?

12

Tehran, Iran

ARMAN ENTERED HIS hotel room, bolted the door, and fell onto his bed, staring at the ceiling. The day had been longer than he ever could have imagined, but it was over. Now, all he had to do was stay in his room and wait until the car arrived in the morning to take him to the airport.

He wished the flight had been right after the conference since the chance of sleeping was slim. Though he lay in a comfortable bed, he felt surrounded by cobras and vipers.

A ring sounded, and Arman gasped, sitting up. The landline phone on his nightstand was ringing. His gut clenched—no one knew he was there. Dr. Hajipour had his cell phone number. Who would call him at the hotel? His pulse started to drum in his ears as the phone rang again. He could ignore it and eventually, they would stop calling. Then

119

again, if the IRGC were checking on him, it would look suspicious if he didn't answer.

He picked up the phone and said hello in his native language.

"Is this Dr. Pirouzi?" a man asked.

"Yes."

"The famous Dr. Pirouzi?"

His chest tightened. "I am not sure if I'd call myself famous, but I am Dr. Pirouzi."

"Doctor, we have an emergent case, and we need your help."

"I am not sure if I can help you, sir. I'm leaving in the morning. Maybe you need to call Dr. Hajipour for help?"

"But our patient asked specifically for you, Dr. Pirouzi."

They'd asked for him? "Who is your patient? How do they know me? What is their emergency?"

"Well, Doctor, the patient is a seven-year-old boy who was riding his bike with one hand while carrying an ice cream in the other. He hit the post in front of his house when his pretty neighbor suddenly stepped out of her door. Blood is streaming from his nose, covering the post. He's still holding the empty waffle cone, but we were able to recover the missing scoop of ice cream dripping down the side of the neighbor's house."

Arman started laughing, remembering the scene with his childhood friend and neighbor, Afshin. "You are a clown—did you know that, Afshin? You scared the shit out of me."

On the other end of the call, Afshin was in hysterics.

"How did you find me, dude?" Arman asked.

"It wasn't easy when you don't tell your friends that you are coming after twenty years but thank God I have connections!"

"Sorry, man, it was an unexpected and tightly scheduled trip. I got here last night and I'm leaving in the morning."

"Well, we are downstairs waiting for you. You better come down or we are coming up to kick your ass, my brother!"

Arman frowned. "What?"

"We're going out, my friend! And we're not taking no for an answer."

Arman smiled. As much as he wanted to stay inside and hide, spending time with friends would take his mind off things. "Give me twenty minutes, I need to take a shower. I'll be there as soon as I can."

13

Tehran, Iran

ARMAN RAN DOWNSTAIRS and his heart warmed to see short, blocky Dariush and tall, handsome Afshin waiting for him in the lobby.

Afshin ran to him and kissed Arman on the cheeks.

"I can't believe you both flew all this way just to see me!" Arman said.

Dariush kissed both Arman's cheeks. "Are you kidding? I wouldn't miss the chance to see how soft you've gotten."

The weight of the day fell away as they laughed, nudging each other with their elbows like they were kids again.

His friends' simple clothing stood out from the modern, crisp trends of the wealthy city folk, but Dariush and Afshin barely looked at the bright shops and tall buildings as they walked to a nearby restaurant. The bright streetlamps glowed above, lighting up the deep indent in Dariush's nose, still more than evident even thirty years after that fateful accident with the bike, the pole, and the ice cream.

Arman slapped his friend on the back. "When are you going to get a nose job? You know, you're probably the youngest guy in history who has had his nose broken for a girl."

Afshin snorted a laugh as Dariush rolled his eyes. They continued happily reminiscing as they reached the restaurant and ordered tea. When it arrived, Dariush cupped his mug, his eyes down.

"We didn't call Ârash to tell him we were coming. I don't think he's in any shape to come out and socialize, even if it's been so long since we've seen you."

Arman nodded. The thought of Ârash's absence, and poor Niki's fate, smothered the previously giddy atmosphere. It could have happened to any of them, and the reminder was sobering.

Arman rubbed his temples. "I didn't even have the courage to call him and tell him I was coming. I don't know how to look him in the face."

Afshin cocked his head, frowning. "You didn't tell him? That is crazy, man. I thought you two were very close."

Arman nodded. "I know, but again, I don't think he's in the right state of mind to meet people now. Plus, I'm leaving tomorrow, so there would not have been time to meet him, anyway. I didn't want to bother him and his family by making him feel obligated to interrupt their mourning to see me."

Afshin stared at his mug before taking a sip of his tea.

"I understand, though," Dariush said. "I'm like you too. I hate these difficult situations. As if I don't have anything to say. What would you even say to a father whose twenty-year-old daughter just died?"

"'Just died?'" Arman said loudly. "Niki didn't *die*, Dariush—she was murdered. What clearer example of injustice do you want? This government is one of the most criminal governments in the world. Who does this to their own people? It's up there with Stalin's regime."

His friends gasped and looked around nervously. Dariush held up his hands and gestured to Arman to calm down and stop speaking.

A chill ran down Arman's spine as he remembered where he was and he lowered his voice. "I am sure very soon this government will get what it deserves."

Afshin shifted his weight, frowning. "And what is it that our government deserves?"

"They need to go, my dear Afshin. They tried for forty-four years and destroyed the country, abused the natural resources, killed their own citizens, and ruined many lives. They simply need to go away."

Afshin straightened, lifting his chin. "Is that what they tell you in America about our government?"

Dariush slapped him on the shoulder. "Let's not talk about the government. It's been too long since we've seen Arman. Let's talk about important stuff... like did you see the final goal in the game against Japan last week?"

Arman nodded. The change of subject was for the best. He didn't wish any ill will toward Iran—in fact, the opposite was true.

Afshin narrowed his eyes and chewed the inside of his lip as Arman and Dariush discussed the latest football games and challenged each other over who was the best player in the Premier League. It was nice to get together again with old friends, but as the hour grew late, Arman pushed his chair back to excuse himself.

"This has been wonderful, my friends. Thank you for taking the time to come out and see me, but my plane leaves first thing in the morning. I really need to go."

Dariush gave him a hug and a kiss on each cheek. "Don't stay away so long next time. We need to keep in touch."

"Definitely," Arman said.

Afshin simply inclined his head to Arman. "Be careful of Western propaganda, my friend. Remember where you came from."

His words—and the lack of a parting hug—grated on Arman's nerves as he stepped out of the restaurant into the cool night air. He looked up at the stars as he walked. The sky looked different here, the air seemed crisper. He knew it was ridiculous; a city was a city, no matter what country he was in, but no matter how long he was away, Iran still somehow felt like home.

He glanced back and saw Afshin on the phone, having a heated discussion with someone. For a second, their eyes met and Afshin looked away with disgust. It was the same look Arman had seen in the eyes of so many photos of terrorists in the "American Propaganda" Afshin had spoken of. The look was hatred, pure and simple.

Arman's stomach soured. Afshin was probably on the phone with Ârash, telling him how Arman had been poisoned by Western thinking. He turned away and kept walking. It wouldn't make a difference. Ârash, more than any of his other friends understood what was really going on in this country. Arman would call him when he got home, apologize for not getting in touch, and hear whatever Afshin had told him.

He started packing as soon as he got back to his room. In three hours he would leave for the airport, and in five he'd be safe on a plane, leaving all of this behind him once again. He'd broken his last promise to never to return to Iran—this time he'd make good on it. As much as the country felt like home, he no longer felt safe there.

14

Tehran, Iran

TWO HOURS LATER, someone knocked on his door. Arman frowned, rubbing his eyes. Dr. Hajipour wasn't supposed to pick him up for the trip to the airport until 6 a.m., and the clock read just after 5 a.m. Pulling himself out of bed, he checked through the peephole and saw a clean-shaven man in a hotel uniform.

"What can I do for you?" Arman asked.

"I am here to check the air conditioner, sir."

His stomach churned. "At five in the morning?" It *was* hot in the room. Still, the request seemed odd.

"Yes, sir. We have a notification that it is down."

"Well, I'm checking out within the hour. You can fix it then."

"Please, sir, I am off at 6. The ticket came in on my watch, and I cannot go home before it is fixed."

Arman sighed. All he wanted was some peace until his driver arrived, but making the poor man wait seemed wrong and exactly what a Westerner would have done.

"Okay, my friend," Arman said, unlocking the door.

The man entered, followed by another man in an IRGC uniform.

Arman gasped, backing away. "What is the meaning of this?"

The IRGC officer gave him a stern look. "You to come with me."

Arman's heart sank. "What if I say *no*?"

The officer gave him half a smile. "This is not a request, Dr. Pirouzi."

It's over.

In many ways, he'd known this was inevitable. Spies much more trained and skilled than he had been caught for far simpler crimes. Yet… if the IRGC knew what he'd done, why not just arrest him at the conference?

A chill ran down his spine, remembering the hatred in Afshin's eyes and the tight grip on the phone as his friend glared at him through the window. That was the one mistake Arman had made—trusting a childhood friend. In Iran, it was hard to tell the rational citizens from those corrupted by the government. He'd been blinded with delight at seeing the

128

boys he used to play football with in the street and forgotten that snakes could be hiding in even the most comfortable of places. His only wish was that he'd been able to send the information hidden inside his tooth to the people who could have used it to save innocent lives.

He felt weak. Those lives... the lives of people Arman had never met, but people who looked like him, sounded like him could have *been* him under different circumstances, were the reason he'd taken this risk. If the information stayed in his tooth, everything he risked would be for naught.

He followed the IRGC officer to a car waiting just outside. As the officer opened the rear car door and motioned for Arman to enter someone shouted his name. Arman stopped and looked over the top of the car. Afshin stood on the other side of the road, arms folded and glaring. Beside him stood Dariush, tears in his eyes, with a hand over his mouth.

His suspicion was correct—Afshin had betrayed him, and even though it looked like Dariush hadn't been involved, there was nothing his friend could have done that wouldn't have incriminated himself, too. The walls of the tall buildings seemed to close in, crushing him. Just a few hours ago, he'd had friends, camaraderie.

Now he had nothing.

15

Tehran, Iran

GENERAL MORADI STOOD tall, gazing out at the crowd from beside the stage. Men in IRGC uniforms and others in turbans as diverse as the many villages in Iran threw their fists in the air, their voices booming through the room, chanting, "Death to America!" Moradi smiled. *Death to America*, indeed. The Supreme Leader had made it clear that "Death to America" meant America's leaders only. That was a shortsighted understanding of the depths of the West's degradation. Moradi considered all Americans infidels who deserved no less than what the American leaders had done to his own people.

The chants of "Death to America" turned to "God is the greatest." Moradi wondered if that was a natural progression or if an enlightened soul was leading them.

The theater overflowed with IRGC officials, *basijis*, and representatives of international organizations willing to give their guns—and their lives—to the cause. Those lives, in the grand scheme of things, were meaningless but necessary. Moradi would use them until the last of their blood was spilled, and they all joined their brothers in the holy light of heaven—while Moradi and those chosen would bask in the glory promised to them by God here on Earth, very much alive. Some might think that unfair, but someone needed to survive to continue God's work.

The lights dimmed, and the room fell silent as the General walked onto the stage. He stood at the podium, making eye contact with as many of his brethren as possible while keeping his expression calm, stern, and commanding. "My comrades, God tells us that if He wants to elevate someone to greatness, even if all forces in the world are against it, they will be great!" He pointed to his chest. "I am here today to testify to this fact."

The room cheered before falling silent again.

Moradi continued. "Forty-five years ago, I was a housekeeper's son in Shiraz. The man whose house my mother cleaned insisted that I go to the same school and get the same advanced, 'progressive' education as his son."

Several people in the middle of the crowd murmured among themselves.

"I was a young, lost teenager, and looking at his façade, I thought he was a great man." He paused, drinking in the energy in the crowd. "I didn't realize what he was trying to do—sending me to a mixed-gender school to sit with girls and learn modern science and other such ridiculousness."

Many people in the audience sneered and called out, "No!"

"You are correct, my brothers. He wasn't doing me a favor. That institution was peeling us away from God one-by-one so the devil could take over—and they were almost successful. That lost, bedeviled man never knew what God had in mind for me."

A hush fell over the room.

Good, they are listening. God's plan needed to be revealed, and they needed to hear and spread the news through their ranks. General Moradi took in their eager faces. "I was lucky that my father still let me go and listen to the local mullah's preaching. He showed me the old ways. The *true* ways. The actual teachings of God, rather than these Western bastardizations."

Men cheered from the rear of the room, many raising guns over their heads.

"Through the mullah, God opened my eyes and I heard my true calling." Moradi closed his eyes and shook his fists. "I would give anything to go back and live through those days again—when we realized what was happening in our blessed land and how the monarchy was trying to corrupt the country by destroying our religion and beliefs." He opened his eyes and lowered his hands. "But they learned, as all infidels learn, that the righteous cannot be contained!"

The crowd roared.

"We showed them our anger when we declared our disdain for the Western decadence they tried to force upon us. We burned the liquor stores, bars, and cinemas."

The crowd chanted, "Death to America" again, their fists waving in unison.

"We raided the houses of government officials and wealthy people who were involved in corrupting our blessed society."

The crowd shouted and raised their hands to God, the noise filling the air.

Moradi waited for them to settle. "When we raided the home of the man who'd tried to force me into a decrepit Western education, my men put him on his knees before me. The infidel looked up and said, 'Naser, I raised you like my own child. Why would you do this?'"

He paused for effect; the crowd was enraptured. Moradi shouted, "I slapped the infidel in the mouth and told him: 'You deserve the worst because of what you were trying to do to me. You were trying to shape me into an unfaithful bastard like your own son. And for that, your punishment is death.'"

The room cheered louder than ever. *Excellent—they agree.* The only punishment suitable for infidels was death.

Moradi held up his palm. "He begged for his life, like all those who fear death, and if it weren't for my father's request, I would have punished him right there. Although he ultimately got what he deserved a few years later when fellow believers found him in Paris."

Many started chanting the ancient words, along with "Death to the infidels!"

"My friends, from those early days, with God's will, I have had the honor of serving Him and our Supreme Leader by organizing the Intelligence Organization of the Islamic Revolutionary Guard Corps, the very righteous men combing the streets, keeping the godly safe."

People nodded, praising the IRGC.

"I spent eight years on the Iraqi war front, making sacrifices just like all of you." Moradi pounded on his prosthetic thigh. "I lost my leg fighting for God! Like any of you, I wondered how God would do this to one of his faithful... and then my mullah reminded me: All things happen for a reason. I simply have not discovered the reason yet."

The crowd screamed, "God is the greatest!"

"Yes, my brothers, God is the greatest, and we must all have faith that if we follow His word, He will steer *us* on the path to greatness." He held his fist in the air. "After my injury, I could no longer be as effective on the battlefield, but I *could* refocus my skills to build and strengthen the Iranian nuclear program." Moradi placed a hand over his heart. "I turned my injury into a blessing and have done all I can to serve God and our great Supreme Leader. This would have not been possible without your help, my dear friends."

The cheers rattled the walls as the crowd shouted its approval.

Moradi held up his palms again for silence. "What I am here to announce, my friends, is that the victory is finally near. As you all know, God wants us, His chosen people, to be a country strong enough to rule the Middle East for the next thousand years. We have worked tirelessly to show Him that we can deliver on this dream."

Anyone still sitting shot to their feet, calling to the heavens and beating their breasts.

"My brothers, we have arrived. We will soon make a proclamation that will entrench Iran as the regional superpower in the Middle East. The protests you see in the streets are nothing but the last dying breaths of the United States as they try to destroy our great nation. Today, from Afghanistan to Iran, from Iran to Iraq, from Iraq to Syria, from Syria to Lebanon, and from Lebanon to the Holy Land in Palestine, we are ready to wreak havoc on the Western infidels."

It was true. All over these great nations, leaders—those chosen by God, like Moradi—were speaking to their followers, rallying them for the final battle promised to them since the beginning of time.

"The United States has never been this weak in the last one hundred years. The devil has overtaken them, running through the streets, poisoning everyone with drugs, alcohol, whores, and *hamjens-bâz-hâ*. Their economy is failing, and they must borrow money to survive. For now, other countries still support them, but soon we will replace their currency with our own, crippling the dollar and making Iran the new world market. The supremacy of the United States will be over."

The crowd nodded along, smiling, their eyes fiery with holy hatred.

"Europe is nothing more than a gathering of a few bankrupt countries. Look at what happened to them when they ran out of gas and their people were shivering and dying in the winter." Harsh winter was a concept some of the men living in Iran couldn't understand, but dying was something most were all too aware of. "In Europe, they don't even have enough people having children. Their lives are so bad that they don't want to have offspring to suffer like they do. They allow their women to take drugs and mutilate their bodies, stopping them from achieving their one and only purpose prescribed by God: to multiply His followers."

The crowd grumbled, shaking their heads. No doubt, many of these men had several wives—hopefully pregnant and ready to birth the next wave of God's army.

"Europe still relies on African and Middle Eastern immigrants to work and help their broken economies survive. The golden days of the West are over, my brothers, and with the help of our allies, Russia and China, the golden days of the East will soon be a reality. The next year heralds the greatest years of the Islamic government. Our announcement will shock the world, and they will fear us as we blind the Western infidels with the sheer glory of God."

More cheers.

"Yes. This is what's been promised to the faithful. And no power in the world can stand in the way of God's will."

Fists rose in the air as the crowd began to chant: "Moradi, Moradi, Moradi!"

He should probably have stopped them. It was wrong to chant any name but that of the Supreme Leader or God. However, Moradi was *His* messenger, and in many ways, Moradi's word was the same as God's.

Yes, Moradi was just as good as God walking on Earth, and he would prove it, right down to the last drop of infidel blood spilled in *their* name.

16

Qeshm, Iran

ARMAN BLINKED THE sting of sleep from his eyes as the car started up an incline. Frowning, he sat up in time to see a sign reading *Persian Gulf Bridge* pass by. He'd heard they'd started construction on the bridge, but hadn't thought about it since the project had been placed on hold during the Pandemic. They continued to go up and Arman took in the play of light dancing on the water below. The Persian Gulf Bridge had been commissioned in 2011 to link Bandar Abbas on mainland Iran to the island of Qeshm—but Qeshm was over six hundred miles from Tehran.

He rubbed his eyes. He had a vague memory of being herded onto a train, but didn't remember getting back into a car. Had he been drugged? He blinked as his vision came in and out of focus. He tried to stay awake, as the scenery flashed between villages with handmade huts and scatterings of more modern buildings, he couldn't be sure if he was dreaming. Was any of this real? Maybe he was still asleep in his hotel room, waiting for his alarm to go off so he could fly home in the morning.

Arman started fully awake as the car rolled to a stop and the door beside him opened.

"Get out."

An IRGC officer hauled him from the car. Heat blasted Arman's face and humidity filled his lungs. The sun was lower in the sky and the bright light seemed to burn his skin. He saw the expanse of ocean and a sick feeling settled in his stomach. He hadn't been dreaming—they really had traveled all the way to the island of Qeshm.

The stifling combination of humidity and warmth coming from the sea thickened in his lungs, making each breath feel heavy. He grew up in the northwest of Iran, in a mountain city called Ardebil with snowy winters, windy springs and falls, and mellow, sunny summers. He wasn't accustomed to heat and humidity. Even when he traveled to medical conferences in places like Florida, he sweated all day and had to crank the air conditioning in his room at night.

The officer shoved him forward. "Get moving."

Arman stumbled to a nondescript white building. It was several stories tall and there wasn't a single window in sight. A white, accordion-like door opened as they approached. Over the doorway, scrawled in thick brown letters on a blue backdrop, were the words *Qeshm Prison*.

Arman dug his feet into the sandy asphalt. "Prison! Why are you taking me to a prison?"

The officer gave a practiced smile that held not a hint of warmth. "It's nothing to worry about. They just want to ask you a few questions."

Arman knew that if he stepped through the door of the prison, there was a very real chance he wouldn't step out again. But what was he to do? Guards in gray uniforms carrying guns over their shoulders stood on both sides of the door, and he could see more inside—he had no choice but to comply.

The officer handed him off as a guard approached. "Dr. Arman Pirouzi. Identification B-12956421."

The guard nodded. "We were expecting you, Dr. Pirouzi." He held out his hand, gesturing through the door. "Right this way."

Arman followed, and the metal accordion door started to shake and screech as it closed behind him. It *boomed* when it reached the wall and the sound of the heavy lock engaging after sent a shiver down his spine.

The guard led him down a brightly lit hallway with white tiles on the walls and ceilings. The floor was covered with the same white tiles, but with a mustard-gold pattern that Arman guessed was probably meant to be cheery.

After turning down several halls, the gold coloring in the tile changed to a leafy green. They walked past dozens of closed, seemingly unlabeled doors before stopping at an open one.

The guard held his hand. "You will stay here until they are ready for you."

Arman trembled. "Ready for what?"

"The IRGC has questions, Dr. Pirouzi. This is fairly routine."

Routine for you, maybe.

Arman entered a bright room with a single, barred window a few inches from the ceiling. The green tile pattern from the hall continued inside, part of the design hidden by a set of bunk beds. A single bucket sat centered in the room beside a drain in the floor.

"You shit here." The guard pointed at the bucket. "You sleep here." He pointed at the bed. "Things are very simple here, Dr. Pirouzi."

"Do I get a phone call? I'd like to let my family know where I am."

The guard smiled. Arman wasn't sure if the man was trying to be reassuring, or if he found the request funny. "There is no need for that, Dr. Pirouzi. They will be here to talk to you soon."

Arman nodded as the guard left the room.

The bucket would take some getting used to, but the cell was far better than he'd expected. He tried to look out the window, but it was too high. It was probably more to illuminate the room without the need for electricity than to provide the inhabitants with a view.

Dinner was some sort of fish, mashed and spread over a thick, crusty bread. Arman told himself he was eating a tuna sandwich, rather than thinking of the bones and other matter that were probably pureed into the paste.

He sat on the edge of the bed, waiting for the elusive "they" who wanted to ask him questions, until the lights overhead winked out without warning.

A small band of moonlight from the window kept him company as he lay back on the mattress and closed his eyes. Things certainly could have been worse. They could have sent him to the notorious Evin Prison, the facility his cousin had been detained in years ago. Bijan had come out a changed man, afraid of his own shadow and lacking the spark of life that once made him the life of any party.

A prison was a prison, though. Arman was locked in a cell, and doubted anyone knew why he missed his plane that morning. The CIA might already be looking for him, but if the IRGC didn't want Arman found, he didn't have much hope they would find him.

The door opened in the morning and a tray with a single round scoop of rice and a cup of water slid into the room before it closed again. The rice was cold, but at least it filled his belly. He sipped at the water, wondering how much longer he'd have to wait before someone came to talk to him. It turned out, not long. He barely finished his water when the door opened again and a guard entered.

The guard picked him up by the collar and roughly hauled him to his feet. "They are ready for you."

"I'm coming, I'm coming!"

The halls were brighter than his room, and Arman squinted as they left the green-tiled section and moved back into the yellow area. They stopped in front of a door, and the guard knocked on the glass three times.

"Dr. Arman Pirouzi," he announced.

"Enter!" a voice boomed from within.

The guard shoved Arman inside. A Persian man in a tailored shirt buttoned to his neck and hanging loose over his khaki pants sat at a small table in the center of a brightly lit room with clean, white-tiled walls.

The door slammed shut behind Arman, making him jump.

"Please, Doctor, be seated," the man said, gesturing to the chair across from him. "My name is Islami."

Islami? It was probably a fake name. Arman kept his eyes down, taking the seat. "They tell me you have questions?"

"I do, Doctor." Islami smiled. "Do you know what Dr. Akbari's job was?"

Arman chose his words carefully. "Someone at the conference told me he was a scientist, but I honestly have no idea if that's true. All I know is that the man came to me for help, and I gave it to him."

"Do you normally do surgery out of the kindness of your heart?"

"When necessary. In the United States, we're made to take the Hippocratic Oath."

Islami sneered. "An oath made to heathen gods."

He'd never thought of it that way, but it was actually true. "It's the meaning that counts. To me, that means I need to help whenever I can. I came here to use my skills to help my people."

"To help your people?" Islami tapped a finger against his lip. "There are many who claim that Akbari's surgery had nothing to do with a heart condition and everything to do with espionage."

Arman lifted his brow, trying to look surprised. "Well, then, they'd be wrong. I replaced a pacemaker and was supposed to bring the defective device to Germany, but it was stolen. That is the extent of my dealings with the man in question."

"You are sticking with that story?"

"Yes, because it's the truth."

Islami's chair creaked as he settled back. "You need to understand, Doctor, that we are the good guys. I promise, you don't want to see the bad guys."

Arman was certain that was the truth, but he had to keep *exactly* to his story, just as the CIA had trained him. Any deviation would be seen as a sign of deception and be grounds for execution.

Islami questioned him for three days.

Every day, Arman was taken to the same room, given the same questions, and he gave the same answers.

On the third day, Islami said, "Well, Doctor, our job is done here. Too bad you would not be honest with us. Tomorrow, you will see the lower levels of the prison."

Ice flooded Arman's veins. The CIA said that if he got caught, his best chance of being released through normal means would be repeating the same story every day. He'd done that flawlessly, just as he'd been trained to do—If he went into the bowels of the prison, he really might never get out.

Arman stood. "I am a United States citizen. You have no right to keep me here. I need a lawyer right now."

Islami laughed. "You were born in Iran and that's your nationality. Plus, being an American with what you have done makes you a spy. And you know what happens to spies?" He leaned closer, the stench of his breath filling the space between them. "They die."

17

Qeshm Prison, Iran

THE NEXT DAY, the lights flicked on before the sun rose. The door slammed open and two guards pulled Arman out of bed and forced a black burlap bag over his head before he was fully awake. He choked on the stench of dust and old vomit as they tied his hands behind his back. A guard pushed and kicked him forward. "Come on. Get going! Faster!"

How the hell am I supposed to move fast when I can't see?

He expected them to steer him left into the interrogation room, but as he slowed near where he expected the door to be, someone shoved him. "Keep moving!"

They promised to show him the rest of the prison—it seemed his time with Islami and "the good guys" had run out.

Arman stumbled down the hall. Light crept in from the bottom of the bag hanging below his shoulders, but aside from that it was blackness.

Another shove. "Keep walking!"

It was difficult to force himself to walk forward blind with his hands tied behind his back. At home, if he woke in the night, he'd hold his hands out in front of him to make sure he didn't walk into something or so he could break his fall if he tripped over Anâr. It made him feel supremely vulnerable, which was no doubt the whole point.

The echo of his footsteps changed, like he'd entered a wide-open space, and Arman slowed. "Keep moving," came the now familiar reply, along with another hard shove. His skin itched as the hair on his neck and arms rose and one of the guards snickered. Sweat dampened Arman's brow. Whatever it was that the guard found funny, he wanted nothing to do with it. As he took the next step, his foot hit nothing but air.

He pitched forward, unable to stop or protect himself with his hands still bound, slamming into a set of concrete steps and stumbling down. Each painful knock of his head on the concrete shot stars into his eyes. His ears rang, and by the time he slammed to a halt at the bottom of the stairs, he couldn't tell which way was up.

Blood dripped down his face, trickling over his lips and into his mouth, flooding his tongue with a coppery tang. He wanted to spit, but with the bag still tight around his face, there was nowhere for it to go.

Footfalls thudded down the stairs, accompanied by laughter. "Doctor, what is wrong with you? Are you drunk?"

Arman groaned. "You did that on purpose."

"Are you trying to say we are torturing you here?"

Arman didn't answer. There were fates far worse than falling down the stairs in a lawless place like this. He was a criminal in their eyes, guilty until proven innocent. That meant he had no rights whatsoever.

Footfalls sounded on the stairs and the stench of the guard's body odor overwhelmed that of blood. With the hot, humid air, it probably wouldn't be long before Arman smelled just as foul.

They herded him down another stairway and into a confined space. A jolt and vibration told him he was in an elevator. When the door opened, the humidity dropped slightly, and the air was cooler, with a musty smell now.

They continued to push him forward and then shoved him down into a chair. Water dripped—the sound echoing off the walls all he heard until a presence loomed over him.

"Welcome to the second phase, Doctor."

Arman cringed. It was Islami again! Were they just playing with him? Trying to make him break and change his story? The CIA covered this sort of psychological manipulation but he had no idea what to expect going forward.

The sound of Islami's boots on the floor overshadowed the incessant dripping. "This is what you wanted. You made us do this. Remember that."

Did he really believe what he was saying, or was this just another tactic to make him feel weak and out of control?

At the very least, Arman had his mind. He knew who he was and what his focus should be. He needed to stick to his story and not relent, no matter what. Giving in to their manipulation was probably what had gotten Niki killed. They'd probably tortured her until she admitted guilt. If he were lucky—if he could hold out long enough—they would have to let him go. The tools the CIA gave him would allow him to get through. In many ways, he knew it was a dream, but he clung to that thin glimmer of hope, nonetheless. At that moment, it was all he had.

A man with wide cheeks and a wider girth pulled the shroud from Arman's head. He grimaced at the sight of Arman's bloodied and bruised face and looked away. Arman almost thought he looked remorseful, if anyone in the IRGC—much less someone who worked in Qeshm Prison—was capable of such a thing.

Islami pushed the other man out of the way and stared into Arman's eyes. "How about we stop playing games like a weak American? We know everything. Now, tell me who Dr. Akbari really is."

Arman took a few deep breaths of the thick, musty air. "If you already know everything, why are you still asking me questions? What do you want from me?"

"We want the names of all your connections. We also want Akbari's pacemaker."

"I told you I don't have the pacemaker. I gave it to a nurse to sterilize it and I never saw it again."

At least that was the truth. Considering it was likely they were the ones who took the pacemaker, it was of the utmost importance to stick to this story. "And I'm sure you already know who my childhood friends are, and you probably know of more family members than I'm even aware of. Other than that, my only connection in Iran is Dr. Hajipour, who invited me here for the conference."

Islami sneered. "You are lying, and do you know what we do with liars?" He straightened to his full height. "We whip them." The man who removed Arman's shroud winced as Islami made a sweeping gesture. "Take him away."

The guard sighed, approaching but not meeting Arman's gaze. "Come on." He walked to the door as two other guards yanked Arman to his feet and pulled him from the room.

Are they serious? Or is this just a scare tactic?

It couldn't be real. Whipping was something you heard about in movies or on the news. It didn't happen to people like him.

Arman struggled against the guards. "Wait! You can't do this!"

Islami snorted a laugh. "Lying to your government is a crime, Doctor. And you will be punished until we hear the truth."

150

Arman dug in his heels, but they dragged him along. He thought of poor, sweet Niki, with all her hopes and dreams, being dragged kicking and screaming down a hallway just like this one. Then again, she'd probably held her head high, defiant to the last. Maybe that was why they'd killed her.

Arman continued to struggle as they took him to a room with several tables, bloodstains clearly visible on the floor. Rats scattered into holes in the crumbling walls as the guards flipped on the lights. Islami had promised a whipping, but there were knives, wires, and drills scattered along the shelves.

They forced him face down on a metal table and held him while they tied his legs to metal bars and pulled off his shoes and socks. Then the first man pulled a lever, and the bed tilted down with Arman's head toward the floor and legs in the air.

The man who looked remorseful earlier held a stick in front of Arman's mouth. "Do you want to bite down on this?"

Islami slapped the stick out of his hand. "No mercy for spies."

Arman gaped at the stick rolling on the floor when a snapping sound filled the room, followed by a dull sting on the bottom of his feet. He gasped, not quite processing before the next snap sounded and a slash of pain tore through the soles of his feet. A shriek filled the room. A cry of such pain and horror that Arman couldn't fathom it. Another snap sounded, and another scream, then another. Arman dimly realized the voice screaming was his own.

The words of the elderly CIA agent, Hal came to his mind.

"While you were unconscious, we fitted you with an epidural pump. On the off chance that they catch you and break your legs, or something like that, press this button implanted under your skin here, on your shoulder."

At the time, Arman had thought it an odd place, but now, bound to a table and unable to move more than a few inches, he understood. He waited for the next slash to tear through his skin before reaching his chin down and pressing the button hidden just at the edge of his collarbone.

Arman started begging and crying. He'd taken lessons on acting frightened and in pain, but in this case, there was no need to act. This was pain unlike anything he'd experienced before. He'd often wondered why people would seem to quickly admit to crimes they hadn't committed—now, he understood. He could see himself admitting to anything to get them to stop.

After a minute, the epidural engaged, and the pain was gone. Arman wasn't sure if it was from the pump or just numbness from the whipping itself, but he didn't care. As relief set in he forced himself to continue wailing and crying with each snap of the whip, drawing on his CIA training. Bile started to build in his throat and he vomited, puke dripping down the side of the metal table they'd strapped him to. He didn't feel pain anymore, but his body was still fully aware of the damage and his stomach revolted, spewing his last meager meal on the bloody floor. As his eyes grew heavy, he moaned and let them close. With any luck, if they thought he'd fainted, they would stop. After all, what fun was whipping someone if they weren't screaming?

A bucket of cold water splashed across his face. He coughed and spluttered as they untied him and dragged him through the halls. The epidural had done its job, making it impossible to move. The guards probably assumed it was due to pain and exhaustion.

They threw Arman into a new cell on the same underground level. The dirt floor, like the whipping room, was stained with blood. Tiny paw prints covered the ground, and a rat scurried into a dark corner and disappeared into a hole where the wall met the floor. In the corner sat a small bucket that smelled like urine and human excrement.

As the door slammed, Arman rested his head against the stone wall, wondering what happened to the cell's previous occupant and deciding it was probably best not to consider their fate. Few entered the bowels of Iranian prisons and lived to tell about it.

As the anesthetic started wearing off, Arman realized what had been done to his feet. It felt like they had chopped his soles with a knife, poured salt into the wounds, and then attached weights to his ankles. He wanted to engage the morphine, penicillin, and anxiolytic implant, but the contents of the small packet hidden inside him were not limitless, and he needed to conserve as much as he could in case they did something worse to him.

He gritted his teeth. Right now, it seemed that nothing could be worse than what he had just experienced, but he knew it wasn't so. The guards here had no mercy and seemed to take pleasure in torment. They surely had dreamed up nightmares no sane person would be capable of inflicting. Arman feared he would soon find out.

The next day, before the lights even turned on, they shoved a hood onto his head and pulled him to his feet. Arman shrieked, buckling as his fresh scabs tore free from his lacerated feet, but the guards simply hauled him from the room and pushed him down the hall. He cried out, his knees buckling from the pain.

"Stop whining like a child!" The guard yanked his arm and dragged him through a door where two men lifted him by the shoulders and slammed him onto a table, this time laying him on his back.

"Tell us what you know about Dr. Akbari," Islami asked from somewhere in the room.

"I told you, all I know is that he asked me for help. I do not know the man."

The shroud was pulled from his head. "Where is the information he passed to you?"

"How do you think he passed me information while he was under anesthesia?"

Islami frowned, considering the question. The frown turned to a sneer. "This is your own fault. You brought this on yourself with your lies."

One of the men threw a piece of white cotton over Arman's face and water quickly followed. Arman choked and spluttered, his body thrashing at the sensation of drowning. After a long, long moment, his implants kicked in. Like magic, he could breathe! *God bless Hal and his ingenuity!* Arman remembered to splutter and cough, doing his best to make it look like he was dying.

They pulled the cloth from his face, and Islami leaned over him. "What did Dr. Akbari give you?"

Arman spit out some water. "Nothing!"

The white cloth returned. Even with the implants, his lungs burned, and he couldn't imagine what kind of pain this would have caused if the CIA hadn't prepared him. The minutes stretched into hours, or perhaps it just seemed that way.

They dragged him from the room again. His feet burned with every step; dirt caked deeply into his wounds. If the IRGC didn't kill him, infection certainly would.

That evening, they gave him a ground beef kebab with a small amount of rice on the side, a lavish meal by prison standards. Soon after, they dragged him to another room lit with bright lights. Every ten minutes, an ear-shattering single-tone alarm sounded, startling him. This went on through the night. In the morning, they gave him breakfast, and then the alarms started anew. Arman held his ears, screaming. Nothing was worth this. The sound quickly became worse than the whipping, worse than the waterboarding.

Soon, his eyes grew heavy despite the noise, and they splashed him with water to wake him. The next time he fell asleep, the guard jabbed him with an electric prod. Time blurred as the world became a kaleidoscope of light, unbearable sound, and pain, until, finally, Islami reappeared.

"Where is the information Dr. Akbari gave you?" he asked.

Arman was so tired he didn't know if he was awake or dreaming. He barely knew who the man was talking about.

Dr. Akbari? Oh, yes. The spy I was sent here for.

Arman smiled faintly, imagining a warm, relaxing beach.

"Yes, that's it," Islami said. "Just tell me where the information is, and I will let you sleep."

Sleep. Yes, he needed to sleep. Nothing else mattered but closing his eyes. He let his weary eyelids fall and another electric shock jolted him.

"Answer, Doctor," Islami said.

Would it really be so bad to tell this man everything he wanted to know? He had already been caught. What was just a little information? Would it really matter?

Islami started to smile, and the horror of that grin was enough to bring Arman back to reality. This wasn't the beach, and the light wasn't warm and inviting. This was hell on

Earth, and admitting any wrongdoing would be the end of him.

Arman shook his head weakly. "I don't know what you're talking about. All I did was replace a pacemaker. Please, you have to believe me!"

The pleading in his voice was real, even if his words were false. He was on the edge of breaking. The pain was one thing, but his will simply wasn't strong enough.

His eyes fluttered closed, and he was vaguely aware of another jolt of electricity running through him, then another horn, and water splashing on his face. But it all seemed distant, fuzzy next to the overwhelming need.

Arman slept.

18

THE ROOM SPUN when he woke, his eyes focusing on the bucket in the corner. He was back in his room. Had the past several days even been real? Or just a nightmare?

I guess it doesn't matter. Everything here is a nightmare.

Something shuffled in the shadows and Arman flinched. Up until now, the rats had stayed away. With the scent of blood, though, he knew it was only a matter of time.

The figure inched closer, making too much noise to be a rat, and a small boy of maybe twelve crept from the shadows. He wore a tattered gray frock and his grime-covered feet were bare. One of his eyes was covered with a stained bandage.

Arman's heart clenched. News stories told of children being tortured in prisons, but he'd always hoped it had been an exaggeration; no people could be that cruel, not even the

IRGC… or so he'd hoped. He saw now that the depths of human depravity were endless.

Arman held out his hand. "It's okay. I won't hurt you."

The child flinched away, scurrying back into the corner.

"I am a prisoner, just like you. My name is Arman."

The boy's one good eye peeked out of the shadows.

"What's your name?" Arman asked.

The child eased out a little further. "Bâbak."

"How long have you been here, Bâbak?"

"I can't remember. It feels like months."

Arman understood that all too well. "What happened to your eye?"

The child's lower lip quivered. "I was at a protest with my sister in Shiraz. The police came. They shot at us." He covered his eye patch. "It hurt."

Arman's stomach twisted. Plenty of women and children had been intentionally blinded by teargas and pellet guns used at close range. Many speculated that the IRGC had been given permission to permanently mark the dissenters.

"Do you know what happened to your sister?"

"No. I remember hearing her scream, but I fell, holding my eye. I cried like a coward for my own pain, while an officer dragged her away by her hair." Bâbak's lips started to tremble again, and tears ran down his cheek. "I'm never getting out of here, am I?"

Arman held out his arms, and the boy scampered to him, clutching his shirt and sobbing. Arman rocked him like his mother used to do when he was upset. He wanted to give the child words of encouragement, but couldn't manage—he didn't want to lie to the boy, not in this godless place.

He held him tightly. "I'm here," Arman said. "You're not alone." It was the only truth, the only comfort he could give him.

The door opened and a new guard stepped in. "Sniffling again, you sewer rat?" He yanked Bâbak off Arman and tossed him to the other side of the cell where he landed in a heap, coughing from the dust kicked up from the floor.

The guard wiped his palms on his trousers. "You aren't worth the space you take up in a cell."

"Leave him be," Arman said. "He's just a child."

"A law breaker is a law breaker, no matter the age." The guard pulled Arman to his feet and shoved him toward the door.

"Again? Can I eat first?" Arman rasped.

When had he last eaten? Or used the bucket, for that matter? He couldn't recall. He didn't feel hungry, which could have been his body's response to the torture. He felt weak, though, and his arms and legs looked gaunt.

When will this madness end?

The door slammed behind him. Bâbak, mercifully, had been left behind. Maybe if they concentrated on Arman, the boy would be saved more pain.

He was dragged down a long, dimly lit hallway with stone walls soiled from condensation and mold. After turning a corner, they shoved him into another room and strapped him to a table on his stomach.

Arman pushed his chin into his shoulder. A second later, a lash stung the bottom of his feet. His wail of pain was very real, as it took some time for the epidural to set in. Like before, he vomited, and they threw water on his face before they tired of whipping him and dragged him back to his cell. They hadn't asked a single question.

Arman lay on the floor, gasping. He tried to swallow, but his mouth and throat were too dry.

A small hand touched his forehead. "Don't die, Mr. Arman."

Bâbak… he had half thought he'd hallucinated the boy.

"I'm all right." Arman pushed himself to a sitting position and examined the open, bleeding wounds on his feet. Even if he found a way to escape, he'd never be able to run.

Bâbak wiped his good eye. "They did that to me, too. I'm so sorry, Mr. Arman. I know it hurts." The child's feet, while dirty and scabbed, were nowhere near as bad as Arman's.

He may not have been able to escape, but maybe Bâbak could. Arman scanned the room, looking for the hole in the wall where the rat had disappeared. The hole was in the dark corner in the rear of the cell. There were other cells to the left and right, but it was possible the wall behind them lead to a hallway or maybe even outdoors. The practical side of him told him this was a fool's errand, but he was tired of waiting for a rescue he knew wasn't coming.

Arman pointed into the shadows. "See that hole near the floor?"

"Yes."

"That's where the rats go. If we're lucky, it may lead to a way out." The chances were slim, but it was something. "If we dig there, it may go unnoticed." It was a risk, but how much worse could it really get if they got caught? Arman pulled himself toward the wall. "Help me."

Together, they started to dig.

They took shifts through the night, one working while the other slept. When Bâbak fell into a deep sleep, Arman continued digging, allowing the child some respite. Arman spread the dirt he scooped out across the floor, making sure not to leave a noticeable pile. His fingers started to bleed nearly as much as his feet, but he ignored the pain. He *would* get out of this hellhole one way or another.

But it was slow going—the dirt was hard, and at this rate his fingers would be shredded to the bone long before they made it through. He needed some sort of tool. Could he possibly get his hands on one of the torture implements? It seemed unlikely.

When the lightbulb overhead turned on, and doors started opening and he could hear the sound of doors slamming from the hall, Arman pulled the bucket to the back of the cell, hiding their work on the hole. Bâbak didn't stir until their door slammed open.

"Time for your slop, swine."

A guard shoved in a tray containing two dollops of what looked like Anâr's canned cat food, and two small metal cups of water. Arman's stomach heaved as he thought about what might be inside the ground up concoction of mystery meat and greens, but Bâbak grabbed a fistful of the wet mash and shoved it in his mouth like it was his first meal in weeks, barely taking time to breathe between bites. Arman sighed and reached for his portion. Whatever it was, it was still nourishment, and he needed to survive if they had any hope of escape.

The mash tasted as bad as it looked, but Arman found himself gulping it down just as fast as the child had, mainly to avoid the taste. The water he drank more slowly. The worst thing he could do now would be to gulp it down and throw up which would only make him more dehydrated. He thought about the hole as he drank, and as the cool metal touched his lips again, he stopped, pulling the cup away and examining it. Though it was hardly a spade, the mouth was wide, and as he squeezed it in his hand, the metal seemed firm—this was something he could dig with. The only question was, would the guards notice a single missing cup?

It's worth the risk.

When the hallway quieted, they set to work digging again, using both cups. As the hole quickly widened, the air in the room seemed cleaner. Bâbak must have noticed it, too, because he dug with more vigor, and Arman even caught a smile on his face.

"What do you miss on the outside?" Bâbak asked.

"My family. My mother and my cat." Oddly enough, he hadn't thought much about Laura.

I suppose that's telling.

"I miss my mother, too," Bâbak said. "And my father. I wonder if they know I am here? Do you think they are trying to get me out?"

Arman grimaced. If Bâbak had been at a protest in Shiraz, he probably lived nearby. His parents may have been searching prisons, but there were many detention centers between Shiraz and Qeshm.

He cupped the child's cheek. "I'm sure they are doing everything in their power to get you out." That, at least, he was sure was true.

A few hours later, lunch was served and the guards left again. No one came to question either one of them or to draw them from their task, and more importantly, they didn't notice the single cup Arman kept. The respite, however brief, was a blessing. It gave Arman time to heal, and more importantly, allowed him to collect his thoughts and quiet his mind. He needed to remember the reason why he risked a trip to Iran in the first place—it was bigger than him and bigger than Bâbak. How many people would die if Iran went to war again?

Arman dug another scoop of dirt from the hole and Bâbak spread it across the floor. He refused to give in. He refused to succumb and tell the IRGC what they wanted to hear. He might die in this place, but as long as he was alive, there was still a chance he'd be able to get the information stored in his tooth to the right people. There was still a chance he could stop a war that would cost thousands of innocent Iranian lives. He could still get home to give his mother her favorite cake for her birthday.

That was his goal. The information was secondary. He'd made his mother a promise, and he damn well intended to keep it.

About an hour after a dinner that looked no different from breakfast and lunch, someone pounded on the door three times. Arman had just enough time to pull the bucket in front of the hole before the door opened.

"Wake up, slobs!" A guard walked in and shoved a hood over Bâbak's head.

Arman pushed the guard away. "Leave him alone!"

The guard punched Arman in the gut before forcing a hood over his head as well. He wrenched Arman's arms back and cold steel snapped around his wrists.

Bâbak sniffled as they dragged him ahead of Arman. They turned left rather than right, and up a stairway, then through another hall and up a second stairway, followed by an elevator.

Where are we going?

The elevator opened, and a cool breeze wafted over his skin. They were outside!

"Push them out," a voice said.

Strong hands gripped Arman's arms on either side, lifting him onto a flat surface.

"Walk," the voice said.

The sound of cars and voices carried from the street below. He was on the roof! How many stories did the prison have? Ten? Twenty?

"Move!"

Arman moved forward hesitantly. The swollen wounds on his feet stung with every step. Was this his execution? Were they forcing him to walk off the end of the building? Was it supposed to look like a suicide?

"Move!"

A whip snapped at his feet, and Arman inched forward another step.

"Touch the ledge."

Arman felt with his foot and found a solid surface, although a small one. The whip snapped again and he stepped up onto the ledge.

"Retract the plank."

"Wait!"

Arman tried to step back but wobbled, off balance. Cars honked below and a gust of wind whipped at his smock.

"What is this!?" Arman demanded. "What are you doing?"

Islami answered. "Would you like to tell me where the information is, Dr. Pirouzi?"

Arman gulped. He wanted to tell. Did it really matter? He wasn't getting out of Qeshm Prison alive. Death might be better; at least the agony would end.

He gritted his teeth beneath the hood. Giving in would mean they'd won. If he was going to die or fall to his death, he'd win the only way he could... by taking his secrets with him.

"Please, no!" Bâbak begged.

"Confess that you were paid by the Americans!" a guard yelled.

"I wasn't!" Bâbak cried. "I swear to God! I was just there to be with my sister." A whip cracked, and the boy cried out again. "Please, I swear it to be true!"

"Leave them both to regret their choices," Islami said.

Footsteps retreated before a guard chuckled. "Which one do you think will fall first?"

"My money is on the brat. I'd also bet he'll scream all the way to the ground."

"Can you hear me, my friend?" Arman whispered.

"Yes," Bâbak replied weakly.

"Keep your head high, and work on your balance. We have plenty of room. We'll be fine."

"I'm afraid, Mr. Arman."

"I am, too. But I'm here. I'm not going anywhere."

Bâbak sniffed and fell silent. Arman thought he heard the child whisper a prayer. Arman hadn't prayed in a long time and he doubted God would listen to him anymore.

The wind changed directions, getting stronger at times. The voices and cars grew louder and softer, and the guards—somewhere not far, but not close, either—chatted among themselves casually as they shuffled cards, playing some game. Were they up there to make sure they didn't fall? Or to make sure they *did*?

As the sun came up, Arman struggled to keep his balance. The heat made sweat pour into his eyes beneath the shroud. His head started to spin, and he swayed. He and Bâbak had stood there for countless hours.

"Careful, Dr. Pirouzi," Islami said. "We don't want you to fall." He laughed. "It's a long ways down."

When had Islami come back? Not that it mattered. He was sure the bastard had a good night's sleep while Arman and Bâbak struggled not to fall.

He could almost feel Islami's gaze on him, but Arman didn't give the man the satisfaction of saying anything. He made up his mind he was going to die and nothing they said or did had much meaning to him anymore.

The sun seemed to burn through the black shroud and stars started to explode in Arman's eyes. His body swayed, and he made one last effort to stay standing before his foot slipped.

He fell, screaming.

"Mr. Arman! No!" Bâbak yelled.

Arman fell for only a split second before slamming into the floor. When his shroud was pulled free to the sounds of laughter, he saw he'd only been on a bucket with fans blowing on him. A speaker on the ground played faint sounds of the city. Bâbak still stood on his own bucket, his knees wobbling until a grinning guard kicked it from beneath him. The child screamed before he, too, hit the floor.

The laughing soldiers dragged them back to their cell, untying their wrists before tossing them inside.

The guard closing the door grinned at Arman. "I hope you enjoyed your last day on this Earth. Tomorrow morning, you will be executed for your crimes."

Arman was sure the sun had started to rise when he thought he was standing on the roof. He couldn't even trust his own senses anymore.

The cell seemed darker than ever before when the guards switched off the light. The walls closed in, and the dripping sound coming from a distant hall sounded louder with each incessant splash.

Soft sobs came from the dark. "I don't want to die, Mr. Arman."

"Neither do I."

Arman massaged his jaw and the fake tooth hidden in his mouth. He'd risked everything for what was hidden there, and here he was, forgotten by the CIA, beaten, and lost. If he managed to get the information out of the country, at least his death would have some meaning. Failure meant more than war; it meant a waste of his life. He could have stayed home, safe, and war still would have come to Iran. He'd have felt terrible about it, but he'd still be alive. He'd still be able to hold his mother's hand when she died and he'd still be there to feed the blasted cat. Now, who would sit with his mother on her deathbed? Would she know Arman had been executed? Would the news break her heart and push her to a faster death?

He rubbed his face. There were so many questions left unanswered, so many things he wanted to do and see in his life. A deep dread and guilt overcame him. He wanted to stop a war, he wanted to save Iranian lives.

Now, how many people would die because of his failure?

A soft breeze swept across his face and he sat up. A tiny beam of light shone from the hole they'd been digging.

"Bâbak! Look!"

"I see it!"

"Come on. We still have a chance!"

Arman moved the fetid bucket out of the way so they wouldn't spill the foul contents and felt around in the dark until he found his cup. They both started scratching at the wall again. After about an hour, Arman forced his hand through and pulled back a wad of tightly packed dirt and roots.

"Can you get in there and see out?" Arman asked.

Bâbak squeezed his head into the opening. "It's a hallway. I think I see a window."

Maybe we aren't underground after all!

"Come on," Arman said. "Help me dig. We are getting out of here tonight!"

The dirt grew softer with each scoop, and Arman realized with a burst of hope that it was turning to sand. The light shining in from the hall lit up Bâbak's grin and they no longer bothered spreading out the piles across the floor—they would be long gone by the time the guards returned.

They opened the hole about fifteen inches wide and the lights came on, signaling morning. Panic flooded Bâbak's face, and they both started punching at the opening. No one had passed by outside to see the hole they'd dug. Possibly it was an unused passage, which would be even better for them once they got out.

The dirt stopped shifting on Arman's side, and he frowned, noticing a straight line from the top of the hole to the bottom. He scooped the dirt back to find a steel support beam.

"We're not getting any further on this side." He started digging on the top, while Bâbak dug on his side.

Someone banged on their door. "One hour until your execution!"

Dammit!

Arman tapped Bâbak's shoulder. "Switch sides. You work on the top or bottom, whichever is easiest. I'll work on making the hole wider."

"Yes, Mr. Arman. Yes!" Bâbak slid to the other side.

Their breaths were shallow and fast as they worked in silence, each handful of dirt bringing them closer to freedom—until another straight line formed on Arman's side. He closed his eyes and sighed.

"What is it, Mr. Arman?"

"Another support beam. We're not going to be able to make the hole wider."

"Then we go higher! Come on!"

Another bang on the door rattled the room. "Forty-five minutes until your execution. Time to make good with God, swine!"

Forty-five minutes—it's not enough time.

Arman looked at Bâbak, then the hole, judging the boy's size. He reached out and stopped Bâbak's arm. "There's not enough time."

"What do you mean? It's working. We can get out!"

Arman pointed at the hole. "It's already wide enough for you to get out."

Bâbak shook his head, his one good eye wide in the light shining in from the hall. "I won't leave you, Mr. Arman!"

Arman grabbed his shoulders. "You must. Go through that hole and run to the window. You need to live to let everyone know what's happening here."

Tears flooded his eye. "But I don't want you to die, Mr. Arman!" The boy clung to him, shaking.

"I have no intention of dying. Once you are through the hole, I will have more room to work. I'll dig from the top and bottom until I get out. But I need you to go and get to safety. I'll meet you somewhere on the outside, far from here." He rubbed the child's cheek with his thumb. "You can do this, Bâbak. You are brave."

"I'm not, Mr. Arman!"

"Yes, you are. Don't waste your life by staying here. Get out and do everything you can to make sure this doesn't happen to another child. Use your life to make a difference."

Bâbak hugged him. "I will, Mr. Arman. I will."

Bâbak clawed his way into the hole as Arman pushed the boy's feet to force him through. He popped out the other side in a shower of dirt and stood, stooping to look back through the hole. He reached through and grasped Arman's hand. "I will never forget you, Mr. Arman."

Arman clutched the boy's fingers. "Nor will I forget you. Now go!"

Bâbak scampered down the hall, and Arman started scraping the dirt at the top and bottom of the opening.

"Thirty minutes until your execution!"

Arman gritted his teeth, caked dirt falling into his eyes. He could still make it. Maybe if he was lucky, he'd see a clear path and find Bâbak outside. They could run together and he could keep the boy safe.

He frowned, hitting a large rock at the top of the opening; there was no way to get through that. He dug his fingers into the bottom, pulling back five more scoops of dirt before hitting another hard, jagged surface.

A guard banged on the door again. "Fifteen minutes until your execution."

Arman sighed, rolling onto his back and setting the cup down.

Fifteen minutes. This was it. He truly wasn't going to make it home. He laughed, taking in the crusted, scabbed wounds on his feet and fingers. At least he didn't have to worry about infection anymore.

Arman rubbed his face. "Oh, Mom," he whispered. "Please know that I did this for our homeland. I did it for our people. We were the lucky ones who'd been able to escape." He shook his head. "This seemed like something I could do for all the people we left behind. I'm sorry I'm not coming home. I'm sorry I can't be there for you. I'm sorry that I can't bring you dessert on your birthday."

A warmth came over him, like a hug from across the ocean. Maybe his mother had known that their final embrace was their last.

Another bang on the door. "Five minutes until your execution. You should use your bucket if you don't want to pee yourselves." The guard walked away laughing and banged on another door, saying the same thing.

Arman shook his head. How someone could find amusement in the death of another human being confounded him. He'd grown up in this culture and had known things like this happened inside prisons, but as a doctor, his job—no, his *calling*—was to save lives. This kind of thinking still seemed foreign to him.

A hinge creaked from the hall. "Time's up, you indecent motherfucker," a voice said through the wall. "Time to pay for your crimes."

"Please, no!" another man's voice pleaded. "I have a wife. A two-year-old son—"

"Then you should have thought of them before denouncing the IRGC."

Another door opened from right across the hall. "Time's up. Do you have any last words?"

"You are all pigs and deserve to rot in hell. You don't deserve to walk on the Earth."

"Watch your mouth."

"I go to a better place. You will all spend an eternity in flames."

A man cried out, followed by the now all-too-familiar sound of a rod hitting flesh and breaking bones.

Arman shivered. He'd always hoped for a quiet end of his days. Maybe dying in his sleep. Hopefully, Anâr would learn to take his food from the CIA agent. He was a good cat and deserved a good home.

The hinges on his door screeched as it swung open. Arman stood, gulping.

"Any last words?" the guard asked.

Arman stared him down. Was this man looking for a reason to beat Arman one more time? *Probably.* He wouldn't give him the satisfaction.

The guard glared. "Fine." He grabbed Arman by the wrist and yanked him into the hall.

Another guard headed into the cell. "Where's the little shit? He's gone!"

"What?" the guard holding Arman said.

"They dug through the wall!"

The guard came out of the cell and flung the metal cup at him before shoving Arman. "What have you done!? We're going to kill you, you piece of shit!"

Arman laughed. "You were going to kill me anyway."

The guard punched him in the jaw. Stars exploded in Arman's eyes and his head whipped back before the man spat in his face. "There are easy and there are hard ways to die, motherfucker."

"No way will be hard, because I go to the grave satisfied that I saved another innocent person condemned in this hellhole."

The next fist lodged in Arman's gut, making him gasp and double over.

"Go find the brat!" the guard yelled. "Call the other cellblocks to look for him." He sneered at Arman. "Then bring the little shit to me. I want to slit the brat's throat and make this American *piece of shit* watch him bleed out."

The drip sounded again, the sound filling the hall as Arman gasped for air, holding his stomach. Hopefully, Bâbak was long gone by now. He hoped the child would have a good life. Maybe he could escape to America and become a doctor, just like Arman had. Whatever the child's dreams were, Arman wished them to come true. If there was a God, He'd see it done. It was a small favor to ask as Arman waited with the others for their execution.

As he slowly righted himself he took in the fresh wounds on the badly battered face of the man next to him and another, maybe half Arman's age, wearing only pants, with long, bloody gashes and welts on his back and chest. Arman shivered, not wanting to think about what might have caused them.

One of the guards placed a hood over the younger man's head and then Arman's. "Move!" He shoved Arman forward.

One of the men in front of him sniffed and sobbed. Arman felt oddly serene and detached. Maybe he'd come to grips with his fate—possibly even from the very moment he'd been arrested. He took solace in the hope that Bâbak had made it out. A young life was worth more than a life already well lived.

His thoughts turned to Niki being dragged down a similar hallway. He hoped she hadn't been scared, even though he could understand if she had been.

I'm sorry, Niki, that we couldn't save you in time. You deserved better.

I'm sorry, Ârash, that I couldn't be a better friend.

I'm sorry, Mom, that I won't be there for you anymore.

And I'm sorry, Laura, for not listening. This may not be any consolation to either of us, but you were right all along.

A door opened on his left and Arman was shoved through. He stumbled before catching his balance. The space seemed vast and wide open. A guard tied his arms behind his back. Sweat dampened his shroud, making the fabric stick to his face. Would he face a firing squad? His mind whirled, searching for answers and finding nothing that would help.

Why it was even a concern, he wasn't sure. Maybe his brain was making one last feeble attempt at being useful.

The guard made him shuffle to his right. Someone banged on metal twice. "Step up on the chair in front of you."

A sniffle beside him told Arman the other prisoner complied. He—maybe more than any of them—had seen that insolence was fruitless.

Someone nudged Arman from behind. "Now you. Up on the chair."

Arman inched forward and felt with his foot until he found the chair. He stepped up and pain exploded from his injured foot as it took the whole weight of his body. The cold metal chair gave his injuries some respite; it wasn't much, but the chill was one last comfort to cling to in this life.

Someone pulled at Arman's shroud, and something slipped over his neck—a rope. Or, rather, a noose.

So, that's how they're going to kill me.

His mind eased rather than reeling in fear. It was the last question in his life that he'd wanted answered, but now that the answer was there, he could face death—and the afterlife—with respect and dignity.

One of the chairs was kicked and a prisoner cried out. The rope around Arman's neck shifted as the apparatus above him squeaked from the sudden jolt of weight and the struggling of the condemned. The first victim gurgled and choked as the guards laughed.

The younger man on the chair next to Arman began to sob.

"Take deep breaths," Arman said. "It will be over soon."

A foot kicked the chair next to him, and Arman could feel the jolt as it clattered against his own. The poor boy choked, thrashed, the apparatus above swinging and creaking from his struggles, until finally the movement slowed, then stopped.

One guard guffawed. "Look! He pissed himself!"

Another voice chimed in. "I'll bet ten thousand *toman* the doctor pees himself, too."

"Nah, I won't take that. He'll *definitely* piss himself. Might shit himself, too."

Arman's heart sank. He wanted to face his death with bravery, but a tear streamed down his cheek. He'd worked so hard, made a name for himself and given himself and his mother a good life, only to die for the amusement of guards who would laugh at his death.

He closed his eyes. "Goodbye, Mom."

The kick against his chair echoed far louder than the first two. Things seemed to slow, his heartbeat drumming in his ears as the cool metal beneath his feet disappeared.

He'd had a good life, despite his unfortunate end, and even though he hadn't been able to get the information out of Iran, he *tried*. If people were too afraid to try, then nothing would change. He'd done the right thing and could take that thought with him to the grave.

His knee hit the floor before Arman fell onto his face. Pain exploded from his nose and blood streamed into his mouth and down his throat. His head pounded and stars shot in front of his eyes as the guards laughed.

"He didn't piss himself! I should have taken that bet!"

Arman shook his head, trying to clear the stars, and a new round of pain burst from behind his eyes and through his nose.

What happened? Did the rope break?

Someone yanked him up by his bindings, sending a jolt of agony through his shoulders. "Get up, indecent motherfucker."

They removed the noose and pulled off the shroud.

Beside him, three metal chairs lay on the floor, and two nooses swung from a metal apparatus above… but there were no bodies.

The guards started laughing anew, pointing at him. "You should see your face!"

"Not so high and mighty now, are you, Doctor?"

Arman's stomach sank, and the room began to spin. It had never been an execution… just another form of manipulation. Another form of torture.

If his hands hadn't been tied behind his back, he might have ripped out the tooth and thrown it at them, giving them what they wanted so they could get on with the real execution and bring his misery to an end. He gritted his teeth and steadied himself as the guard's laughter etched into his brain.

These men are insane.

Anyone who gleaned so much pleasure from the suffering of others should have been in a mental institution, not given free rein over the lives of others.

"Come on." One of the guards pulled him toward the exit. "You are going to wish you really *were* dead before the day is over."

Arman puffed out a laugh before he could stop himself. If their goal was to make him lose his mind, it might be working.

19

Tehran, Iran

GENERAL MORADI POURED himself a cup of tea and settled on the couch as the Western news agency began broadcasting the United States President's speech to the newly created European United Front.

Moradi sneered. "United Front" was a falsehood in and of itself—the organization was nothing more than a cult of anti-religious Western extremists publicly meeting to plan the genocide of God's holy army. They would not succeed. God had chosen His people, and His people would inherit the spoils when the West imploded in an inevitable fiery doom. Moradi and His army would storm over their crushed bones and build a new nation. He snickered as the cameras panned over the delegates, who wore simpering expressions. Little did they know their time on this earth was coming to an end.

President Brown took the podium and began his speech by coddling the other nations of the West. Did he know how weak he looked? They all looked weak, cowering in a high-security building, deciding the fates of countries they had nothing to do with and could never understand. "And then we have countries like Iran," Brown crooned, "who refuse the peace offered by those in this room, and who defy the International Atomic Energy Agency guidelines by continuing their efforts to obtain military-grade uranium."

Look at that pathetic crowd, Moradi boiled, *how full of fear they are. They knew Iran is the heart of God's chosen.* All Moradi needed was a weapon and the chance to use it, and they would wipe the Western threat from the world.

The American infidel continued his rant. "News arrives every day, chronicling the protests in Iran, and how instead of celebrating the right to speak one's mind, they kill their own people in cold blood rather than listening to them and being a part of positive change."

Positive change? The frightening thing was the West actually believed the lies spewing from their lips. They'd allowed the devil in and had been manipulated into believing the degradation of morality was not only a virtue, but a God-given right. How could they not see the work of the devil right underneath their noses?

Moradi sipped his tea. It mattered not. Their self-righteousness left them with their throats bared, begging to be slit. Their deaths would be on their own hands. The West needed to be cleansed so a new, *moral* world order could rise.

The crowd applauded for something the infidel said before the condemned man continued. "For the past week, Iran has been arresting not only protesters, but even dual nationality citizens who have done nothing wrong. Dr. Arman Pirouzi, invited to speak at a medical conference in his home country, was arrested hours after teaching his lessons and is now being held in an Iranian prison. Dr. Pirouzi was in the country only one day and had done nothing but share his wisdom with up-and-coming Iranian doctors for the betterment of medicine in the country of his birth—and now he is being punished for his generosity."

Moradi frowned. However erroneous his myopic understanding of right and wrong was, if he was speaking the truth, the arrest of the Iranian doctor was not something the General was aware of. He tapped his fingers on his lips. He had followers in the medical field whose goal it was to seek out doctors who'd left for the West in hopes of bringing them back home in order to protect the knowledge of God's chosen people before the Western eradication. These medical professionals were to make sure they were invited to prominent events to show the misguided how strong Iran was—they weren't meant to be arrested.

President Brown looked directly into the camera. "We are publicly calling for the release of Dr. Pirouzi and *all* those illegally detained."

Interesting. Why would they have picked out this Dr. Pirouzi in particular? Why did this one man pique the interest of a leader drowning in the troubles of his own country? Moradi leaned across the couch and picked up his phone, dialing his assistant. "Tell me what you know about the arrest of Dr. Arman Pirouzi."

There was a brief pause and the sound of a keyboard tapping. "Dr. Arman Pirouzi is located in Qeshm Prison. He is being questioned due to his association with Dr. Akbari."

"Dr. Akbari?"

"Yes, sir. Dr. Akbari was on government watch for suspected collusion with Western governments. He committed suicide when our agent went to arrest him."

"And this Dr. Pirouzi has not been executed?"

"He has not admitted guilt, but the interrogators seem certain he will eventually admit to his crimes."

Moradi nodded. Most detainees confessed to crimes eventually. Interrogation tactics stripped away the devil's work and allowed them to admit their guilt, even if many backpedaled, saying they'd been coerced into confession. Still, this man had been a guest and had taught in an Iranian hospital. He could be a valuable ally if he was, in fact, innocent.

"I would like to speak to this Dr. Pirouzi myself. In person."

"Very good, sir. When?"

"Tomorrow."

20

Qeshm Prison, Iran

THE HARD DIRT felt like a pillow beneath Arman's cheek. He was so exhausted after his mock-hanging yesterday that he barely had the strength to lift his head. He drifted, half asleep, his eyes closed.

Tiny, cold hands pressed against his cheeks and Arman opened his eyes to see Bâbak's smiling face. "Get up, Mr. Arman. You have to get out of here!"

"I can't. I'm too tired."

"You must, Mr. Arman. You must!" Bâbak's eye widened, and he gasped as someone jiggled the door and the hinges creaked.

Arman tried to push up off the floor. "Run Bâbak!" He blinked, finding himself alone.

The door swung open and a guard stepped inside. "Time to go."

Arman stared at the empty corner of his cell. Bâbak had seemed so real.

"Hey!" The guard kicked him. "I said it was time to go."

Arman rolled over. "What fun do we have in store today?" He shouldn't have been so flippant. It would likely get him beaten, but he was beyond caring. He glanced back to the space where Bâbak had been. Hopefully it had only been a dream, and not the child's ghost.

The guard leaned on the side of the door. "You're going back upstairs."

Arman blinked. He must have misheard, or had finally suffered brain damage. Why would they bring him upstairs?

The guard kicked him again. "I said, get up!"

Arman pushed himself to his feet, each movement triggering a deep ache in muscles he'd never known could ache before. "I'm coming, I'm coming."

The guard shoved him down the hall and up the stairs. The air heated with each step, quickly becoming stifling. Arman huffed a mirthless laugh. He couldn't believe he was already missing the cool air in the dungeons below.

After moving down a long hallway, the guard pulled him through a door into a humid room. "Here." He shoved a bucket in Arman's hand with a cloth and a grimy bar of soap that looked like it had been used and abandoned on a shelf to mold. "Go shower. You stink."

Arman pulled the bucket to him. *Are they serious? A shower? A real shower?* He gritted his teeth to keep from bursting into tears. He hadn't bathed since he was taken from his hotel. How long had it been? Weeks? Months?

Backing away before they changed their minds, Arman peeled off his filthy, blood-crusted smock and dropped it to the floor. If they made him put the fetid material back on, the shower would be meaningless, but at this point, even a moment of cleanliness was a blessing.

The spigot spewed black goo at first, which faded to a muddy hue, and finally a tea-like color. It wasn't perfect, but it was better than nothing. Arman eased underneath the stream and let the cool water flow over his skin. Lines of black grime flowed around his toes, circling the drain. He rolled his shoulders, rinsing the filth and mold from the soap before lathering it in his hands. There was no musky scent, no essence of pine tar or eucalyptus, but the plain, white suds were the most luxurious he'd ever felt as he rubbed them over every pore and lathered them through his hair.

"Enough!" A man approached, paying no heed to Arman's nakedness—not that he retained any real sense of modesty after all he'd been through since arriving in that horrible place. Arman turned off the water and stepped out. To his surprise the guard handed him a white towel that appeared to be freshly laundered and a stack of actual clothing instead of another loose-fitting smock that barely covered his frame. Arman quickly dried off and slipped on the pants and shirt, which, surprisingly again, seemed new.

"Good enough," the guard said. "Let's go."

He yanked Arman's arm and led him to another room with a single chair centered beneath a light swinging overhead. A chill ran down Arman's spine. Was this another form of torture? Making it seem like they were being kind, only to snatch it away at the last moment? They pushed him into the chair and a man wheeled up a tray of knives, blades, and scissors. Arman shouted and squirmed, trying to get away.

"Stay still, you fool!"

Two men held him down while the third scraped the long blade up his throat and across his beard. Arman froze, closing his eyes with relief. It wasn't torture—they were just shaving his filthy beard. Once done, they cut his hair. They gave him no mirror to check his appearance, but Arman couldn't care less. With his skin clean and face smooth, he felt *human* again.

"Come. Time is up."

A guard shoved a bag over Arman's head and pushed him through the hall. A man yelled somewhere far away, sounding like he was in pain. What new nightmare was this? Had this been a ritual cleansing? Were they purifying him before sending him to meet God?

They stopped and the hood was pulled from his head. Arman stared at a door. The guard reached over his shoulder and knocked. "Dr. Arman Pirouzi, as requested."

"Enter!" a voice boomed from within.

The guard opened the door and Arman stepped inside before the door closed behind him. A man with thick, gray hair combed to the side and a short beard sat behind a desk, scribbling on a piece of paper. He placed the sheet on top of a stack, grabbed another, then perused it for a moment before scrawling a signature and adding it to the stack. Then he placed the pen down and raised his eyes.

Arman gasped, taking a step back as he met the gaze of one of the most notorious war criminals the world had ever seen—*General Naser Moradi.*

Moradi's gaze narrowed and Arman became hyper-aware of a mark on the general's forehead, muddying his otherwise flawless appearance. Arman knew the story, that the dark indent on the general's forehead was from hours upon hours of kneeling for daily praying, head pressed to the ground on a hard clay disc called a *turbah,* a symbol of the earth. Both doctors and scholars claimed it was impossible for a mark to appear on the forehead simply from praying a lot, and many believed such marks were fabricated by pressing something hot, like the back of a spoon, on one's forehead, all to make it look like they prayed endless hours each day. Whether real or fabricated, the mark was in sharp contrast to the death and torture hidden beneath Moradi's deep, barren eyes. If the eyes truly were a window into a person's past, this man had spent no true time with God.

Of course, if Moradi caught anyone saying he was anything but one of the most pious men in the land he'd probably label that person an infidel and have them executed on the spot. *Because that's what pious people do*, Arman thought bitterly. *At least the extremists.* They blamed others for their failings and killed them to prove themselves right and silence further dissention.

Moradi stood and walked toward Arman. He was shorter than Arman expected, and rounder in the belly, with a pronounced limp—possibly a war injury. Moradi shook Arman's hand. "Hello, Dr. Pirouzi. It looks like they have been treating you well." Arman almost laughed. Was this the trick? Did they torture people for weeks and then clean them up before they met people from the outside? Was the shower and fresh clothing supposed to make it look like he had been on an extended vacation?

Moradi returned to his seat behind the desk, his limp even more pronounced from the rear. "I hope it hasn't been so bad for you, Doctor. After all, you are our guest."

Arman tried to deliver a smile but couldn't manage.

Moradi examined him. "Do you know what your verdict is?"

Verdict? A verdict meant there had been a trial. All Arman had been subjected to was torture and questioning. He took a deep breath. "No. I haven't done anything wrong."

The General laughed. "You know what you have done." He leaned back in his chair. "Doctor, I am going to tell you two stories." Arman was sure he didn't want to hear them, but anything that kept him from actual torture was a blessing. "I am sure you have heard of the good cop and the bad cop." Moradi adjusted the pages on the table. "Today, depending on your answers, I am going to play both."

A chill raced over Arman's skin—one of far too many chills since arriving in a place with such a hot climate.

Moradi continued. "The first story goes back to forty-four years ago. My parents used to be housekeepers of a *Baha'i* before the revolution. This man pretended that he loved me like his son, but he had traitorous intentions. He tried to turn me away from God." He grimaced. "When I understood what he was trying to do to me with his pretentious kindness, I raided his house with a group of believers. He begged for his and his family's lives. After all those years, I felt for them and I let them go. But I didn't do it until he gave me the list of all *Savak* agents in the city of Shiraz. See, we had a deal. He kept his promise, and I kept mine. Although, years later, he was assassinated in the streets of Paris. God will always find a way to punish infidels when needed."

His murky smile told Arman everything he needed to know—the assassination had not been random, but targeted, and Moradi probably orchestrated it. Arman wondered if Moradi had the entire family executed on the same day or if some were left to mourn and warn others about what happened to anyone with progressive thinking. Arman did his best to keep his face serene. He was dealing with a monster.

Moradi smiled. "The second story happened about ten years later. I was on the front line fighting with Iraqis at the time. We were defending our country. Do you know what they used to call me?"

Arman shook his head.

"They called me 'the tank hijacker.' I used to go after midnight to the Iraqi front line and kill the guards and steal anything I could find. One day, I came back with a tank. That is when the nickname started." Moradi sat back, steepling his fingers. "Near the end of the war, I discovered the Supreme Leader had accepted a ceasefire deal. The government was running out of money, equipment, and, most importantly, volunteers to fight on the front line." He tapped his fingers on the desktop. "They estimated that we would lose the war in six months if the situation was not rectified." The tapping paused. "However, I also learned that the Supreme Leader had been diagnosed with cancer and he had about six months to live."

It felt like the temperature in the room had increased just from the general's intensity.

"Acceptance of the ceasefire and the power void created by his death were enough to take the government down. That's when I received a call from one of my friends, who was the head of Evin Prison in Tehran. He told me I was needed to help him with a task crucial for the future of our culture." Moradi's eyes lanced Arman's. "We had more than ten thousand political prisoners in the country, mainly in Evin Prison. Many of these people were set to be released in the next couple of years. Out there, any whom the prisons had failed to rehabilitate and bring back to God would be a threat to the government. So, the plan was to bring them in one-by-one and ask them if they accepted the government's rules and ideology. If the answer was no, they would be executed, even if they had a few days left of their sentence."

Arman nodded slowly. He remembered the horrific news stories.

Moradi leaned on the edge of the table. "The problem was some of these infidels were virgin girls and, as you know, virgins are pure and go straight to heaven. We couldn't have that. If they went against God in this life, they didn't deserve the eternal reward afforded to the rest of us."

Arman gulped. He knew where this was going.

Moradi leaned toward Arman. "I went to Qom and asked one of the high-ranked mullahs to give me a fatwa so he could enter the prison and wed the women to the prison guards." His smile broadened. "It was quite a gift for those guards. A new wife each night." His eyes darkened. "And the next morning, the traitorous women went to hell where they belonged."

Arman swallowed down the bile building in his throat. If they were legally married, it would not be considered rape. Some of the men probably married more than one woman a night. It was bad enough that the women were surely tortured in the prisons trying the get them to confess, but to be brutalized one last time before their deaths… it was evil beyond human comprehension.

Moradi smiled at the horror on Arman's face. "Do you know why I am telling you these stories?"

"I have no idea."

"I want to make it clear that I will do whatever needs to be done for our cause. For the Supreme Leader. For God. I demand the same standard from all my followers."

"*Your* followers?"

Moradi's grin widened. "I told you about the assassination of my father's former employer. I told you about hijacking tanks, and I told you about giving those infidel bitches what they deserved. God has granted me the ability to do anything in my power to foster His cause. Now understand this, Dr. Pirouzi: The only way you will get out of here is with full cooperation. Do you understand?"

Arman's shoulders sagged. He'd hoped this might be the end of his torture, but it seemed like it was only the beginning. Moradi slammed his fist on the table. "Do you understand!?"

Arman nodded, fear pumping through his veins. "Yes. Yes, I understand."

"Good." Moradi sat back. "Now, let me ask you a few questions. Where is the information you took out of Akbari's pacemaker? Who introduced him to you? And finally, why did he kill himself when we went to arrest him?"

Arman gasped, then immediately wished he hadn't. "M-my patient killed himself? Why?"

The General slammed the desk again. "You know why. What was in that pacemaker?" So, Akbari was dead. It was horrible, but also probably the only reason Arman was still alive—they had no one else to torture for the information. Arman looked at Moradi and saw him for what he was—an old, pathetic fanatic in decline. He smiled, amused at the thought that this *powerful* man had come here in person to try to get the knowledge Arman had.

Moradi picked up a sheet of paper, perused it, and placed it back down in the same pile he'd taken it from. "Today is your lucky day. We have a message from your president stating that if we kill you, he will disclose classified information regarding our nuclear program that will undoubtedly make the Security Council authorize military action against Iran." Arman tried to keep his face neutral, but the shock still showed on his face. All this time, he'd thought the CIA and the United States had forgotten about him.

Moradi swiped his arm across the desk, scattering papers on the floor. "We are not idiots, Doctor," he roared. "You come to this country and somehow end up removing the pacemaker of the chief scientist of our nuclear facilities. The next day, the hospital's security reviews the recording and notices that you took something out of the pacemaker during the surgery. And now this message from your president! I would kill you right now if it didn't mean serious consequences for our government. Instead, I am going to make sure that you'll enjoy the next days *thoroughly* until we reach an agreement with your president."

That meant they would make him miserable, but at least he'd survive. The United States had Moradi in an unescapable situation. He looked trapped, and Arman felt a burst of pride at how *helpless* the demon looked—and he had contributed to it. Arman sat a little taller. "My country does not negotiate with terrorists."

The General stood, circled behind him, and slapped his head hard. A high-pitched buzz filled his ear, his cheek tingling with warmth from the handprint as warm blood trickled from his ear.

Moradi stormed out the door. "Take this piece of shit to his cell and let him think about his pathetic life!" Two guards entered and pulled Arman to his feet. The moment he was out of the office, a hood was pushed over his head and he was dragged down the hall. He stumbled forward until someone gave him a hard shove and he careened down a stairway, crashing and bumping until he slammed to a halt on a landing. Groaning, Arman lay there stunned as footfalls stomped down the stairs.

"What happened, Doctor? Are you really that clumsy? Let me help you." A boot met Arman's ribs. He coughed. Another kick to the stomach rolled him over. Then a kick to the back. Then the head.

The world started to spin. He should have told Moradi what he wanted to know. Then, at least, this torture would have been over.

21

Tehran, Iran

FIFTEEN-YEAR-OLD Masoumeh Moradi pulled at the edges of her hijab as she turned up the television. Faces of protestors flashed across the screen before the photo of a man in a lab coat appeared next to a newscaster. "Dr. Arman Pirouzi, an expatriate visiting Iran under the guise of speaking at a conference, is being detained in an undisclosed location. The esteemed General Moradi reports that Dr. Pirouzi is a guest and is being held for questioning under suspicion of espionage. The United States Government is demanding Dr. Pirouzi's release, falsely claiming that he is being tortured."

Masoumeh frowned, focusing on Dr. Pirouzi's kind eyes as his picture faded from the screen. Her father certainly wouldn't hold someone prisoner unless they'd done something wrong, but the doctor's eyes seemed good, joyous even... filled with God's love. Certainly, that couldn't be faked. She heard some of the story several weeks ago, how the medical community was excited for his arrival and about the generosity of his teaching and the time he spent answering their questions. What caused even more excitement was Dr. Pirouzi performed complicated surgeries while the doctors and students watched, and he then answered questions about his techniques.

That kind of teaching wasn't available in a textbook. Masoumeh wished she were older and could have been there to see him perform surgery firsthand. She only hoped his arrest wouldn't stop more doctors from coming to Iran and sharing their knowledge, though she knew it likely would. If things didn't get better by the time she was old enough to go to school—assuming her father *allowed* her to go to school—no one would want to come to her country and she'd be left with only the knowledge currently available in Iran, which was subpar compared to the advancements in the West.

The door opened and her father entered.

Maman came in from the kitchen. "Good evening to the mighty General Moradi." She smiled and gave him a hug. "How was your day?"

"Better now that I am here with my two favorite ladies."

"Baba!" Masoumeh ran to him and gave him a hug.

He kissed her forehead. "How are you, my wonderful gift from God?"

"I'm good! Maman taught me how to make *sholezard* today."

"Well, that sounds delicious. Why don't you go clean up and get ready to eat?"

"Yes, Baba!" Masoumeh scampered to her room.

Raziyeh Moradi wrung her fingers, hoping Masoumeh wouldn't bring up the protesters again. Even the mention would anger her father greatly. When her daughter ran to her room, Raziyeh released her hands, glad Masoumeh was more excited about dessert than focused on the recent unrest. Moradi followed Raziyeh into the kitchen. Today had been an insightful, if not discouraging day, and Raziyeh wasn't sure she should bring up the conversation she'd had with their daughter to Moradi.

Masoumeh had confided to her that she hoped to go to university and study to be a great scientist. She wanted to find cures for disease and put Iran on the map for medical advancements. Of course, the great General Moradi would be behind anyone in Iran making medical advancements, but perhaps not by a woman, because in his heart he knew a man could do better.

When Raziyeh's father told her that she would be given to General Moradi in marriage, she was horrified to find out he was thirty years older than her. He had proven to be a dutiful husband, though, as well as a good father. Still, she dreaded the day when her daughter found out her dreams were controlled by a man who loved her but still didn't think she had the capability of adding value to society other than procreation.

Once Masoumeh was behind a closed door, Moradi gave Raziyeh a kiss. "Hello, my joy." He reached into the cabinet and grabbed three plates and utensils, arranging them on the table.

"You don't need to do that," Raziyeh said. "You work hard all day long."

He kissed her on the head again. "Nonsense. The best part of my day is always helping you."

The sound of the television drew his attention away from her. "And the Supreme Leader vows that he will never forget that in the last drone strike, we lost ten of God's soldiers, including Colonel Sardar Shafighi, a close friend of the Supreme Leader's right hand, General Naser Moradi."

Moradi grimaced, and Raziyeh wished she'd turned the television off. Their time together when he first came home was always a blessing. It reminded her of when they were younger and he didn't carry the worries of the country's future on his shoulders.

His glare softened slightly as he turned to her. "I will have my revenge soon. Sardar's death will not go unanswered." Declaring someone's imminent death usually released some of his tension, but to Raziyeh he still seemed like his thoughts were distant.

"What bothers you, my husband?"

He pursed his lips, as if deciding how to answer. "I was contacted by the mullah."

"Sheikh Rahimi?"

He nodded. Sheikh Rahimi had been a longtime friend of their family and Sardar's family, as well as being their blessed mullah. "He told me that I have a responsibility to Sardar's family."

"Of course you do. We were all close."

His gaze turned to her. He looked upset, but then a coldness swept over his features, like any time he was forced to do something he didn't want—usually for the good of God or the country. Raziyeh tensed. It never meant anything good.

Moradi straightened. "The mullah directed me that it is God's will that I take Sardar's oldest daughter as a second wife."

Raziyeh blinked in surprise. "But you told me I was all you wanted. You said you'd never take a second wife."

He stood. "Don't you think I know that?"

She shrunk away. She should have known better than to question, but she had to speak her mind. "You are sixty-two. That girl is only sixteen years old."

Moradi nodded. "The mullah said that she will birth me many sons for God's army."

Raziyeh flinched. Many *sons*. She had only birthed him daughters. Was that what this was really about? Was she about to be forced to share her beloved husband so his blood could spawn more soldiers?

Tears streamed from her eyes. "This isn't fair. I love you."

He hugged her and kissed her forehead. "It's what God wants, so we will comply."

Raziyeh shivered. The girl was far too young, but also very beautiful. She couldn't help but wonder if this edict from the mullah had come as a pleasant surprise to her husband. Perhaps it had even been orchestrated by him.

Masoumeh ran into the kitchen. "Are you ready to try my *sholezard*?" Her mother's tear-filled eyes widened before she turned away, wiping her face. "What's wrong?" Masoumeh asked.

"Nothing, dearest. Let's eat."

As they ate, Masoumeh's thoughts turned to Dr. Pirouzi. Her father was an important general, and he probably knew the truth about what was going on.

"Father, do you know of the man detained as a spy? Dr. Arman Pirouzi?"

He glanced at her, then back to his plate. "Of course."

"What did he do?"

"We don't know yet, my dear God's gift. We think it has to do with a procedure he did on someone, but we don't have any evidence. We are trying to make him talk."

That sounded ominous. "How are you trying to make him talk?"

"Well, there are techniques that we can use."

Masoumeh flinched. "Like torture?" She'd heard rumors, but she knew her father was a good, godly man—she saw it every day. Certainly, he would not be involved in anything bad.

"I wouldn't call it torturing, but we do have ways to make him talk."

Masoumeh lowered her eyes. Anything that would *make* someone talk had to be uncomfortable, which sounded very much like torture. "I thought torturing was forbidden in our religion."

Her father's eyes flashed, becoming dark and ominous. He stood, looking a thousand times taller than normal. "You wouldn't understand. You are just a girl."

"Then help me understand. Torture is not allowed. It's in the book."

Her mother grabbed her arm. "Masoumeh!"

Her father slammed his fist on the table. "I will not be questioned, especially by a woman. Our people are chosen by God. Iran will be the seat of God's power in the Middle East and beyond. To achieve that, we need to protect our government at all costs. That includes my own family. There is no red line when it comes to doing God's work."

Masoumeh lowered her eyes. "Of course, Father."

But how could they be doing God's work if they were doing things that were directly forbidden by God? And maybe even more disturbing, although she'd never say so out loud, was that he called her a *woman* with palpable disdain in his voice. How could she go from being a "gift from God" to being spoken of with no more affection than a dog in mere minutes?

As her father shoved food into his mouth, Masoumeh glanced across the table. Her mother's eyes seemed to plead with her to hold her tongue, so she remained silent. Still, her father's angry words hung in the air, and for the first time in her life, she felt sick to her stomach just looking at him.

"I am done." Masoumeh's father threw his utensils on the table and stood, storming from the room.

Masoumeh wanted to remind him she made dessert, but decided it wouldn't taste as sweet if he were in the room. Her mother seemed oddly somber as she watched him leave and close himself in his office.

Masoumeh took her mother's hand. "Why were you crying when I came in?"

She forced a smile. "Oh, my dearest, they were tears of joy. God has chosen me to be part of a great test of faith."

Masoumeh tilted her head. "A test of faith? How so?"

"The mullah has chosen a second wife for your father. This is a great blessing because she will give your father many sons. You will finally have brothers." She forced a smile. "I am grateful for this test, and I am happy to help him with this."

Help him? By doing what, standing back while he takes another woman to his bed? The West had many faults, but growing up in a family with one mother was something Masoumeh had grown accustomed to. Her mother's smile seemed plastic as her eyes filled with tears again. "We will support your father in this and welcome his new wife as a sister."

A new sister? Would she be living with them? "Who is this woman?"

"Sardar's daughter, Ra'ana Shafighi."

Masoumeh's mouth fell agape. "What? She is only a year older than me!"

Her mother stood. "I am aware of that, but she is in her birthing years. This is probably why the mullah tells us God wants her in a place where she can be productive."

"Productive? She's a girl, not a sheep. She's being brought here to breed!"

Her mother placed her finger over Masoumeh's lips. "Keep your voice down."

"Or what?"

She pressed her entire hand over Masoumeh's lips and moved closer, whispering, "You heard him. 'We need to protect our government at all costs.' That includes his own family. 'There is no red line when it comes to doing God's work.'"

Masoumeh frowned and whispered, "What are you saying?"

"Your father has done unspeakable things to his own friends and family in the name of God. He loves us with all his heart, but he will put God first, always."

Normally, Masoumeh would have thought that was a good thing, but it appeared that she and her father had a much different definition of *God's work*.

22

Imam Hospital, Qeshm, Iran

"YOU NEED ME to see a new patient now?" Dr. Zhina Farzin glared at her boss. "It's the end of my shift. You can try to save a dying man just as easily as I can."

Dr. Taghavi smiled at her, adjusting his thick-framed glasses. "Being in charge has its benefits. Now, I get to go home on time and let you take care of the constant stream of scum coming from Qeshm Prison." She held his gaze. The hospital's closeness to Qeshm prison was the whole reason she'd accepted this transfer. Qeshm held some of the vilest criminals in the country. Murderers, rapists, and even worse— traitors.

Zhina sighed. "I've only been here for a week, and I've already lost three patients from that prison. How does that look on my record when so many of my patients die?"

Taghavi took a sip of his drink and started walking toward the exit. "Then it would be a good idea for you to make sure this new patient doesn't die." Zhina rolled her eyes to the ceiling. If the guards realized how bad of a state their prisoners were in and brought them to her earlier, there would be a much better chance of saving them. Of course, with some of the injuries, it was quite possible that bringing the prisoners to the hospital was just a public relations stunt made to make it appear the government cared about the poor souls housed within.

Zhina, maybe more so than anyone on the outside, knew that this was the furthest from the truth. Some of the injuries the guards claimed were "accidental" seemed like anything but accidents. For instance, how could so many prisoners have lacerations on top of previous lacerations on the soles of their feet? And why were so many of them infected, like they had walked through sewage? How was it possible so many of them seemed to have fallen down the stairs? Was there something about the prison that made people inadvertently clumsy? Of course not, unless heartless men with guns caused clumsiness.

She pushed through the hall to the critical wing. Things were bad enough with the violence on the streets and innocent people getting caught in the crossfire of radical extremists and protestors. A nurse handed her a chart. "Dr. Farzin, thank goodness you're here. This one is in rough shape." They usually were, or the prison doctors would have taken care of them, at least enough to get back to the torture.

She hung the chart on the wall and continued reading while she adjusted her hijab. The patient had a shoulder injury and multiple rib fractures due to accidentally falling on 'multiple objects.' She had a feeling those objects were boots worn by IRGC guards. This poor man, labeled "Prisoner B-12956421," also showed the typical signs of falling down prison stairs and Qeshm Prison's infamous infected slashes on his feet.

She sighed. How could they be allowed to get away with things like this?

It was shaping up to be a very long day. Surveying all this man's injuries by herself would take hours. It was patients like this that had forced her to make a horrible choice less than six months ago. Her husband complained that his dinners were never ready when he got home from work and that the laundry wasn't done in a timely manner. She explained that sometimes she was unable to leave work on time, but he didn't care and he told her he needed a wife, not a doctor. So, he divorced her and took a younger wife, one ready to serve him at every waking moment.

A quiet, subservient wife simply wasn't who she was, even before she became a doctor. She wanted an equal relationship, one where they shared duties and appreciated each other. She thought her husband was that kind of man, but you never really knew what a person was like until you lived with them.

The nurse shifted her weight. "They also said that he needs to be in good condition for interrogation tomorrow." Zhina laughed. The gall of these people! They wanted her to save him so they could turn around and throw him down another staircase. It would almost be more humane to give these men lethal injections rather than send them back to the hell waiting for them in that awful prison.

The nurse lowered her eyes. "I'm sorry. They ordered me to make sure I told you that they wanted him back as quickly as possible."

Zhina placed her hand on the woman's shoulder. "I'm sorry. It's not your fault."

Zhina was a specialist in physical therapy and rehabilitation, which was another reason Dr. Taghavi started assigning her to the prison cases. Taghavi only wanted to treat patients and be done with them. He wanted nothing to do with long-term care and quality of life, which, she had to agree, seemed unnecessary if she was only sending prisoners back to be executed. Still, she'd do her best. If anything, it would at least give the poor man hope.

She opened the door and approached the bed, freezing as she stared into the beaten, swollen face of *Dr. Pirouzi, the American doctor on the news*. She grabbed the edge of the bed to steady herself as the room started to spin. *It had been nearly twenty years since she'd seen the man.*

"Dr. Farzin!" The nurse gripped her shoulder. "Are you okay?"

Okay was a relative term. Her heart skipped a beat and her breathing became ragged. This man was the entire reason she accepted this transfer. His name was all over the news. Still, part of her didn't think it was possible that she was standing in the same room as Arman Pirouzi. They met at medical school in the United States and started dating soon after.

They'd been filled with so many hopes and dreams and had fallen in love, planning to start a family in the United States and make history with their medical advancements.

So many plans… until her father's stroke during the last few months of medical school brought them all crashing down. Her father needed long-term care, and her mother had been unable to do it on her own. As their only child, it was Zhina's duty to return to Iran and help. She begged Arman to come back to Iran with her after they graduated. All the dreams they had could still be achieved there.

Arman begged her to stay in America.

"Iran is our past," he said. "The United States is our future. This is where we'll be able to make the advancements we've been dreaming of."

Zhina wasn't ready to sacrifice her duty to her family, and Arman wasn't willing to give up on the dream of the United States.

"I'm sorry," Arman said, "but I promised I'd never go back there. My life is here, now."

Leaving Arman was the hardest thing she'd ever done. He'd broken her heart, so much so she didn't think twice when her mother said they'd found her a husband. She met Ali, they went out a few times, and he seemed nice enough. Their first few years together were fine, at least until she started residency in an underserved hospital in Qeshm island.

"Dr. Farzin, are you sure you're okay?"

Zhina shook away the mental fog. "Yes, of course. Let's get him some fluids, and I want to examine all his injuries while he's still unconscious." That was at least one simple kindness she could give him. If he was awake, moving him to different rooms would have been painful. Also, with this many broken bones, there was no way she'd be returning him tomorrow. He'd need considerable therapy.

They probably only wanted him conscious, not perfect, but she'd do her best to keep him at the hospital. She might not be able to free him, but she would make him healthy and keep him out of that prison as long as possible.

23

Imam Hospital, Iran

SOMETHING BEEPED PERSISTENTLY. Arman groaned, trying to turn over and pull the covers over his head, but he couldn't move. *Why can't I move?* And what was that *incessant* beeping? His eyes fluttered open, and the blurry overhead light stung his eyes. The smell of antiseptic filled the room, and the air tasted clean and cool.

Had the prison been a dream, or was *this* the dream?

Someone leaned over him, blocking the light, and two beautiful brown eyes focused on him.

"Can you hear me?"

Those eyes spoke to him more than the words, but they did not belong to a woman in a hijab. They belonged to a woman he knew, bright, alive, and free, a doctor with a long, black ponytail and dreams even grander than his own. He warmed inside, remembering happier days. "Zhina? Am I dead?" His voice was raspy and dry. How long had he been asleep?

"Shh." She dabbed a cold towel over his brow. "Let me get you some ice chips."

Ice chips? *Definitely heaven.*

The ice felt like glorious freedom, but unless the USA had rescued him while he was unconscious, he still wasn't free. He glanced around the room. "Hospital?"

Zhina nodded. "You are in Imam Hospital, just a few miles from Qeshm Prison." Arman closed his eyes. So, it hadn't simply been the worst of nightmares.

She stood and grabbed his chart. "I did a thorough exam and took multiple X-rays while you were unconscious. You have a brain hemorrhage, a broken shoulder, and three cracked ribs. You're also severely dehydrated and malnourished. That's on top of needing intravenous antibiotics for a growing infection in both of your feet. Frankly, I'm not sure why you're not in worse shape." She leaned down closer. "With the exception of some odd devices that I felt under your skin but accidentally forgot to mention in your chart." She stood again.

So, she was still the same old Zhina he'd known so long ago. Maybe there really was a God if He'd landed Arman in her hospital by happenstance.

Her expression saddened slightly. "What are you doing here, Arman? You told me you'd never step foot back in Iran."

"Well, you said you got a good look at my body. That means you probably have a pretty good idea of why I came back." Or who'd sent him. That kind of hardware wasn't easy to come by, even for a doctor.

She stared at him before she began to pace. "It's been so long, Arman."

"Twenty years. Before becoming a guest at Qeshm Prison, I could have told you the months, weeks, and days it's been since I've seen you, but being imprisoned has a way of making a man lose track of time."

She stopped and stared before beginning to pace anew. "I heard about Niki."

Arman nodded. "That was one of the reasons why I agreed to come back."

"Maybe you shouldn't have."

"This is bigger than me. It's bigger than both of us."

She put her arms around herself like she was giving herself a hug. "Things are so bad here; you have no idea."

Arman ached to tell her he wished she would have stayed, that they would have gotten married and started a family and made all the medical advancements they'd both dreamed of. But there was no use in dwelling on what could have been. "Has there been any communication with the United States? Are they lobbying for my release?"

Zhina shook her head. "I have no idea. The guards brought you in here with no name, only a prison number. You were just another nameless face they wanted me to patch up and send back to them. It's driving me insane." She crossed the room and stood beside his bed again. A firm resolve crossed over her features. "Whatever you did, or they *think* you did, doesn't matter to me. How can I help you?"

"You already have by not mentioning my implants. Anything else would only put you in more danger." He sighed, looking around the room. The hospital seemed fairly modern, the equipment only a few years behind what would be common in the United States. "It looks like you have a good life here. I don't want to make things worse for you."

She pulled on the ends of her hijab. "Look at me. Do you remember me telling you how these things used to strangle me? It's no different now. Yes, I'm a doctor, but I still don't have my freedom. Not like I did in the United States."

Arman knew that no matter what he said, it would be the wrong thing, so he decided to get away from the topic. "How are your parents?"

"They're both gone."

Arman's heart clenched. She'd loved them so much—so much she'd given up her freedom for them. "I'm sorry." But did that mean she was alone here? "A husband? Children?"

"I'm divorced. No children."

If they met under different circumstances, it would have been wonderful news. They could pick up where they left off and maybe rekindle the life they could have lived together. But Arman was fooling himself if he thought he'd ever get out of

Iran alive. If the United States hadn't come for him by now, they likely never would.

Her gaze remained glued to his. "Please tell me how I can help you."

"We both know that there's no way you can help me that wouldn't put a target on your back. I can't ask that of you."

"Yet you can ask that of yourself? I'm sure you've seen the news. You knew what you were walking into when you stepped foot back in this country, yet you still came."

"They'd kill you if they found out we were even having this conversation."

"Niki was willing to die for what she believed in. The government is staying in control because people are afraid. *Women* are afraid. Niki did the right thing to stand up for what she believed in, and I should too."

Arman closed his eyes. He should say no. He should curse at her, tell her that he never cared about her, anything to make her walk away. But she knew him too well. She was all he had, and without her, he was as good as dead.

He tried to keep his face stern. "I'm afraid you'll get hurt or killed."

"You're American now. You shouldn't be making decisions for the women in your life." She tugged on her hijab again. "I'm dying here, in this life. I've been sheltered for so long. Let me do the right thing. Give me a reason to wake up in the morning. Give me a reason to feel good about myself.

Give me something to look forward to, not just for me, but for every little girl who wants to rip off her hijab and burn it."

Niki had said that if she didn't stand up for what was right, who would? Maybe Zhina was right. Sitting idly by while atrocities happened did nothing. Everyday people, not politicians and dignitaries, needed to do something to make a difference. For Arman, that meant getting the information stored in his tooth to the right authorities to hopefully stop a war.

"The only way I think you could possibly help me is to find a way to let the United States government know where I am. I'm sure they'd be very interested in seeing me safely returned." He opened his eyes wide, hoping to make her understand it was imperative he got back alive, not just for himself, but to complete his mission—although he dared not say that out loud.

She paled slightly, then nodded. "I can call someone or send an e-mail."

Arman shook his head. "No. That would be too dangerous. Any digital footprint or call record could be traced back to you and you'd be arrested." He rubbed his eyes, and the tubes in his hands caught his blanket, tugging them painfully. "Trust me, many of the screams I've heard at night in the prison belonged to women. The guards would not have mercy on you. In fact, it would likely be even worse for you than it has been for me."

Zhina started pacing again, tapping her fingers against her lips. The gesture sent him right back to medical school. She used to do it while they'd studied together. They would drill each other on definitions, and whenever she had to think, she would pace. She was just as beautiful now as she'd ever been, even in the hijab, though he wished he could see her hair. Hopefully she hadn't been forced to cut it off.

Zhina stopped and spun toward him. "I have an idea!"

He'd seen that look in her eyes before... the grim determination of a woman with an idea and no way to stop her from carrying it out.

Hopefully, the idea wouldn't get them both killed.

24

Dusatku Village, Qeshm, Iran

ZHINA STEPPED OFF the wooden planks erected over the
dunes, and her shoes sunk into rich, warm sand. The breeze
carried the scent of fresh, salty air as waves lapped the shore.
Sun glistened off the water as she made her way down the
beach to the small village that had become like a second home
to her.

As she neared the makeshift huts, the pleasant sounds of
someone playing a jirba filled the air. The man holding the
tanned goatskin smiled at her between breaths. She clapped in
time to the music as he blew into the yellow skin, squeezed the
sides of the flower-patterned bag, and beautiful music came
from the pipes attached to where the goat leg had once been.

Zhina smiled. She found it wonderful how all parts of an
animal were used in this culture. They'd found a way to create

music with nothing but the gifts of nature, right down to the boiled reeds sculpted by artisans, natural twine, and wax.

It felt like a lifetime ago that she'd been on this beach, enjoying a relaxed evening, when someone cried for help.

> *An Afro-Iranian woman ran onto the wide stretch of sand, shouting for a doctor. Zhina knew most doctors would turn the other way rather than help people in a community too poor for a doctor's services, but that wasn't who she was. In Iran, she wasn't held to the Hippocratic Oath. In Iran, it was considered an oath to a heathen god, but no matter the oath's origins, Zhina believed in its principles. She had medical training most could only dream of, even accomplished doctors in Iran, and it would be wrong of her to look the other way if a person was in need.*
>
> *"I'm a doctor!" Zhina shouted.*
>
> *The woman looked relieved. "It's my neighbor. She's having a baby and it won't come out!"*
>
> *Zhina worried. The area was inhabited by mostly Afro-Iranian fishermen, descendants of slaves in ancient times who remained clustered together as tradesmen ever since. Most of the women couldn't afford hospitals, so they simply relied on midwives or neighbors to get them*

through childbirth. In normal circumstances, that was fine, but a breech birth could be a death sentence for both the mother and the baby.

The small hut was filled with people when Zhina entered. Almost a dozen women crowded around a pregnant woman lying on the dirt floor. "I found a doctor!" the woman she met on the beach announced.

A man with lines of worry creasing his brow approached. "My name is Isâ. I thank you for being willing to help. Just tell me what you need."

Zhina pushed up her sleeves. "I'll need water to keep things clean, and we need more air to breathe. Everyone but immediate family needs to leave." She looked at the terrified faces as the woman on the ground screamed. "And everyone needs to stay calm."

After three hours, Zhina placed the crying baby girl in the arms of the father, and then worked with a local midwife to try and stabilize the mother. She'd lost too much blood, though. If they were in a hospital they could start an IV or maybe even call an interventionalist like Arman to stop the bleeding. Zhina would have had medical equipment and other trained doctors to help her. But as it was, all she could do was place the baby in the mother's arms and *give her a chance to hold her child once before she died.*

As the mother's eyes fluttered closed for the last time, the father wiped away his tears, taking the baby into his arms and speaking to her, "You are truly a gift from God." He smiled as his new daughter's tiny fingers wrapped around his thumb. "Your mother was a wonderful woman, and I will teach you all about her."

"I'm very sorry for your loss," Zhina said. "I did everything I could."

He nodded. "Without you, I would have lost both of them. I am forever in your debt."

A few months later, Zhina returned to check on them and discovered the child had a club foot. The father, Isâ, started to cry. "I hoped it would fix itself!"

"It's not a death sentence. The treatment is pretty straightforward. She will have to wear a cast, and then the muscles will need to be stretched once a week, and then a new cast put on. It's a long process and will take probably ten weeks, but after that, she can wear a brace for a while, and eventually, she'll be running like any other child."

Isâ gaped. "Ten weeks? Ten casts? I don't have that kind of money."

Zhina smiled. "I need the practice, and I love fish. How about I come once a week for a good meal and change out the cast and do therapy while I'm here?"

Isâ beamed. "I'm a fisherman. I can get you all the fish you want."

The treatment had gone well, but the therapy, even after little Mona had learned to walk, had been slow. Zhina ended up visiting regularly for years until her new husband and her job kept her away. She'd given therapy routines to Isâ, instructing him to do them with little Mona every day, even if the child started to do better, in the hopes that one day no one would even be able to notice a limp.

Isâ hugged Zhina, thanking her for the years of help, telling her, "I will be forever in your debt."

Zhina slowed as she walked through the small huts lined up on the sand. She'd never intended to call in this debt, but Isâ was the only person she could think of with the ability to help her. The humble, simply dressed fisherman lifted his head as she approached and a wide smile burst across his face. He ran over to greet her.

"My friend!" he said, giving her a tight hug. "It is so good to see you!"

"And you," Zhina replied. "It's been too long."

He tugged her to the hut. "Come, let me get you some fish."

Zhina laughed. Elsewhere, fish was considered a luxury, but in this village, it was their livelihood. The sea offered them unlimited food without having to use their meager earnings to buy what they needed to survive.

After a delicious meal and catching up, Zhina rested her hand on the table. She needed to stop with the pleasantries and do what she'd come here to do. "You told me a story once, how your boat got caught in a storm, and you were lost at sea for some time."

"Five days! I thought I was dead!"

"But you were picked up by an American ship, and they brought you back home."

He nodded. "Yes, I got lucky. Once you get far out to sea, there are many ships."

Zhina nodded. The Iranian government often complained about the Western warships "plaguing" their waters. "I need to ask you a favor."

Isâ sat straighter, detecting the change in her tone. "Anything."

"You are under no obligation to say yes, and it would not affect our friendship."

"I will say again: *anything*. You gave up time for me and my daughter for years. That is a debt I am more than ready to repay in any means within my power." She looked down. Isâ was such a kind and giving man. She'd seen him help repair his neighbors' huts and give fish to those who were sick, helping them survive until they were well enough to return to their own boats. He lived a meager life here, but a good one. It was wrong of her to ask him to risk himself.

She stood. "I changed my mind. I need to go."

Isâ grabbed her arm. "Sit and tell me what you need."

Zhina lowered her eyes. "You are a good man, and you have a young daughter."

"A daughter I would not have if it weren't for the kindness of a stranger who could have ignored our cries for help. Now, tell me what you need."

She met his gaze. "This request will mean risking your life."

He stared at her. "And whatever this is… it is important to you?"

She nodded. The sounds of children laughing carried through the window. Isâ glanced out, smiled, and then returned his gaze to Zhina. "If anything happens to me because of this request, or any other mishap, would you do me the honor of taking Mona as your own?"

Zhina's eyes widened. It had been years since she'd considered having children. In many ways, she hadn't been happy enough with her ex-husband to bring a new life into the world, and work had always seemed more important. But she dearly loved Mona already. She couldn't think of the child with anyone else.

She smiled. "Yes, I would be honored to be her godmother."

Isâ gripped her shoulder. "Then make your request."

Zhina studied the lines on her palms. It was too much to ask, but she had no one else. She swallowed down the dryness building in her throat. "I need you to take your boat back out into the Persian Gulf and find another American ship."

He frowned, and she understood why. The last time he found himself in the vast expanse of the Persian Gulf, it was an accident. His boat was small and meant for local fishing runs, not the deep sea. Going out there purposely to find Americans would also mean he'd have to go out on his own, without a crew. In the Persian Gulf, that was risky enough, even if there wasn't the fear of getting caught.

Isâ shook his head, as if trying to ward off the shock. "Why would you ask this?"

She bit her bottom lip. "There is a doctor in my hospital who has been detained in Qeshm Prison. His name is Arman Pirouzi. He has information that the Americans need, but they don't know where to rescue him. I need someone to give them his location."

Isâ's eyes went wide as he gaped at her. "He is an American spy. A traitor to his people."

Zhina tilted her head. "You and I both know that the media tells us what they want us to think, not the truth."

Mona walked in and reached for a small bucket by the door. Her simple cotton frock was soiled and her bare feet were caked in dirt. The little girl looked up and smiled. "Dr. Zhina!" Leaving the bucket, she ran to Zhina, giving her a hug. The child was damp and smelled like salt water. "I was able to run today, just like you always said I would!"

Zhina smiled, messing her hair. "I knew you would."

Mona hugged her again. "Father always said that God sent you to us to give me feet to walk on. Thank you." Her eyes widened. "But I have to meet my friends back on the beach!" She spun, grabbed the bucket, and ran off.

Isâ watched her go. "I have a confession. All those years ago, I acted surprised when you told me she had a problem with her foot, but I already knew."

"Why didn't you tell me?"

His eyes started to tear, and he wiped them. "All the other doctors said she'd never walk. One even suggested sending her to God early to avoid living in a world that would not accept her." Zhina stared in shock. How could anyone tell that to a father? Too many people here would rather give up on a child than do the work to help them flourish—especially if that child was a girl.

Isâ smiled. "Then, once again, you appeared, as if God heard my prayers." He lifted his chin, firm resolve in his eyes. "I owe you my daughter's life. I will help you. Whatever danger it is to me is nothing. Just tell me exactly what you want me to say."

25

Persian Gulf

ISÂ ADJUSTED HIS engines, heading for the small dot on the horizon. Normally, he'd do everything in his power to avoid the massive warships posturing on the edge of "international waters." Before, when he drifted out to sea with no engines, the first reaction from the soldiers was to point guns at him. Luckily, there was someone on board the massive ship who understood him and believed he was in trouble and not there to do them or their ship harm. Hopefully he'd be as lucky today, although he had taken the time to learn some English since that frightening day on the off-chance he ever needed it. The sound of his own nervous laughter was lost in the constant churn of the sea. Never in a million lifetimes had he thought he'd travel this far out on purpose.

He steered directly for one of the larger, newer-looking ships, and asked God to watch over him and protect him.

Selfishly, he also prayed for protection even if Zhina wasn't right about her spy. Certainly, God would look out for a man trying to help a friend, even if their reasons might have been misguided.

Gritting his teeth, he climbed up on the bow and waved his hands in the air.

A voice boomed from a speaker on the ship. "Unidentified craft, keep back one thousand feet for your own safety."

Isâ gulped. The phrase could be taken in more than one way—while it was true sailing near the massive ship could be dangerous for his tiny boat, it was also a fact that in this political climate, the Americans looked at everyone as a possible threat. In a time when religious extremists looked at themselves as saviors for the cowardly act of strapping bombs to their chests, Isâ could understood their caution.

Still, without a megaphone of his own, he needed to get closer. He pointed his boat straight at them and engaged the engines.

"Unidentified vessel, your actions have been taken as a threat! Back off, or you will be fired upon!"

Isâ gulped. He was a good swimmer, but this far from shore, he'd never make it back, even if he had the opportunity to jump out of the boat in time. Not to mention, it would take weeks, if not months, for him to build another boat. That was a long time to go without food, even if his neighbors helped in the interim.

He reached down and lifted the red, white, and blue blankets he'd tied together, waving them in the air. He wished he had an actual American flag, but this would have to do. Hopefully, they understood his message and didn't blow him up out of extreme caution.

Two rubber boats, both larger than Isâ's little lenj, dropped into the water and started heading in his direction. He cut his engines and held his hands in the air as the first pulled up alongside him and the men inside pointed guns at his head.

"I'm friend," Isâ said, hoping he had the pronunciation right.

"What do you want?" one of the soldiers asked.

"I have message. I need to give to American captain."

"About what?"

"A prisoner. I know where is Dr. Arman Pirouzi."

One man talked into a radio on his shoulder. The man tilted his head, listening to someone respond before saying a few words back and then directing one of the soldiers to board Isâ's boat. Isâ dropped to his knees and placed his hands over his head as they searched his boat and patted him down. He didn't protest. This would have been a perfect way for an extremist to make his way onto their ship and do irreparable damage.

After what seemed like an eternity, one of the soldiers took the controls of his boat and steered it toward the

American ship. It rose up like a massive city in the water, even larger than the ship that had saved him so many years ago.

After Isâ told the captain everything Zhina had asked him to, they gave him a few bars of a sweet, crunchy cereal and a bottle of water, then escorted him to a small, metal room with a table and a single chair. Once inside, they locked the door without further comment. Isâ looked around the metal walls which were devoid of any decoration. They wouldn't have given him food and drink if they were going to torture him or worse, execute him. At least, he hoped that was true. There was so much propaganda on how heartless the soldiers of the United States were. He'd heard horrible things through the years, but the soldiers who saved him last time had been kind. Hopefully he didn't use up all his luck back then.

After some time, the door opened, and a soldier entered. "We've confirmed that there is a Dr. Pirouzi in prison, and he is someone that the president is interested in saving."

Isâ nodded. "He has information."

The man narrowed his eyes. "He is a United States citizen, being detained against his will. That's all that's important."

Isâ nodded again. In case they were wrong, and Isâ was a spy of some kind, it was important for them to say as little as possible, both for their own safety and that of Dr. Pirouzi.

The man kept his face stony. "Can you get to Dr. Pirouzi?"

"Me? No. But my friend—she can get to him."

"Good." The man handed him a paper bag. "This is a satellite phone. If Dr. Pirouzi can't keep this hidden, then have your friend keep the phone and we will communicate through her. It is imperative that Dr. Pirouzi remains on Qeshm Island. If they bring him inland, there will be no way we can get to him without being discovered."

Isâ nodded emphatically. "Yes, yes, I understand."

"We're going to call in a SEAL team to come up with an extraction plan. He needs to be ready to go at any time."

"Yes. Yes, I understand."

They placed Isâ back in his lenj after the sun went down and the rubber boats pulled him away from the massive ship and set him free. He drifted farther away, then cast out nets to catch even a small amount of white halva, just so he wouldn't be coming home empty-handed. When the nets were stowed, he headed back to shore. When he got home, Mona was already asleep and Zhina sat at his table, staring into a mug of water. She stood, her eyes wide and expectant.

Isâ gave her a weary smile. "It is done."

26

Imam Hospital, Iran

ZHINA LEANED OVER Arman, massaging his leg. Sometimes, she cursed her own skill. His muscles were responding well to the treatment, which meant she'd have to clear him soon and he'd return to prison. With prisoners, getting better quick was a bad thing. She gave him a practiced smile. "You're doing well. At this rate, you'll be walking fine soon."

"Why do you make that sound like a bad thing?"

She leaned closer. "It's been two weeks, and there's still been no call from the Americans. I can't keep you here forever."

He placed a hand over hers. "Afraid you'll miss me?"

How can he make jokes at a time like this?

She pulled her hand away. "I'm afraid you'll be dead!" She glanced over her shoulder to make sure they were alone. "I don't even want to think about the horrible things they'll do to you."

"They have already done plenty."

"You cannot be so shortsighted as to think it can't get worse. The prison calls every day for updates. Someone was here yesterday, reviewing your charts." She clawed at the top of her hijab. "They're pressuring my superiors to speed up your treatment." Silently, he reached out and caressed her cheek with his palm. The simple touch brought back memories of college with him in the United States. Things had been so much easier back then. They were both safe, with their whole lives ahead of them, and dreams of taking on the world. Now they were prisoners in the very world they both thought they'd escaped from. Zhina closed her eyes and sighed. "I don't want to lose you again."

Arman smiled. "I have no intention of getting lost."

She gave him a half-hearted smile back. Even after all this time, he was the same old Arman. Even after torture, he still had the same stubborn optimism that had made her fall in love with him all those years ago. Zhina held his gaze. "What will we do if the Americans don't come?"

Arman's smile only widened. "'We?' I like the sound of that."

She sighed. "I'm serious."

He grasped both her hands. "So am I. If the Americans don't come, we'll just save ourselves."

"How?"

"We'll figure it out." He caressed her cheek again. "Together." It was such a simple thing to say, and he seemed so sure of his words, but the world was much bigger and more horrible than either of them had ever imagined. Optimism alone wouldn't save them. The door slammed open and Zhina jumped, pushing Arman away.

"Dr. Farzin!" A nurse ran in. "There is an emergency. An IRGC officer was in a car accident. He has a broken pelvis, and he is bleeding badly. They keep giving him blood, but his blood pressure is still dropping."

Zhina frowned. "Why are you coming to me? I'm specialized in physical medicine and rehabilitation."

"They told me you had some training in medical school on the subject."

She huffed a mirthless laugh. She'd taken that elective simply to spend more time with Arman, hoping he'd notice her. It worked, and he tutored her just so she could pass the class. That was the day she decided she was destined for physical therapy.

The nurse twisted her hands. "They want all available doctors to review the information and assist, if possible."

"Very well." Zhina opened up her computer.

"You are taking the call here?" the nurse asked.

"Yes. The Wi-Fi is better in here." She glanced at Arman. "You don't mind, do you?"

Arman started doing his arm exercises on his own. "Not at all. Just let me know if I'm doing anything wrong with my exercises."

The nurse backed out of the room and Zhina grabbed her laptop and set it on the tray table. She entered the online meeting. Several doctors' faces lined the screen on the right while the surgeon talked. Zhina tilted the screen so Arman could see.

"I am at a loss," the surgeon said. "No matter how much blood we give him, he's not responding."

"Blood loss shock." Arman leaned closer to the screen. "He must have internal bleeding."

Zhina lifted an eyebrow, surprised he was showing interest, given that the patient was a member of the very organization that had been torturing him for weeks. A few of the other doctors discussed ideas for treatment, but Arman shook his head, murmuring, "None of that will work. Is their training really that far behind the United States?"

The surgeon frowned. "He has small fractures of pubic rami. The bone fragments have severed an artery. His fracture isn't that bad—it will heal itself in time—but it won't matter if we can't stop the bleeding."

Another doctor spoke. "I'd just cut the pelvis open and search for the artery. The patient has nothing to lose."

The surgeon shook his head. "There are far too many organs in such a small space to find the artery in time. I can try to ligate a larger artery feeding that area, but there are so many collateral branches in the pelvis that people keep bleeding after ligation." He rubbed his face. "I'll try to save him, but his chances are slim. It is a shame to lose a young man like this, but that is how it is going to be, I guess."

Arman stopped doing his exercises. "They're going to let the patient die? This is ridiculous. I can help him!"

Zhina glanced at Arman, then back to the screen. She hit her mic icon. "You need an interventionalist."

The surgeon nodded. "I agree, but this man doesn't have the time. The nearest interventionalist is at the trauma center on the mainland and we have nobody with that kind of skill on the island."

Zhina glanced at Arman again.

He sighed. "Ask them if they have a sixty-centimeter Cobra catheter and a glide wire."

Zhina asked the surgeon, who nodded. "Yes, but like I said, we have no one qualified to use them."

She took a deep breath. "Get the patient into surgery. I have an idea."

27

Imam Hospital, Iran

ARMAN HELD THE armrests tightly as Zhina pushed his wheelchair down the hall. When they made it to the surgery center, the staff gasped. He would have been shocked, too, if another doctor had wheeled a patient into the surgery prep area. Zhina slowed him to a halt and locked the wheels on his chair. "This is Dr. Arman Pirouzi. He is an interventionalist from the United States under my care. He has generously offered his help."

Arman tried to stand but fell back. "I'll just need a little help." He winced. "I'm not quite myself these days." A few of the people in the room whispered, and Arman caught the word *prison*. It had probably gotten out how he'd received such extensive wounds and broken bones. He understood their trepidation. If he were in their place, he'd have been nervous too.

"Here." Zhina offered a hand to get him to his feet, and he leaned on her as she helped him get into fresh scrubs and wash his hands and arms before they slowly limped into the operating room. Arman hated that he needed help, but Zhina assisted him with such attention and ease, he felt no embarrassment. They did have an extensive past. When they dated, he had no doubt they'd marry one day. Maybe she was the reason so many of Arman's relationships since had failed... everyone else was simply not Zhina.

Arman blinked at the bright lights. Crisp white tiles covered the floor, wall, and ceilings, and the medical equipment gleamed on a nearby tray. The surgeon adjusted the patient's meds and turned to Arman. "You have a few moments, but then we need to get started." He looked down at the patient. "Mr. Rostami, this man is an interventionalist. He's the only one who can save you."

Arman limped up to the bed and gasped at the same time the patient's eyes widened. Arman's heart skipped a beat as he looked into the eyes of the man who'd offered him a stick to bite down on seconds before they'd started to whip him—the only man in the blasted prison who'd shown any sign of compassion, even if it was slight. The man on the operating table was a member of the IRGC. He'd seen and done things that would drive most people insane with guilt. He'd stood there while Arman was tortured. The monitor beeped as his heart rate increased.

Arman forced a slight smile. "Interesting place we find ourselves in... you have to place your life in the hands of a man who unfortunately is not as steady as he normally would be, after being... *questioned* with such vigor in Qeshm Prison."

Rostami's bottom lip started to quiver. "Please..."

Part of Arman very much wanted to hear him beg for the mercy that he himself had not received. However, this man *had* tried to help him, maybe in the only way that had been possible. Treating him without compassion would only serve Arman's own ego, and this man had very little time. Arman leaned in closer. "I trust from the look on your face that you remember who I am?"

Rostami nodded.

"I will be honest with you. Despite speaking at a conference here, I do not have a license to practice medicine in Iran. But, I have done this procedure countless times in my practice in the United States. If you want to refuse my treatment, I will walk away, but I'm here now, and I'm willing to help."

Rostami grimaced. "W-why would you want to help me?"

"We are very different people," Arman said. "I have taken an oath to help people whenever it is in my power. If I stood here and watched you die, I would not be able to live with myself." Rostami closed his eyes, no doubt thinking about how many times he'd stood by as someone had died painfully. He'd probably never imagined himself on the other side of things. Or maybe he had—perhaps that was the reason he tried to bestow some mercy in such a merciless place.

Arman stood taller, steadied by Zhina behind him. "What is your decision? Do you accept my help?"

Rostami opened his eyes and nodded. "Yes. I want to see my son again." *The man has a family?* Odd how the worst people could lead a double life. His family probably had no idea what he did when he left the house every day.

Arman stepped back and nodded to the anesthesiologist. Within moments, Rostami started to look groggy again. With this sort of injury, it would be safer to keep him partially awake rather than add the extra complications that came with full anesthesia. Zhina squeezed Arman's shoulder. "I'm here. Just let me know what you need."

"Just keep me from falling over." Arman chuckled, and the assembled nurses and doctors looked uneasy. Unfortunately, it wasn't a joke—his legs were already trembling from the strain of remaining upright. Gritting his teeth, Arman allowed muscle memory to kick in and went to work. They didn't have an ultrasound machine to help him access the patient's artery, but luckily he'd trained for just such an occasion. He remembered his mentor from the old days: "If an interventionalist can't access an artery by palpating it, they are not a real interventionalist." He and his young coworkers used to laugh at his ideology. After all, if there was technology meant to make their lives easier, why not use it?

Still, out of respect—and maybe out of fear of the man— they'd never used the ultrasound machine when their mentor was in the building. Now Arman was thankful for all that extra training. It was almost as if the good doctor had known that all of them would face such an instance at some point in their careers.

A nurse wiped Arman's brow as he used a needle to access the artery in Rostami's groin. After palpating the area and finding a weak pulse, he injected local anesthetic and then picked up an eighteen-gauge needle. Those around him shifted, trying to get a better look as he held the artery between his fingers and inserted the needle at a forty-five-degree angle. Blood started gushing out forcefully and a nurse gasped.

"That's all right," said Arman. "That's a sign that I'm in the artery. In this case, bleeding like that is good."

He advanced a wire through the needle into the artery and took a vascular sheath from the tray. One of the doctors watched closely over his shoulder as Arman exchanged the needle with the sheath. Arman asked the doctor, "Have you seen this done before?" The man shook his head. "The sheath I just inserted is basically a small plastic tube with a valve that gives me constant access to the artery while still preventing bleeding." He took a smaller tube with a curved tip from the supply tray. "Now, I will use this catheter to access the bleeding artery in the pelvis."

From there, it was an old routine. Luckily, Rostami was a younger man with little calcium buildup in his arteries. This allowed Arman to advance the wire into the aorta without issue, and with the Cobra catheter he'd selected, he easily made his way to the blood vessel that fed the pelvis on the opposite side. When everything was situated correctly, he injected contrast, and moments later, a big blob of contrast dye appeared outside of the artery. He nodded, pointing his chin at the screen. "See there? That's the bleeding. You see how fast that blood is pouring out of the artery?"

The surgeon nodded. "It's coming out too fast. Can we stop it?"

They could certainly try. "We need to block this right now," Arman said. "He only has minutes. I need *five-millimeter coils*, stat."

The surgeon shook his head. "They have them on the mainland, but not here."

Arman gaped. Iran's medical facilities were behind the West, but they shouldn't have been *that* far behind. Keeping medical advancements in city hospitals and not allowing them to filter to facilities catering to poorer people was unconscionable. Then again, this was Iran—he should have expected the worst. Arman gazed at the monitor. *How the hell am I going to close this artery and stop the bleeding without coils?*

Only the beeping of Rostami's heart monitor answered him. With each beat, more pumped from his ruptured artery, bringing him one step closer to death. Situations like this had been death sentences in the past... but they hadn't always been. A particularly interesting chapter in his medical history books exploded in his mind, a chapter about innovative doctors working with what they had to save lives.

Arman turned to a nearby tech. "I need a new wire and a sterile wire cutter. Stat. This man has moments to live." The man ran from the room, the door swinging behind him. Arman's gaze met the surgeon's. "Stay ready. I'm going to need you."

The tech used his back to push the door open moments later. "I have the wire cutters and wire."

"Excellent." Arman nodded at the surgeon. "Cut the wire into three pieces about two and a half centimeters long." He scanned the screen, watching the blood still pouring from the artery. His own pulse started to drum in his ears, but he refused to let panic set in. He needed to be calm and collected if he was going to save this man's life.

"Here." The surgeon handed him the one-inch segments.

"Good. Now watch." Arman took the pieces and spun them around his hemostat until they each formed a small, individual spring. "Here is how they used to coil the artery before the invention of manufactured medical coils." For the first time since Arman had taken that class, knowledge of *medical history* proved useful in practice. Pulling on all the information he thought he'd never need; Arman took each self-manufactured spring and forced it through the catheter hub. Then he advanced his wire and pushed the coils into the blood vessel.

The doctor nodded. "Fascinating."

Arman had to agree. It was why he'd chosen this profession in the first place. Too many were afraid to even try to save these patients due to the complexity of the procedures. Arman looked at each surgery as a challenge, and if he won the challenge, the patient lived. In the games life played, his job had the ultimate effect on people's futures... or lack thereof.

He jerked his chin at the interested doctor. "Can you mix the gel foam with contrast for me?"

"I don't know how."

"I'll teach you."

The man started mixing and Arman gave directions until the perfect consistency was obtained.

"The last step," Arman explained, "is to inject the gel foam into the damaged artery, sealing the leak." He continued the procedure, watching the readings closely.

"His blood pressure is already rising," the nurse said. "You did it!"

Arman nodded. Steadying himself, he removed the devices and set them on the table before placing a wad of gauze over the wound. He looked at the nurse. "Hold pressure on the groin for twenty minutes, gently releasing the pressure every five minutes or so." He turned to the surgeon. "The artery has been repaired. You can continue with the bone fixation." He swayed, grabbing the edge of the gurney and Zhina caught him.

"Come on. I need to get you back to your room," she said.

"One moment." Arman made his way to the front of the bed and leaned close to the patient's face. "You're safe now. They are going to start your surgery. You will be able to walk in a couple of days. I wish you luck, my friend."

Rostami blinked, his eyes foggy and his lips quivering. "Thank you."

Arman gave him a curt nod. It was a small bit of charity, and more than the man deserved, but Arman always kept his patients calm and informed in the past. It didn't seem right to treat this man any differently, despite their history. He may have treated Arman like an animal, but Arman refused to fall to his level. He'd keep his humanity intact, no matter what it took.

28

Undisclosed CIA Operations Center

SWEAT DAMPENED ZARABI'S shirt as he stood outside the door to the CIA conference room.

"You okay, kid?" Agent Barlow asked.

"Yeah. I've just never had to do a presentation for the director of the CIA before."

Barlow laughed. "The President will be in there and you're worried about the Director of the CIA?"

"Yeah, well, the President will only be on the monitor, and the director of the CIA is the one who will fire me if I make a fool out of myself."

.Barlow patted him on the back before pushing him through the door. "Then how about you don't make a fool out of yourself?"

Within the conference room, people spoke in hushed tones, some standing, others already in their seats. The director of the CIA pulled out a chair at one end of the table, and on the far end, stood a screen on a rolling cart displaying the presidential seal. The director called the meeting to order. "The President is on the line, people. We're here to discuss the possible extraction of one of our civilian assets, Dr. Arman Pirouzi. We are operating under the assumption—based on information provided from a contact in Iran—that Dr. Pirouzi has the package and only needs to get out of Iran in order to deliver it."

Zarabi took a deep breath. "The extraction should be a standard covert op. The challenge is that we have confirmed reports that the Chinese have provided a state-of-the-art radar system to Iran. We have to proceed under the assumption that they're using that technology to watch all points of entry, including the ships in international waters."

"I trust you have an idea?" the director asked.

Agent Sara Matika stood, adjusted her tailored navy-blue suit, and walked to a screen next to the table. "On April 19, 2017, an oil rig belonging to Delta Martin Service, an affiliate of the United Arab Emirates, was hit with a freak storm and separated from its anchoring space in the sovereign waters of Sharjah." She clicked a remote, and a picture appeared of children playing on a beach with an oil rig in the background. "After two days, it washed up on the beach near Ramchah Village in the southern part of Qeshm Island. The Emirati never took action to recover it."

"The Iranians are okay with that?" the director asked.

"Normally, no. But in December 2020, the rig went up for auction, and they've been dismantling it for steel and selling it or reusing it, quite probably for munitions warehouses and weaponry."

"How is this supposed to help us?" the Director asked.

"We're suggesting we find an outdated oil rig. There are dozens that are either abandoned or in the process of being shut down after their locations stop being profitable." She pointed to a screen as a simulation of a drifting oil rig appeared on a map. "We can hide our SEAL team inside, haul it close to Qeshm Island at night during an inward tide, and then release it to drift to the shore."

"That's crazy," a man said, shaking his head. "They'd be sitting ducks, with no means of escape if discovered."

Another man settled back in his chair, crossing his massive arms over his equally large chest. "Not crazy at all." His dark, deadly eyes scanned the room. "Lieutenant Commander Steve Scott. I'll be leading the SEAL team earmarked for this extraction. My guys have reviewed Agent Sara's plans, and there's more than enough room in an abandoned rig to hide, even if it were searched."

The director of the CIA steepled his fingers, staring at the screen. When the simulation started over again, he turned to Lieutenant Commander Scott. "What are the chances of this working without casualties?"

Scott stood and pointed at the oil rig on the screen. "Once we cut the anchors and haul it close enough, the tide will do the rest. The oil rig will end up grounding near Qeshm Prison.

Once we have the asset, the Navy will have two modified Boomin' Beavers on hand to get us out. They may spot them, but by then it will be too late. We'll be out before the IRGC even knows we were there."

The CIA director scanned the room. "I trust this is our best option?"

Everyone nodded in agreement.

The director of the CIA stared at the screen again. "Mr. President, this involves sending the US military into Iranian territory. Do we have your permission to make this a go?"

The presidential seal dissolved into the face of the President of the United States. "You have my permission. There's too much at stake." He leaned closer to the screen. "Lieutenant Commander Scott?"

The SEAL stood and saluted the screen. "Mr. President, Sir!"

The President nodded at him. "At ease. This will be a deniable mission. As far as anyone can know, the United States was not involved with this operation in any way."

The SEAL saluted again. "Understood, Sir!"

The President scanned the room, looking grim. "Bring Dr. Pirouzi and your men home safely."

The Director of the CIA slapped the table. "There you have it, people. Operation Trojan Horse is a go."

Agent Barlow patted Zarabi on the shoulder as they exited the conference room. "That wasn't so bad, now, was it?"

Zarabi rubbed the back of his neck. "I may have aged a few years, if I'm being honest. If I do too many more meetings like that, I might look as old as you."

"Very funny, hotshot. There's still a lot to do. Let's get that oil rig as close to that prison as we can. Then we'll call the contact and really get this ball rolling."

A few days later, a company reported that one of their oil rigs had broken free of its moorings and was floating into the Persian Gulf. They were monitoring the situation but assured international news agencies there was no danger.

Zarabi dialed the satellite phone, and on the second ring, a man answered. "Alo?" The man coughed. "I sorry. What is word… hell-oh."

Zarabi smiled at the accent so similar to his father's. "Is it safe to speak?"

"Bale… I mean… yes, safe."

The man sounded terrified, and with good reason. He could be executed for having that phone, let alone talking with the CIA. Zarabi switched to Arabic. "Excellent. We are sending in a small team to extract Dr. Pirouzi. They will be there tomorrow, weather permitting."

"Yes. Yes. Good," the man replied, still speaking English.

"We might need help distracting the IRGC and disguising the extraction team to make them look like locals."

The man laughed nervously, then also switched to Arabic. "Disguise, I can do. But if you want to look like us, send people with dark skin. White people will stand out here like a sore thumb."

Zarabi jotted down the note. Lieutenant Commander Scott's dark skin certainly fit that bill, but it was a good idea to make sure that the rest of his team did, too. "Understood. There will be more details to come. If you can think of a distraction, we'd greatly appreciate it."

"I will see what I can do."

Zarabi nodded. "Thank you, sir—and Dr. Pirouzi, I'm sure, thanks you as well."

The man switched back to English. "I no do for doctor, but yes. Understand."

Zarabi hung up the phone. Interesting. If he wasn't doing it to help Dr. Pirouzi, then what was his motivation? Not that it really mattered, in the end.

"Do we trust this guy?" Barlow asked.

Zarabi sat back in his chair. "We don't have much of a choice."

29

Imam Hospital, Iran

A COMMOTION IN the hall roused Arman from his hospital bed. The room spun and his legs, shoulders, and ribs throbbed in pain. Standing for so long during the surgery had set him back significantly. The door swung open, crashing against the wall as a man in an IRGC uniform stormed into the room.

"Sir!" a nurse shouted. "Our patients need to rest!"

"He's rested long enough." The man grabbed Arman by the collar and hoisted him from the bed.

"Dr. Farzin!" the nurse shouted from out in the hall.

Arman's muscles screamed in pain, and the second his feet hit the ground, he crumpled to the floor.

"What are you doing?" Zhina yelled as she ran in. "This man is in a delicate time in his recovery!"

The officer glared. "We only need him to be able to sit up straight. Can he do that?"

Zhina gaped. "Well, yes, but—"

"Then get him into a wheelchair. Someone wants to talk to him."

Zhina's eyes were full of horror as she met his.

"It's okay," Arman said. "Fighting won't do any good."

Zhina and the nurse helped him into a wheelchair while the guard stood and watched, doing nothing to assist. Once in the chair, the guard took over, speeding Arman through the halls, banging into doorways and even walls each time he turned a corner until they stopped at the hospital director's office. Arman frowned. What would the hospital director want to speak to him about? The guard knocked twice. "Dr. Arman Pirouzi, as you requested."

"Enter!" a voice boomed from within. The door opened and Arman could do nothing as the guard wheeled him in and set him in front of a wide mahogany desk that looked far too rich for a hospital office. Behind the desk was not the hospital director, but General Moradi. "You look surprised," Moradi said.

"I'm not used to visitors," Arman managed, his mouth going dry. "My days usually start with breakfast and a few hours of therapy."

Moradi leaned on the desk. "Are you ready to talk?"

"I told you all before, many times," Arman said. "I have nothing to say. I came here for a conference and I was stolen from my hotel room. I have done nothing wrong."

"Sticking with your story, are you?"

"It's not a story, it's the truth."

It *was* the truth from Arman's perspective. He'd agreed to help the CIA to stop a war that would cost countless Iranian lives. There was no way to consider that wrong.

Moradi looked bored. "Bring in the other prisoner." A chill settled over Arman. Had they arrested Zhina? Had the IRGC found out she'd helped contact the Americans? His dread only worsened as they dragged in a man and slammed him into the wooden chair beside Arman. The sound sucked out of the room, replaced by the thud of his heart in his ears as he stared into the swollen and bruised eyes of his childhood friend, Ârash. Arman's vision swam and his world became a kaleidoscope of memories.

The day the bomb dropped on their street...

Digging to find Ârash's mother...

Holding Ârash back from the rubble as he screamed, locking their fingers together as a show of solidarity...

Holding Niki for the first time after she was born...

The vacation in Istanbul where they'd all gotten drenched in a rainstorm, and Niki laughing about it...

The devastation in Ârash's voice when he told Arman on the phone that Niki had been executed for protesting…

And now this.

Hadn't Ârash been through enough? If there really was a God, why did He see fit to torture some people more than others?

The General placed his palms on the wooden desk. "So many say the CIA is the most advanced intelligence agency in the world. I say Iranian intelligence is far more reliable, getting information and people needed to perform any task with the utmost speed." Moradi smiled. "It took them only a few hours to discover that the only person in Iran with whom you had consistent contact with was this man. And also his daughter, who, interestingly enough, was recently executed for treason."

Ârash lifted his head. "My daughter did nothing wrong."

"Our courts found differently. And I'm sure they will do equal diligence while sorting through your past." The General turned his gaze on Arman. "I am tired of playing games with you, Dr. Pirouzi. Tell me where the information you extracted from Akbari's pacemaker is hidden, or your friend here will meet the same fate as his treacherous daughter."

Arman clutched the arms of his wheelchair. "You're going to say he did something he didn't do? Is that what our government has become? Nothing but lies and manipulation?" He looked to Ârash and then back to Moradi.

"This man has done nothing other than be a good friend and an even better husband and father. He does not deserve this!"

"And what do *you* deserve, Dr. Pirouzi? You were the one who removed the pacemaker. You are the one committing treason."

"I took out a man's faulty pacemaker and replaced it with a working one. They were supposed to give me the pacemaker to return to the German manufacturer, but someone took it. I don't even have it! If the pacemaker is your concern, find the people who stole it and leave me and my friends alone!" Moradi probably knew exactly where the pacemaker was—he may have even been the person who had the device stolen. Still, Arman needed to be careful not to deviate from his story in any way. He took a steadying breath, trying not to cower under the scrutiny of Moradi's heartless eyes. It wasn't just his life in jeopardy now, but Ârash and Zhina's as well. Arman had fleeting thoughts of giving in while being tortured, but now that someone else was in danger, Arman was really considering telling them about the false tooth. He would die, and horribly, but at least it might save his friends.

"I am tired of your lies, Dr. Pirouzi. This man's blood will be on your hands."

Arman pushed himself to his feet, but his legs buckled, and he fell back into the wheelchair. "How do you sleep at night? You kill people in cold blood and place the blame on others? You are a psychopath and your God knows the truth." Arman trembled with fear and rage. "You claim to be a good man with that false impression on your forehead, trying to fool people into thinking you spend all your time praying. Well, I know differently. One day, you will be held accountable for your crimes. Not just here on Earth, but when God denies you access to heaven."

Moradi threw his head back and laughed. "Believe me, Dr. Pirouzi, I am more moderate than many others following the path of God's chosen."

"If you really believe you are one of God's chosen, you are more delusional than I thought."

Moradi folded his hands on the desk. "There are many extremists calling for your immediate execution. They want to use you as a warning to anyone else who might try to thwart God's work."

"You have no idea what God's work is," Arman spat.

Moradi leaned toward him. "If you do not believe that I am doing God's work, then you are sorely mistaken. I am on a path prescribed by Him. God has called me to be the next Commander-in-Chief of the IRGC." Arman gaped. The Commander-in-Chief was barely one step below the Supreme Leader. In some ways, the position held even more authority. If Moradi ascended to that kind of power, he'd be all but unstoppable. "There are many in the government who are not as pious as I am, Dr. Pirouzi. They are on the path of their own ambitions. They want to see themselves in that position, rather than me." Arman shifted in his wheelchair. He couldn't imagine anyone worse than Moradi, but Qeshm Prison had shown him the depths of human depravity went deeper than he'd ever wanted to know.

Moradi sat back. "My elevation to the place God intends for me depends on protecting Iran from those who will do the country harm. Dr. Akbari was so ashamed of himself that he took his own life rather than admitting what he'd done. His fate is now in God's hands." He pointed at Arman. "But your fate, Dr. Pirouzi, is in *my* hands. Whatever information Akbari intended to share was passed on to you. Once I extract that information and save Iran from whatever you're planning, then I will be the undisputed candidate for the position." He punched his own chest. "I am ready to sacrifice myself to God's will."

Did he really believe it? Or was it just an act to trick people into following him like some sort of prophet? Arman wasn't sure which was worse.

"I have worked many years to get here, Dr. Pirouzi. God has called me to do whatever is necessary and I will eliminate anyone who stands in my way." The man's eyes were deadly serious. He truly believed that he was killing for the good of God. "This is my last challenge before ascending, and I will not allow a treasonous pig like you to come between me and the destiny God has deemed mine."

Arman turned at a *click* and found the guard standing behind them had a gun pointed at Ârash's head. Ice flooded Arman's veins as he gripped his wheelchair tighter.

"Make your choice, Dr. Pirouzi," Moradi intoned. "God gives me permission to do what needs to be done. And to answer your other question—I sleep well at night. You are the one with the choice here. You can change your mind and serve

God and this man will live. Or you can stay on a treasonous path, and he will die. What is your decision?"

Arman's head spun. Everything seemed so simple when he started this journey. He hoped to save Iran from war, but he had done nothing but fail. He was going to die here. And no matter what he decided, Ârash would probably die, too, just for knowing him. There was no way out that didn't lead to blood. Arman looked over at his friend. He dearly wanted to believe that there was a way to save him. If he held out for the Americans, Moradi would end Ârash's life without a second thought. But maybe, *possibly*, Moradi was telling the truth and he would let Ârash go if Arman gave up the information. Then Arman would be the only one to die.

Maybe that was his way out… giving his friend a chance and hoping that Iran would not be plunged into war. Of course, he'd be dead then and have no idea what happened.

Arman steadied himself, prepared himself to make a deal with the Devil when Ârash nudged his chair. His friend locked his two index fingers together, just like they'd done as children. They'd made a pact that day that they'd never give up and always stand together against those who'd dropped the bombs—now it seemed the bombs hanging over them were held by the man sitting behind the desk. The certainty in Ârash's eyes was astounding. After all they'd been through, Ârash still trusted him, despite the lies he'd no doubt been told. He supported his friend, even if it meant both their deaths.

A wave of strength and certainty washed over Arman, and he sat a little taller as he turned back to Moradi. "I keep telling you, all I did was a surgery. I met Dr. Akbari for the first time that day when he asked me for help. We were never even alone together. Ask anyone who was there."

Moradi nodded to the guard who pulled Ârash to his feet, bashed him in the head with the gun, and then kicked him in the stomach when he fell.

"Stop!" Arman jumped from the chair, but his legs gave out, dropping him to the floor beside his friend.

Ârash spat blood on the gray tiles and looked at Arman, his eyes still filled with defiance. He clearly wanted him to keep fighting, but Arman didn't know how much more he could take.

I'm not strong enough to watch my friend die.

Moradi stood and pointed at Ârash. "Charge that man with treason and set up a public execution for him tomorrow. I want him humiliated in front of everyone he knows."

Arman choked back a sob. "Please, he has nothing to do with all of this."

Moradi crouched beside him. "He has nothing to do with *what*, Dr. Pirouzi? Is there something you'd like to tell me?"

Arman rolled onto his back and stared at the ceiling as Ârash was dragged from the room. It was too much. He couldn't sacrifice his one true friend. "Tell me what you want me to do."

Moradi smiled, the triumph in his eyes terrifying. "I will set up a television interview three days from now. There, you will confess to all the crimes you have committed and ask the Supreme Leader to pardon you."

Arman snorted a laugh. "The Supreme Leader would never pardon someone who'd confessed."

"That's up to him and God."

Arman closed his eyes again. He was so tired. *I just want this to be over, one way or another.* "And Ârash?"

"After your confession, he will be free to go."

Moradi could be lying—he probably *was* lying. But it was Ârash's only chance. Arman's life was over, either way. Ârash had a slim possibility, but it was still a chance, and it was all Arman could do for him at this point.

"Alright."

30

Home, Qeshm, Iran

ZHINA TUGGED AT her hair, poring over the maps she could find online, looking for any possible route to smuggle Arman out of the hospital without the IRGC catching them. The interview and confession would be nothing but political propaganda. The people of Iran who hadn't been fully brainwashed by the IRGC knew these spectacles for what they were. The others really thought the IRGC was doing God's work.

She sighed. As soon as Arman confessed, he'd be tried and publicly executed. She had less than two and a half days to save him and no idea how to do it.

A knock sounded at her door. One tap and then three—it was Isâ. Zhina opened the door and her friend slipped inside, checking the windows to make sure no one was watching.

"The Americans say to expect their men soon," he said, not wasting time on a greeting. "But they cannot say when. I do not like how they won't commit to a time. I'm starting to fear for your friend's chances of escape."

"I know. We may need to get him out on our own." Zhina rubbed her face. The island was crawling with soldiers. How could two unarmed civilians challenge that?

"They want us to create a distraction to give the Americans some cover. It sounds like these SEALS are very tough. Maybe tougher than the IRGC."

Zhina nodded. She'd heard about them while in the USA. They were considered heroes to most, though when she returned to Iran, they were spoken of in less favorable terms, like mercenaries or hired guns. Perhaps that made them the perfect people to stand up against the IRGC.

"Let's say they do get here in time," she said. "What could we possibly do to create a commotion big enough to hide enemy soldiers arriving on our shores?"

Isâ sat. "I had a thought about that. A Baba Zaar lives near my village. I gave him fish once when I had a particularly good day, and he was very appreciative of my generosity. I think he would help."

"A spiritual healer? The government hates them almost as much as they hate the protesters."

"Yes, but with all the government has done to the Mama Zaars and Baba Zaars, I'm sure they'd be willing to help."

"How? They're peaceful people."

Isâ lifted a finger. "They're peaceful people able to call many together with very short notice. If they could do a large Zaar ceremony, with all the drums and singing, that would be more than enough distraction, and it would be easy to cover and hide the Americans as soon as they step foot on our shores."

Zhina considered it. Although most ceremonies only had a few dozen people, she'd seen a few grow quite large. Isâ's idea definitely had merit—but only if the Baba Zaar agreed. The faithful took their ceremonies very seriously and the Baba might see it as an affront to their beliefs to hold a Zaar ceremony without there being anyone to actually heal. Still, the ancient Zaar ceremony was deeply ingrained in their culture, and its entrancing rhythm and spiritual fervor could create the perfect diversion—if they could manage it.

"I think it's a good idea," Zhina decided. "But as tough as the Americans will be, I don't think it's feasible that they'll get to Arman on time. We need to find a way to get him away from the IRGC before Moradi gets his confession. We'll hide Arman in the villages if we have to and then let the Americans get him off the island once they get here."

Isâ shrugged. "I only know my own world. I don't think I can be much help coming up with a way to get him out of a building as big as that hospital."

Zhina patted his shoulder. "No worries, my friend. Your plan is excellent." She started packing her bag. "While you talk to the Baba Zaar, I'll head over and talk to Arman." She zipped the bag closed and straightened. "We will wait for the Americans if we have to, but I'd rather meet them outside and give us a better chance to escape."

Isâ nodded. "Hopefully, we can still pull this all together before the telecast." He looked down. "And if for any reason you don't come out of the building, I will show the Americans where to go."

Zhina smiled. He was so brave. If she and Arman didn't make it out, there was a good chance they'd already be dead, yet he still planned to help, even in the worst-case scenario. "You are a good friend."

"I do nothing anywhere near the help you have already given me. We will free your friend. You'll see."

Zhina nodded firmly. His positive attitude was infectious, though her stomach still churned as she thought about the obstacles they still had to overcome.

31

Imam Hospital, Iran

ARMAN HELD HIS leg straight as Zhina adjusted the Velcro fasteners on his new soft supports. "The IRGC finally approved these leg braces," she said. "They don't want to have to worry about having you in a wheelchair anymore. This is good timing for us." Arman nodded. It certainly was. Even after all his therapy, his legs could feel strong one moment and then give out from under him the next. The braces gave him a chance to escape without falling and risking both of their lives. Organizing the Zaar ceremony was an excellent idea, and he planned to personally thank this friend of Zhina's the first chance he got if the man was able to pull it off.

Still, Arman wasn't happy with just the thought of escape. If they fled, they would be leaving so many others behind to face fear and prosecution, including his own best friend. He couldn't let him meet the same fate as Niki and her predecessors. He leveled his gaze at Zhina. "We can't leave Moradi in power. The man's ego and ambition have no bounds. He will destroy this country and every good citizen in it."

"What do you suggest we do? He has the entire IRGC behind him."

"That doesn't matter. Ârash knew he was about to be executed, yet he showed me our childhood sign." Arman locked his fingers together. "He wanted me to fight, so I need to fight. No matter the risk. I have a chance to make a difference not just for me, but for Iran." He looked out the window as soft, fluffy clouds drifted by. Niki used to stare at clouds as a child. She had a vision, a vision that had been cut short before it had time to blossom. "Niki would have fought. She died because she wanted a better Iran than she grew up in. Maybe I can give that to those she left behind."

"Wasn't that why you came back in the first place?" Zhina asked. "You need to get home and give the Americans the information they need—that's the only way to keep Iran from getting dragged into another war."

"Yes, it is the only way to stop the *immediate* threat, but Moradi represents a threat to the future. He won't stop at the IRGC. He wants to rule everything. He will single-handedly destroy any chance of Iran becoming a safe place for the people."

Zhina dragged her fingers through her hair. "What are we supposed we do without weapons?"

"We're in a hospital, there are weapons everywhere."

"What do you mean?"

Arman sighed. He'd kept the depth of his predicament a secret from her. He didn't want to frighten her more, but she needed to know if they were going to come up with a plan that had a chance to work. Taking a deep breath, he folded his hands and leaned toward her. "I know you want to get out of here before the interview, but I've decided to go through with it."

Her eyes widened. "If you confess, you're as good as dead."

"I agree. That's why we're going to use the interview to our advantage."

Zhina frowned. "How so?"

"First, you need to make sure the hospital insists you are at the interview in case there are issues with my health. Tell them I've been having fainting spells."

"That shouldn't be hard. You were barely conscious for the first few days after you arrived, and the guards told us you had episodes of unconsciousness while in prison."

Maybe the torture he'd endured for so long would be the ticket to his freedom. "You could say I'm showing signs of hematoma from multiple impacts to the head."

"That's already documented, although I did clear you. So saying you have signs isn't even lying." Her brow furrowed. "What?"

Zhina shifted her weight. "According to the news, Moradi will be there for the cameras. No doubt he wants the glory of showing he was the one to extract your confession."

Arman nodded. "That's great. I was hoping he would be."

"I still don't understand how this helps us!"

"When the interview starts, I'm going to pretend to pass out." He pointed to Zhina. "You will pronounce me dead and grab a defibrillator."

"Are you insane?"

"Hear me out—make sure Moradi is close to me. I'll grab his leg and when you shock me, it will shock him too, stopping his heart."

"You *have* lost your mind. That will stop *your* heart, too!"

"Yes, it will." The horror in her eyes was almost comforting. It had been too long time since he'd seen it in someone's eyes. "Have your friend Isâ tell the SEALs that there will be a big commotion and that will be their signal to enter the hospital. Once the bullets start flying, it should be a large enough distraction to keep the IRGC occupied while you resuscitate me."

"You're talking about purposely stopping your heart. What if I can't revive you?"

Arman looked down. It was a valid question. If he died due to his hastily concocted plan, it would leave things no better off than if he'd died in prison. The information needed to get to the right people—who delivered it didn't matter. He reached into his mouth and extracted the false tooth.

Zhina gasped.

Arman held her horrified gaze as he offered her the tooth. "You need to give this to the Americans."

She looked at it and frowned before returning her gaze to him. "What?"

"This is what they're looking for. If I die, this information still needs to get to the CIA."

She glanced over her shoulder. "The IRGC runs snap inspections all the time. If I'm found with that, I'll be executed." She folded Arman's hand over the tooth. "The information has been safe all this time. There's no need to place it at risk now. Keep it hidden. If the worst happens, and I can't revive you, I'll know where it is, but let's plan on you walking out of here and giving it to the Americans yourself."

Arman closed his eyes. Part of him wanted to be rid of it, to leave the responsibility to someone else. But she was right—he had to see this through. He placed the tooth back in his mouth.

"Alright."

Zhina stared at her hands. "There's only one defibrillator per floor."

"I don't think anyone would question you grabbing one if it was an emergency. Just make sure you're near one when they call for you."

She stared at him for a moment, her eyes pleading. "You do realize that the chance of successfully resuscitating you after a three-hundred Joule shock is only about fifty-fifty."

Arman lifted his chin. "I'm already marked for death. The way I look at it, I'm going from a zero percent chance of survival to a fifty percent chance." He shrugged. "Pretty good odds if you ask me. And a hundred percent chance that Moradi will die. To me, that's worth the risk."

"You're asking me to kill you." Zhina looked down, holding her head. "Please don't make me do this."

Arman cradled her cheek in his palm, bringing her gaze back to meet his. "If you ever loved me, you'll know how important this is. Please respect that I have decided this is the right thing to do. It's time for me to make a sacrifice, just like Niki did."

"But you have a great life back in America. You have so much to lose."

"My mother is dying and may already be dead. My girlfriend left me and I had to give my cat to a stranger." Arman shook his head. "My goddaughter has been executed and my best friend is in prison because of me. I have nothing left to lose."

Tears welled in Zhina's eyes. "What about me? I lost you so long ago, and I finally found you again."

He laced his fingers between hers. "That's why I'm trusting you with my life. No one else here cares about me as much as you do. I know you'll fight for my life." He kissed her hand gently. "And if things don't work out, I know you're strong enough to deliver the package. You will be in charge of my legacy if I die. *You* will save Iran."

She closed her eyes. "This is too much."

She was right in many ways. He'd never expected to see her again, much less when returning to Iran for this mission. Maybe it was fate that had brought them back together to continue where they'd left off.

"Hey." He stroked her cheek. "These last few days with you have been the best of the last twenty years."

She shook her head. "You're just saying that."

"No. It's true. I've been looking for happiness, getting tied up in relationship after relationship, but they all failed. Do you know why?"

She wordlessly shook her head.

"Because they weren't *you,*" Arman said. "I understand that now. You are the love of my life. You are worth fighting for." He gripped her hand tighter. "*We* are worth fighting for."

Tears spilled down her cheek. "You do realize there is a good chance neither one of us will survive this."

"I do. But we have to at least try."

32

Qeshm Mosque, Iran

ISÂ WIPED SWEAT from his brow as he waited to see the village elders. Dust swirled in the street as he stood outside the plain, white-walled building less than a kilometer from the beach. He hadn't come here in years… not after the discovery of Mona's club foot. He hoped the elders wouldn't hold that against him. He couldn't let something like a lapse in faith get in the way of his task. The Americans contacted him just before sunrise to confirm the arrival of the rescue team sometime within the next few days. "Weather permitting," they'd said, although Isâ wasn't sure what that meant. With Arman Pirouzi's public confession scheduled in just two days, it was cutting things far too close.

The doorway cracked open, and a light-skinned inlander boy wearing a patch over one eye peeked out. "Are you Mr. Isâ?"

Isâ fidgeted with his sleeve. "I am."

The child held open the door for him. "The elders will see you now."

The interior of the mosque did little to cool Isâ's skin as he stepped into the wide-open space normally set aside for worship. The tiles inlaid in the floor spread out in a repeating pattern of burgundy, blue, gray, and white that transfixed him as a child. As an adult, he was still amazed, now understanding the time and artistry in placing each tile with such care.

"Isâ!" Aziz, the chief elder, approached with open arms. "It is good to see you."

Isâ smiled as they hugged. "It is good to see you, too."

The rest of the elders greeted him with similar enthusiasm. Isâ helped many of their families when they needed. Luckily, the sea always provided him with more than enough fish to share. Isâ never really felt like a hero; it just happened to be that his nets were full on days when his friends needed help the most.

"What can we do for you, my son?" Aziz asked, leading him past the tall, white pillars to a small space in the center of the room, where they sat down on the tile. The boy filled cups with water from a clay pitcher intricately carved and accented with red and yellow paint and handed them to the elders and Isâ. Isâ looked at each of them. They were simple folk, like Isâ, dressed in soiled, long shirts, and some of them missing teeth after a life well-lived. These men held so much respect in their village. They were good men of God. Certainly, they would understand and accept his request.

Isâ held his head high. "You all know that the IRGC is holding an American doctor, accusing him of crimes against the government." The boy balked, spilling water as he poured. He collected himself, soaking up the spill with his own robes before continuing his task.

Aziz nodded to Isâ, not seeming to notice the commotion. "Yes, the news is everywhere. They are going to make an example out of him, just like they did with those protestors. The poor children."

"Do you agree that he is probably innocent?" Isâ asked.

"Likely he is. Any God-fearing man knows the IRGC looks for criminal behavior anywhere they do not have control and if they do not find what they are looking for, they fabricate it."

The others nodded in agreement.

Good. Hopefully, they would be sympathetic to the doctor's cause. "I need you all to make a promise to God right now, to not repeat anything I am about to tell you to anyone other than those in this room." The elders glanced at each other, frowning before they mutually agreed. Isâ looked over at the boy.

"He's no trouble," Aziz said. "Believe me, that child is no friend of the IRGC."

The boy kissed his fingers, placed them over his heart, and looked at the sky. "I swear to God." In this holiest of places, Isâ figured that was good enough.

He took a deep breath before continuing. "The Americans are sending a team of soldiers to free Dr. Pirouzi and they need our help."

Aziz gaped at him. "How are *we* supposed to help? The IRGC already looks at us as troublemakers. Don't forget what they have already done."

Isâ nodded, remembering the story. The IRGC had sent in a spy posing as a homeless man. He had gotten close to the wisest of the elders, gaining his trust, and then used that trust to poison him. At first, the others only suspected the homeless man—who'd disappeared the same day—until a week later, when they saw the same man on the television, his tattered clothing replaced by a uniform as he stood proudly next to General Moradi. "As long as the people respect the elders more than the government, the IRGC will see this mosque as a threat."

The existence of the elders—a governing body that the people looked to before the Supreme Leader—*was* a huge threat to the IRGC's control over Qeshm Island. Any time the Afro-Iranians asked for things other Iranians took for granted—like fresh water—the government accused them of being troublemakers and separationists.

Isâ made a fist and slammed it into his palm. "We've lived too long under their thumb, worried for our lives just because of our heritage. It's time to take a stand for what's right."

Aziz shook his head. "I appreciate your youth and enthusiasm, but this is not a good idea. If the government finds out we were involved, the IRGC will take out their anger on the entire village."

Heads nodded as the elders spoke softly to each other.

Isâ wiped his brow again. He'd promised Zhina he would be able to get their help. He needed to find a way to convince them.

The Baba Zaar held up his hand, and the murmuring stopped. He was a man of few words, but when he did speak, those words were respected. The Baba leaned on the edge of his staff. "For the past forty-four years, we have tried our best to work with the government in the hopes we could have a normal life, but we are still treated like pariahs in our own country. Since we are Sunnis and speak Arabic, those in power look down on us like we are something less than 'true' Iranians." The Baba held out his hand to the boy with the eyepatch. "Even young Bâbak here has felt their wrath. They blinded him for protesting, for asking for women's rights." He looked around the room. "Can you imagine the reaction of those we serve if we blinded them for having an opinion?"

People mumbled, looking down.

"We took Bâbak in because he was far from his home. It was the right thing to do, even though we knew it could bring the wrath of the IRGC down on us."

None of the elders spoke.

"I see no reason to change our ways now," the Baba said, turning to Isâ. "What would you ask of us, my son?"

"Nothing that would get you in trouble, Baba. I only ask that you do what you always do—heal someone in need."

"Who?"

"It doesn't matter. What I'm proposing is a large Zaar ceremony. I mean no disrespect to anyone's beliefs, but I can use the gathering as cover to help the Americans enter Iran unnoticed. Then they can slip out just as easily, with the blessing of your drums and chanting."

Aziz shook his head. "That would be no better than the IRGC defiling our religious beliefs with their hate and rhetoric. These ceremonies are not for amusement, they are for healing those who cannot be healed. We cannot fabricate an ancient ceremony for any reason."

The Baba held up his hand and the room once again fell silent. "I disagree. Not that we should fabricate a ceremony, but that we cannot have one for any reason." He rubbed the edge of his cane. "There are many coming to me every day to be healed. Most do not have proof that modern medicine was unable to help them, so we have not called for a ceremony." He scanned the room. "I say we invite all those needing a healing to hear the sound of our drums and the songs of the ancients." He shrugged. "If a few Americans happen to walk by while good people get healed, that is not our concern."

Aziz frowned. "That would have to be a huge ceremony. When are the Americans coming?"

Isâ winced. "I don't know. They will tell me when it is time. All I know is that it will be within the next two days." At least, he hoped so. If not, they would need the villagers' help even more because they'd have to hide Dr. Pirouzi from a very angry Moradi with an entire army at his disposal.

The men started to murmur again, and he saw more than a few shaking their heads. Isâ understood their hesitance—what he was asking was a large undertaking, and not giving a solid timeline made things even worse. "They will most likely come under the cover of night. When I know they are coming, I can raise the Dangerous Tide flags on the beach."

"We haven't used those flags in years," Aziz said.

Isâ nodded. "Yes, that is exactly why raising them would be a good signal. And there is no harm in people staying away from the water for a time."

Aziz shook his head. "But that still gives us only a few hours to pull together the ceremony. How can you expect us to get that many people together so quickly, let alone notify the sick?"

The Baba smiled, using his staff to get to his feet. "It will be a challenge, but we have done more with less. We can let the sick know there will be an event when we feel the time is right. It isn't even a lie—we are waiting for the time to be right. They don't need to know what time we are waiting for." He snorted a laugh, showing a wide gap in his teeth. "In the meantime, we can prepare ourselves. We only need one patient for a Zaar, but I guarantee you... if we announce an open ceremony, many will come and join." His gaze carried over the confused, unsure faces. "The worst that can happen is a few extra people get healed."

"That is not the worst that can happen," Aziz said softly.

The Baba placed his hand on the elder's shoulder. "You need faith, my friend. Let's get started." He smiled at Isâ. "You will have your ceremony, my young fisherman, and it is my greatest hope that our song not only gives you the distraction you need but also touches *your* heart."

Isâ huffed out a relieved breath as he left the mosque. He couldn't believe they'd actually agreed!

"Mr. Isâ!" Bâbak, the boy with the eyepatch stood in the doorway, waving him back.

"Yes?"

Bâbak looked left and right. "The man you want to save. Is it Mr. Arman?"

"His name is Arman Pirouzi, yes."

The child beamed. "He is my friend. He is a good man. He helped me escape the prison."

Isâ gaped. "He did?"

"Yes, yes!" Bâbak's grin widened. "God brought me here for a reason, don't you see? God steered me here so we would meet. I want to help Mr. Arman like he helped me."

Isâ smiled down at him. "He really must be a good man if you'd risk yourself for him."

"He is, Mr. Isâ, he is! Please, let me help."

Isâ placed a hand on the boy's shoulder. "I'd be honored to have your help. And I think I have the perfect job for you."

33

Qeshm Coast, Iran

ISÂ'S DAUGHTER, MONA, shook him from his sleep. "Baba! Baba! Come look!" He blinked, rubbing his eyes, startled that the sun was already coming up. How could he have slept so late? Even if he hadn't been on the lookout for the Americans, he would have missed the early morning catch! "Baba, come on!" Mona grabbed his hand and pulled him from the bed. "You must see! You must see!" Isâ rubbed his eyes and pulled on a shirt as he followed her outside. A cold breeze rolled off the ocean as the morning sun glistened on the water, backlighting a massive steel structure floating just offshore. Huge mechanical arms jutted out at sharp angles from the structure's base, one with a cable and hook dangling and swaying with the waves. A massive framework in the center rose high into the sky, like the metal frame of high-rise buildings Isâ had seen on television once when he'd entered

285

the city. Beneath the crane arms were giant boxes bigger than Isâ's entire house. He gaped at it. The structure looked like it could rise out of the ocean at any moment, like the war machines of the American movies he and his brother snuck out to see when they were younger and less afraid of being caught.

Trucks and emergency vehicles with swirling lights lit up the beach as a coastal patrol vessel pulled up onto the sand, carrying three men wrapped in blankets.

"Baba!" Mona cried. "Were those men in the giant boat?"

Isâ nodded. They must have come from the thing, for he saw no other ships aside from the coastal patrol. He grabbed two bottles of water. "Stay by the house."

"But I want to help!" Mona said. "I can run now, like everyone else."

Isâ kissed her head. "I know you can, but I want you back here until I'm sure it's safe. Then we'll look at the giant boat together when the sun is all the way up, okay?"

Her big brown eyes filled with disappointment, but she nodded. For so long, she'd been on the sidelines, watching other children play, unable to keep up. Now that she was stronger, she waited for something exciting to happen so she could show her new strength. Now that day had come and he was telling her to stay behind. He'd make good on the promise to show her the giant craft—as soon as he made sure it wasn't dangerous.

Isâ ran to the shore. "I have fresh water to drink!"

A coastal patrol officer waved him closer. "You live here?"

"Yes. My name is Isâ." He pointed to his hut. "I live right over there, I'm a fisherman."

"Did you see this oil rig come to shore?"

So that was what that monstrosity was. "No. I was asleep. My daughter heard the commotion and woke me up."

An Indian man stepped off the boat and pulled the dark blanket around his shoulders tighter. "You hold water? For please, we thirst," he said in broken Arabic.

Isâ held up the bottles. "Here, my friend. I only have two, though, so please share with your friends."

The man reached out, took the bottles, and then shook his hand. "Thank you, Isâ."

Isâ gaped, surprised the man used his name. The man's grip was stronger than he would have expected for a person who'd been lost at sea, but there was also something hard and square pressed in his palm, cutting into Isâ's skin. A note of some kind? Isâ's eyes widened. He'd been told to expect the arrival of the Americans. Was this them? He glanced up at the massive oil rig. It certainly was more conspicuous than he'd expected. His heart started to beat madly. Isâ knew some spoken English, but he couldn't read it. What if the note wasn't in Arabic? What would he do?

An IRGC soldier appeared at their side, glaring at the man wrapped in the blanket. "What is going on? Why are you here?"

The man flinched and pulled away, taking the note with him. Isâ's heart drummed against his ribs. They could have been caught! The man took a sip of the water, slipping the note back into his own pocket. "We float in sea for three days. We do maintenance on rig, prepare rig for a new crew, but storm hit and broke cables, set us adrift."

"Why didn't you call for help?" the officer asked.

"Believe me, we tried," said another sailor with a dark complexion and a thick accent. "We were able to let the Emirates know we were experiencing inclement weather, but soon after, we lost all communications, and within an hour, we were adrift."

One of the other men added, "We have never been so happy to see land. Where are we?"

"Iran," the guard said. "Qeshm Island, to be exact."

"Well, we are very grateful for your hospitality."

Three more boats headed out toward the rig, each filled with soldiers.

Sweat beaded Isâ's brow despite the slight chill in the air as the weight of the unread note in the man's pocket suddenly weighed him down. "What are they doing?"

"Searching the rig," the officer said. "We need to make sure our borders are secure."

Isâ's bottom lip trembled. If the American soldiers were hiding on that rig...

The Indian man patted Isâ on the shoulder. "Don't worry, we accounted for everyone still on board. We weren't about to leave a friend behind." He made eye contact with Isâ a few moments longer than would have been customary. Was it true? Were these men, who looked small, beaten, and frail, the great American hero soldiers sent to save Dr. Pirouzi?

While the stranded men sat and waited on the beach, Isâ fetched more water but all the while, his eyes were trained on the rig. Finally, the IRGC soldiers got back in their boats and came back to shore.

"The rig is clear," one said. "We found signs of storm damage and no one else was on board."

Isâ looked over at the three stranded men again. Maybe this *was* the American team. But they looked like they needed a hospital themselves, not like they could rescue a man from one. He gritted his teeth, wishing the IRGC had not shown up when they had. If he'd had time to read that note...

The soldier waved the men to their feet. "Come. The Emirates have already been notified of your arrival. We will take you somewhere safe until they arrange passage home." If this was the American rescue team, their plan had already gone seriously awry. The IRGC might take them to the prison— they might even put them through questioning. Then they would need to be rescued themselves or have to break themselves free before saving Zhina's doctor friend.

Isâ's plan required a much more discreet arrival and the Zaar ceremony as cover. There was nothing he could think of to save these men who had arrived in such a completely unmissable way.

"Thank you, kind sir," the Indian man said before turning to Isâ. "And thank you for water. We appreciate the help."

"Yes," the other man said. "We were very thirsty."

The first man shook his hand again, pulled him into a hug, and whispered, "Wait for phone call."

"Come!" the IRGC soldier said, pulling the man down the beach.

The man looked back at Isâ over his shoulder and Isâ nodded, hoping they had not counted on him to do the impossible and free them, because if this *was* the American rescue team, the operation had failed before it had even begun.

34

Qeshm Coast, Iran

ISÂ PACED IN his hut, sweat dampening his shirt. He was just one man. How was he supposed to get those men out of prison? He had no idea what to do. If he'd only gotten that note! A buzz shook from the dresser cabinet near him. Isâ pulled open the top drawer and retrieved the phone from the Americans. "Alo?"

"Mr. Isâ, this is Agent Zarabi of the CIA. Is it safe to speak?"

"Yes. Yes." He looked out the window where all but one of the trucks had departed. "Oil rig offshore. Three men save," Isâ said in his best English.

The American switched to slightly accented Arabic. "Yes, we are aware. I trust the oil rig has been searched, and they've cleared the structure?"

"Yes, but they brought the men on board to the prison."

"They are not your concern. The Emiratis are already en route to pick them up and bring them to safety." Isâ heaved a sigh of relief. That meant they were *not* the soldiers sent for the rescue. "Have you arranged a distraction to hide the extraction unit?" the agent asked.

"Yes. But—"

"Then all you need to know is this… Get in your boat at one-thirty in the morning. Make sure you are not followed. Then sail your boat out to the oil rig and dock on the ocean side at two o'clock in the morning."

"Why? What do you want me to do?"

"Identify yourself as Isâ. Make sure your face is uncovered. That's all you need to know for now."

The line disconnected before Isâ could ask questions. What was he supposed to do on an empty oil rig?

As the sun set and Isâ tried to keep himself busy, his gaze remained locked on the derelict rig stranded over a thousand feet from the beach. What could they possibly expect him to do with it? He certainly couldn't drive it, and chances were there were no instructions on board the vessel or the IRGC would have found them when they inspected the place.

As the night grew late, he tucked Mona into bed and sat down at his table. Part of him wanted to ignore the CIA's request and be done with all this American secrecy, but he made a promise to Zhina, and while he would not take a risk for the Americans, he certainly *would* take one for her.

At one-thirty in the morning he pushed his boat from the mooring and let himself drift until he was far enough from the shore before starting the engines, giving himself just enough push to direct his boat around the back of the oil rig. He docked as directed, his presence shielded from the shore.

The rig towered over his tiny boat, hovering above the surface of the water like a gargantuan creature waiting to consume him. He tied off beside a long metal ladder. The water slapped against the steel, warning of terrors on the horizon, as if the sea itself knew tonight may see horrors no one in his small fishing village had dreamed of.

Taking a deep breath for courage, Isâ ascended the ladder, only to be greeted by the barrel of a large gun. "Identification," the man holding the gun said in Farsi.

Isâ swallowed back his fear. "I am Isâ, the humble fisherman."

Someone shined a light in his face while another held up one of those tablet computers similar to Zhina's. "Clear," the man with the tablet said. "Welcome aboard, Isâ." Isâ squinted in the light. Three dark-skinned men in mottled black and gray clothing stood around him, while three more stood on elevated walkways above.

Isâ gaped. "This is impossible. The IRGC searched the ship. They are very thorough."

"Yes, they were. They searched every locker and every corner of the ship. What they didn't consider was that these rigs are built to float." The man knocked his knuckles on the hull. "And parts of it are hollow."

Isâ continued to gape—he had no idea. "How many of you are there?"

The man with the gun gestured to his compatriots. "This is my team. I'm Scotty. This is Techie, the guy who greeted you is Retro." He looked up to the others. "And in the rafters, we have Nichols, Spiner, and Carnegie. No ranks on this mission. If anyone asks, we're civilians."

"B-but there are only six of you. There are at least a hundred IRGC officers on the island, not to mention the military."

Retro laughed. "Sounds like a party."

"They won't have a chance," Techie said, placing the tablet into a bag hanging over his shoulder.

Isâ looked them over—at least they were all dark-skinned. Three of them could pass as IRGC, while the other three could easily be mistaken for Afro-Iranian, like Isâ. Still, with the numbers of IRGC on this island, it wouldn't be enough. None of them looked concerned, though. Either they were not good at math, or he had not used the right words to describe the situation.

"We are Navy SEALs, son," Scotty said. "All we need is cover for the initial approach. Once we're off the beach, we'll disappear."

"The elders in my village agreed to a large Zaar ceremony on beach. They know of your arrival, and with many people there, you can blend in and hide."

The man called Carnegie jumped from the platform above and landed a few feet from Isâ. "What's a Zaar ceremony?"

Isâ scratched his head beneath his hat. How did one describe a Zaar? "It is religious ceremony. Very loud. Lots of people."

The man called Nichols climbed down the ladder and approached. "It's a little more than that. A Zaar ceremony is a traditional healing and spiritual practice that has roots in various countries in the Middle East and East Africa, including Iran, Egypt, Sudan, Somalia, and Ethiopia. The word 'Zaar' itself means 'possession' in Arabic, and the ceremony is believed to be a way of healing and exorcising evil spirits or negative energies that might be afflicting an individual." He smiled at Isâ. "I have to admit, the Zaar is one of the cultural phenomena that has always fascinated me. I'd be very interested to see one in person."

Scotty adjusted his gun. "This isn't a vacation, Nichols. This is a snatch-and-grab. We get in, we grab the doctor, and we get out—hopefully without being detected."

"I get that," Nichols said. "But you can't begrudge me watching as I run by."

Scotty glared. "Mission first."

Nichols held up his hands. "Of course. I'm a SEAL."

Scotty glanced between Isâ and Nichols. "Tell me more about this ceremony so I know what to expect."

Isâ wrung his hands. "We do have modern medicine in Iran, but there some things that doctors can no heal. Those people go to Baba Zaar for help."

Scotty cocked his head. "Baba Zaar?"

"It's kinda like a witch doctor," Nichols said. "It's a combination of an exorcism mixed with Voodoo. Really potent stuff. It's fascinating."

Scotty nodded at Isâ. "Go on."

Isâ nodded back. He half-expected the man to laugh. At times, Isâ laughed about it himself, so he wouldn't have blamed the SEALs if they thought the ritual foolish. Isâ had lost faith after his wife died—after the elders told him it would be best to allow Mona to die early rather than face a lifetime as a lame woman, unable to earn her keep. Zhina—and modern medicine—had helped Isâ in ways that ancient religion couldn't. Still, he'd never tell the elders that and disrespect such an important part of his heritage.

Isâ wrung his hands again. "They believe spirits called *jinn* attach to humans and cause problems. The Zaar ceremony lures the jinn out and ask them to leave."

Nichols nodded. "Yeah, it's so fascinating. The healing philosophy is based on the effort to free the body from the evil spirit that's causing the ailment. The Baba Zaar undergoes years of education, usually by his father if his dad was a Baba Zaar. Then there is a ceremony to become a Baba Zaar, and they test them and make them take oaths and stuff. This is serious stuff, and if this Baba Zaar offered to help, he must really hate the IRGC."

Isâ grimaced. "They have not been kind to the Afro-Iranians on Qeshm. The Baba Zaar will not allow us to defile the ceremony, but they willing to have the ceremony and look the other way if men walk by who are no familiar."

Scotty leaned against a storage crate. "Okay, I get it. Big, important religious ceremony. But what does it look like? How hard will it be to blend in?"

"There are constant drums in different rhythms," Isâ said. "They repeat the rhythms and chant until the jinn inside the patient starts to dance."

Scotty frowned. "Dance?"

Nichols beamed. "Yes, it looks like convulsive movement in the patient. It shows them that they've connected with the jinn. When the dancing starts, the patient is covered with a linen sheet, and herbs are burned around them to help keep the patient engaged. This goes on for hours before the Baba Zaar takes the patient to a quiet place to cleanse the jinn and ask them to leave."

Scotty narrowed his eyes. "Cleanse?"

Isâ bit his bottom lip. This was the part where most non-believers would balk. He didn't want these foreigners to think less of his elders.

"Remember what I said about the voodoo?" Nichols continued. "They need fresh blood. Usually it's a chicken. They coat their canes and stuff in the blood." He shrugged. "I don't get the appeal, personally, but there's tons of research that says this helps people. You can't refute science, even if the science doesn't seem all that scientific."

"All this is really supposed to help people?" Carnegie asked.

"Hell, yeah." Nichols nodded. "The Zaar ceremony is deeply rooted in cultural and spiritual traditions and is often regarded as an important form of therapy, particularly in communities where more conventional medical treatments may not be readily accessible or as effective." He shrugged. "While some view the practice as spiritual and therapeutic, others might interpret it as superstitious or unscientific. But like I said, it seems to help people, so I find it incredibly cool."

Carnegie shoved him. "Why do you always sound like a textbook?"

Nichols shoved him back. "Hey, I read. Opening a book wouldn't hurt you once in a while."

"Why would I waste my time when I can just ask you, and you know everything already?"

Isâ twisted his hands, hoping the men were joking. "Important thing is that Zaar ceremonies are common. The

IRGC will no think it odd that a large Zaar ceremony suddenly start on beach."

Scotty stared out at the water, considering. "I like the part about lots of people and lots of chanting and drums. The noise will make great cover."

"Not to mention the possibility of hiding under the sheets," Nichols said. "But that would only be a last resort, because that would probably be a bit disrespectful."

Isâ nodded, thankful that they were considerate of his people's religious beliefs.

Scotty looked over his men. "That's the plan, boys. We hang tight until the chanting starts, then we use the cover of the ceremony to walk right past the IRGC, extract Dr. Pirouzi, and walk him out right under all their noses."

"Will it really be that easy?" Isâ asked.

"No. It never is, but that's what we're going to do nonetheless."

Isâ gulped. The man spoke with such assurance. Hopefully, his bravado was warranted and no one got hurt. Isâ would feel terrible if anyone's life was ruined because of his plan to help a man he didn't even know. All he needed to do now was get back to the beach and plant a flag in the ground, letting the Baba know that tonight was the night for the largest Zaar ceremony this island had seen in years.

35

Imam Hospital, Iran

ARMAN HOBBLED DOWN the hall, pulled along by IRGC officers. His new leg brace helped, but he still felt weak. Hopefully, if their plans went well, he would be strong enough to make it out of the hospital to the relative safety of the Navy SEALs. The officers shoved Arman through a door marked *Video Conferencing.* He stumbled, grabbing the wall before a muffled grunt called his attention to the back of the room. He gasped, finding his good friend Ârash gagged and tied to a chair. "Don't look so surprised," General Moradi said. "He is here to make sure you confess your crimes to the world and confirm that you were not tortured in order to get this confession. If you stray from this in any way, you will be wearing your friend's blood. Do you understand?"

Ârash's gaze locked with Arman's. He couldn't move, but his eyes were as defiant as ever, just as they had been when they were both children. It was clear the man had no intention of just sitting back and taking it, and he wanted Arman to know it.

"I understand," Arman said.

Ârash was an added complication, but maybe it was a good thing. If Ârash was left behind, he'd no doubt be executed. Now, if things went according to plan, maybe they could all escape together.

The cameraman wiped sweat from his brow as he made final adjustments to his equipment and opened the window, muttering about the heat. He must have been from the mountains—the weather was no warmer tonight than any other time on Qeshm Island. As he walked away from the window the sounds of drums carried from the distance a dull, regular beat—the Zaar ceremony. Soon, the whole night would be filled with chanting and—hopefully—enough people to hide the Americans and aid their escape.

General Moradi slapped the table with his palm. "We begin." He pointed at a metal chair next to the Iranian flag. "You will sit and prepare to tell the world what you have done." Arman counted back from ten, but it did little to settle the churning in his gut. A guard walked across the room and stood behind Ârash, the threat clear. Arman needed to make sure Ârash didn't become a casualty during their escape plan.

The drumming became louder as more people joined the Zaar, though it didn't seem to be getting any closer. Maybe they were staying near the beach to give the Americans the cover they needed. He couldn't do much more than hope the soldiers would make it to the hospital in time.

Arman sat in the chair and General Moradi stood beside him, the flag visible behind his right shoulder. The cameraman focused on him, counted down, and nodded as he began recording. Moradi lifted his chin. "In the name of God, the beneficent, the merciful. Greetings, righteous people of Iran." He paused, no doubt imagining people shouting to the skies and praising God—or perhaps praising Moradi himself. In the General's eyes, they were one and the same. "Today, we praise God and the Supreme Leader with excellent news on the progress of our holy war against imperialism. We have caught one of the most dangerous Western spies to ever step foot in Iran. Dr. Arman Pirouzi came to us under the guise of teaching medicine, but he was in fact meeting with a spy, intending to sell intelligence that is crucial to the survival of not only Iran, but God's holy church." He pointed at Arman. "This man represents one of the greatest threats to our government we've seen in years, and despite reports from Western media, there has been no torture involved in bringing him to this point. Dr. Pirouzi is here to testify to this truth and tell us why he has decided to turn on his comrades in the West for the good of Iran." Moradi punched his own chest. "Under my direction, we have seen this ungodly criminal brought to justice, and I am here to bear witness for you and for God, as he confesses his crimes."

Moradi held up his hand, and the camera turned to Arman. Across the room, Ârash struggled in his seat, grunting against the gag in his mouth. He didn't need words—his eyes said it all... *fight*.

But fighting wasn't part of the plan—not yet at least.

Arman turned and looked into the camera. "I-I am Dr. Arman Pirouzi." He swayed, half-closing his eyes and parting his lips. "I-I..." He fell over, hitting the table and dropping to the floor.

Ârash screamed through his gag, his chair scraping against the tile.

Arman lay motionless with his eyes closed. He wished he could tell his friend that he was okay, that this was part of the plan, but maybe it was better this way, since Ârash's reaction was unrehearsed and very real.

"What's going on?" Moradi yelled. "Turn off the camera, you fool!" Boots stomped across the floor. "Go find his doctor, you imbeciles!"

More stomps and the door opened and closed. *Good.* The guard and possibly also the cameraman were gone. Hopefully, they'd stay gone.

Across the room, Ârash continued to shout into his gag. Moradi paced the room, grumbling to himself. The door opened and closed.

"What happened?" Zhina's voice filled the room before Arman was rolled onto his back. She placed her fingers on the side of his neck. "He has no pulse! How long has he been like this?"

"I don't know, a few moments?" Moradi growled. "He's been there as long as it took that imbecile to find you."

Zhina squeezed Arman's hand. He appreciated the support, but he hoped that no one had noticed.

"I need help with the defibrillator." She released Arman's hand. "Bring the box closer and open it up for me."

Moradi growled. "How *dare* you try to command me, you little—"

"If you want this man to live long enough to get your confession, you'll help me. If not, let him die. It makes no difference to me."

Arman gritted his teeth to keep from smiling. Zhina still had her fire.

"Fine," Moradi growled, stomping across the room.

Arman felt Zhina's palms on his sternum, and slight, rhythmic compressions. To anyone trained, it would be clear she wasn't doing real compressions, but it would be enough to fool Moradi.

"Here," Moradi said, slamming the defibrillator to the floor next to him.

Zhina stopped the simulated chest compressions. "Good. Open his shirt while I get the machine ready."

"You want *me* to open his shirt?" Moradi asked.

"I certainly can't ask the man tied to a chair to help! If you want Dr. Pirouzi to live, help me!"

Excellent—she'd found a reason to make sure Moradi was close. Hopefully, he'd stay there.

Moradi tugged vigorously at Arman's shirt; he was probably worried his chance of getting his coveted confession was lying there dying.

The door opened and a new voice filled the room. "General! What happened?"

Shit, the guard is back.

"Rip his shirt away," Moradi said. "She needs to get to his skin."

The guard started tugging on Arman's other side. So, Moradi was on his left and the guard was on his right. If he only successfully jolted Moradi, they'd have to deal with the guard who no doubt had a gun. He had to get them both.

Arman tried his best not to take a deep breath for courage as Zhina placed the contacts on his chest. It was the last step before she sent an electric shock through his body that would stop his heart—and hopefully kill the vile beasts next to him. Arman gritted his teeth—he would get only one chance.

"Okay." Zhina sounded uncertain. "I-I'm going to do this."

Arman slitted his eyes open to see both Moradi and the guard release his clothing and stand, one on either side of him. They each remained close, perhaps out of morbid curiosity.

Zhina met Arman's gaze through his hooded eyes. "Three. Two. One."

Arman reached out and grabbed ahold of the guard's leg and then Moradi's. Oddly, the General's leg was cold and hard. Arman's eyes went wide.

No!

"Clear!" Zhina called, placing the paddles on Arman's chest.

He felt searing pain as his body convulsed, then nothing at all.

36

Imam Hospital, Iran

ZHINA HELD BACK a sob as Arman's body jumped beneath the paddles. Her heart ached as he went fully limp.

What have I done?

The guard fell to the floor with a *thump*. Moradi cursed, staring down. His eyes turned manic, and he started laughing before reaching down and prying Arman's hand off his leg.

"You piece of shit she-devil!" He snarled, pulling up his pant leg. "Look at the glory of God!"

Zhina backed away, stunned. The man had a prosthetic leg—the jolt had grounded and never reached his heart!

General Moradi tilted his head back and laughed. "Years ago, while I was purging the Earth of infidels, I lost my leg in battle. At the time, I could not understand why God would do this to me. Now, I understand that it was not a punishment—it was a blessing. He took my leg all those years ago to save me in this very moment." He raised his fist to the sky. "I *am* His chosen one!" His smile faded and he pointed at Arman. "But I need this piece of shit to fulfill my ultimate destiny. You will revive him now so he can confess and take me one step closer to my holy legacy." He grabbed Zhina by the scarf around her head and shoved her. "Hurry, woman! If he dies, then you die with him."

Zhina stumbled back, tripping over the medical case she'd brought in. It burst open, spilling syringes and vials of medicines she'd brought with her to revive Arman.

The General snarled at her. "I am too close! I will not let you and your ungodly ways steal my destiny from me!"

An empty sixty cc syringe rolled across the floor and rested at Arman's side.

"What are you doing, woman?" Moradi spat. "Save him!"

Zhina unfroze, scooping up her supplies. She injected Arman with epinephrine and started chest compressions.

He looked so pale, his skin already turning cold. She'd done this to him—she'd killed him and he had trusted her to bring him back. They risked everything for this one chance and Moradi still lived.

If Zhina managed to revive him, the General would surely torture him before killing them both. It would probably be more merciful to let Arman die, but she couldn't bring herself to do it. He'd been lost to her, and she'd just found him again. She couldn't let him go, even if it was the right thing to do.

She grabbed the paddles and shocked him again. Moradi took a large step back as she did, though Zhina was fully focused on Arman. There was no heartbeat.

"No!" She started chest compressions again. He couldn't die. A few hours ago they had their whole lives left to live. Together. That dream was lost unless she found a way to save him.

She grabbed the paddles again and placed them on his chest again. His body jumped, and Zhina burst into tears as Arman's eyes opened.

37

Imam Hospital, Iran

A BLAST OF light hit Arman's eyes as they fluttered open. He was on the floor. A man lay beside him, his eyes open and unfocused, a final expression of surprise frozen on his lips.

Zhina's face came into focus.

Zhina… It had been so long since he'd seen her. They'd had so much fun at school. He hadn't thought he'd ever see her again. Was he dreaming? Was he dead?

Dead. There was something about death that felt right… like he expected it. Was this what was supposed to happen?

Zhina wiped tears from her eyes. *Why is she crying?*

"I saved you." Tears continued to stream from her beautiful eyes. "Thank God, I saved you."

Just like she promised to do.

Arman blinked and rubbed his head. Why was everything so foggy?

Across the room, Ârash wiggled in his seat. White plastic ties bound his wrists and ankles to the chair. A gag covered his mouth and a trickle of blood ran from his nose. Why was Ârash here, and who had tied him up?

A deep, booming laugh filled the room. "I win!" A man stood above Arman in military fatigues, leaning on his knee as he jabbed a finger at him. "Now you will give me the confession you promised."

Confession?

"I'm sorry." Zhina swept back sweat-damp hair. "It didn't work."

It didn't work?

The man started laughing again, and a whirlwind of colors and sounds slammed into Arman's mind. The man. Fatigues. A general. General Moradi.

Alive.

No. It couldn't be.

The laughing grew louder at Arman's shocked expression. "Did you think it would be so easy to kill me?" Moradi asked. "I am God's hand on Earth. I stand here because He sees all. He knows all!"

Arman gasped as everything became clear. Their plan had failed—the bastard was still alive.

General Moradi turned toward the door. "Rostami! Get in here!"

Arman clenched his fists as Officer Rostami entered the room with two other guards and the cameraman. Their eyes met. Rostami's face was a picture of stoic IRGC calm, unlike the panic in his eyes on the operating table when he'd asked Arman to save him.

Rostami's jaw tensed as he turned to Moradi. "General."

Moradi pointed at Zhina. "Arrest this woman and pull this other piece of shit off the floor and put him in the chair. I will have my confession tonight if I have to cut his friend's fingers off one at a time."

Rostami nodded. "Of course, General." He looked back to the guards. "You, get the woman, and you, grab that piece of trash on the floor and get him back in front of the camera."

Arman closed his eyes and gritted his teeth. It was too much to hope for mercy from the man—once an IRGC officer, always an IRGC officer.

There had been a chance with only one guard in the room, but with three, plus Moradi, and who knew how many more guards outside, their dreams of escape and saving Iran from this terrible man had come to an end.

"Let go!" Zhina struggled as the guard hauled her away from him.

The other guard grabbed Arman by the arm and yanked him up before shoving him back in the seat beside the flag.

The room spun around him as reality sunk in. In the depths of Arman's mind, he'd expected to see home again. He'd held out hope their crazy plan would work, but his luck ran out at the worst possible time. Now he, Zhina, and even Ârash would feel the consequences of his failure.

Moradi rolled up his sleeves and punched Ârash in the face. Blood tricked down Ârash's nose, but he still defiantly held Arman's gaze. Arman wanted to resist too, but he simply didn't have any more fight left in him.

"I'll do it." Arman jerked his arm out of the guard's grip. "I'll say whatever you want. Just leave him be."

The chances of Ârash being set free, even if Arman confessed, were probably zero, but he had to try. Arman and Zhina's fates were already decided, but Ârash was an innocent, a pawn used to leverage the confession. Moradi might take pity on him, if there could be any pity in a man without a soul.

Arman sat behind the table and stared into the camera as the videographer adjusted the lens. He blinked away wetness, staring down at the short statement taped to the table until it came into focus. It was simple, really. All he had to do was speak these words into the camera, and all his torture, all his suffering, would be over. He'd probably be shot by a firing squad or maybe hanged. Either would be fairly painless, at least compared to the continued torture. And he could always bite the implant in his jaw and steal the satisfaction from General Moradi.

Maybe I should just bite it now and get it over with. Then he could rob Moradi of the confession as well.

A gunshot echoed through the room and the guard dragging Zhina toward the exit dropped to the floor. She stood frozen, gaping at him as he lay at her feet, red spreading across his chest.

The guard beside Arman cursed and reached for his gun as another deafening shot rang out. He dropped, and behind him stood Rostami, his weapon raised, the barrel smoking.

"What's going on!?" a new guard yelled, stepping into the doorway.

Rostami spun, firing. The guard ducked away, the bullet hitting the doorframe in a shower of splinters.

Gunfire erupted from the hall. Zhina screamed, dropping to the floor and a stray bullet hit the cameraman as he attempted to do the same.

General Moradi ignored the gunfire, his eyes fixed on Arman as he lunged for him. "You piece of shit! This is not over! I will have my confession!"

Arman stumbled back, tangled up in his chair. His leg exploded in pain as Moradi slammed into him, shoving him back against the wall.

"Help Ârash!" Arman yelled. Zhina ran for Ârash, still tied to the chair and screaming into his gag.

Moradi threw a punch, and Arman dropped beneath it, the General's meaty fist hitting the wall. The man let out a roar of rage as Arman scrambled away, his fingers brushing a large, sixty cc syringe on the floor, forgotten since spilling out of Zhina's bag. He snatched it and pulled himself to his feet with the side of the desk.

General Moradi lumbered toward him, his gaze falling on the syringe. His lips twisted into a sneer. "You think you can kill me with a needle? I have killed more soldiers—real men—with my own hands than you could imagine."

Arman clenched his jaw, working to keep his eyes focused. He pulled the plunger on the empty syringe, filling it with air.

Moradi stalked closer. "I am going to break your miserable legs and your scrawny arms. Then, while you lie there and watch, I am going to slowly kill that bitch and your sniveling friend." The veins in his neck pulsed with each angry word. "While your soul weeps, I will get my confession. Then, and only then, will I allow you to die."

Moradi leaped for him, arms outstretched. It took everything Arman had to just stand there and not try to dodge out of his grasp. Instead, he focused on those thick veins, lifting the syringe and allowing the General's own momentum to drive the needle into one. As soon as it met flesh, Arman pressed the plunger, injecting a burst of air straight into the General's jugular.

Moradi tore the syringe from Arman's hand, throwing it aside. He wiped at his neck, rubbing the tiny smear of blood between his fingers. "You want to hurt me with a pinprick? You will have to do better than that." He pounded his chest. "I am *His* chosen. I am the one who will…" Moradi hesitated, clutching his chest. He glared at Arman. "What did you do?"

Arman supported himself on the edge of the desk. "That was for Niki and all the young girls you have killed."

Moradi fell to his knees, clutching his throat. "Can't. Breathe."

It was something any good interventionalist knew—air in a vein was deadlier than any wrong medicine.

Arman stood over him as he slumped to the ground. "Air, oddly enough, can stop you from breathing if it gets into your veins. It's a pity you ran into that syringe."

Moradi grimaced, reaching weakly for Arman. "I'm… going to kill you…"

Arman watched the man's hand drop, limp. "No, I don't think you are."

He backed away and shuddered as a chill swept through him. He'd made an oath to protect lives, not take them, but in this instance, he had done a public service. The monster lying on the floor killed so many and would have killed even more. Too many people had been too afraid to stand up to him. Now, maybe others would realize they had the power to do the right thing.

Arman was shaken from his thoughts by Ârash's hand falling on his shoulder. His friend turned him around and pulled him into a hug. "I am glad you are not dead."

Arman laughed. "Me too. But we still have to get out of here."

"Get down!" Rostami yelled.

Another gunshot ripped through the room, the bullet splintering the wall behind Arman, who crouched along with Ârash and Zhina.

Rostami fired two quick shots out of the doorway and Arman heard a *thud* as a body dropped in the hall. Rostami peeked out into the hall, then back at Arman, his brows tight.

"It's usually better to duck *before* the shot."

Arman gave him a weak nod. "Thank you, my friend. We'd already be dead if you hadn't helped."

"And I'd be dead if you hadn't proven to me you were the kind of man worth saving. Check the other bodies for guns."

Arman patted down General Moradi but found nothing on him; he'd counted on others to carry weapons for him. Arman stared down at his pale face and wondered if Moradi would be lauded as a martyr. Another ambitious man would no doubt take his place, but at least this particular zealot had been stopped. Hopefully the good people of Iran would get things in order before someone as charismatic and extremist reared his head and replaced Moradi.

Arman looked away and leaned his forehead against the cool wall. He had dealt with plenty of death in his career, but it had never come from his own hands.

"Nothing," Zhina said, patting the cameraman's jacket.

Arman cursed, *"Shâns-e-goh!"* ("Crappy luck!")

Ârash stood up by the last guard, holding a black handgun. "I found this!"

Rostami glanced back from where he stood at the door, watching the hallway. Arman heard shouts and footfalls getting closer with each passing second. He gestured for Ârash to step forward, then plucked the gun out of his hand, flicked a switch, and handed it back. "The safety is off. Just point and shoot. Make sure no one you care about is between you and the target."

Ârash's eyes widened. He was a pacifist, like Arman. Neither ever dreamed they'd be in a position like this. Ârash gulped and leaned against the desk, his eyes wide with a mixture of fear and determination. Zhina picked up her first aid kit and clutched it to her chest.

Rostami lifted a finger to his lips, urging silence as the footfalls in the hallway grew louder. Arman's heart pounded in his chest and Rostami's gaze met his, the officer's eyes conveying a silent message: *Stay calm. Stay quiet.*

Arman looked at his friends, who gave him silent nods. They were putting their lives in Rostami's hands, whatever the man's plan was.

An IRGC guard burst into the room, gun in hand. "General Moradi!"

Rostami moved with lightning speed, striking the man's throat with a powerful blow. He gasped, his weapon falling to the floor before he collapsed.

Chaos erupted as the other IRGC officers outside shouted, firing through the doorway indiscriminately—they must have realized Moradi was dead and no longer were concerned about hitting him. Arman grabbed Zhina and dove for cover behind the desk, his wounded leg throbbing against his brace as he moved.

Rostami snatched the fallen gun and returned fire. He shouted to Arman over the din. "The hallway directly across from this room looks clear." He looked over his shoulder to Zhina. "Can you get them out from there?"

Her eyes widened before the fear turned to resolve. "Yes."

Rostami gave her a curt nod and plucked something from the downed man's belt before returning his attention to the door. "I'll provide cover while the three of you get out of here."

"What about you?" Zhina asked.

His face was a mask of determination as he let his gun hang on the sling and Arman saw what he had scavenged—a grenade. He pulled the pin. "When this goes off, run for it. I will be behind you."

He released his grip. A lever sprung free from the grenade and clattered on the floor. Rostami waited only a second before lobbing it into the hall. Screams and a rush of footsteps were cut off in an earth-shaking *boom* that sent plaster dust raining from the ceiling.

"Go!" Rostami yelled, leaning out the door and opening fire.

Adrenaline pumped through Arman's veins as he grabbed Zhina and locked fingers with Ârash. If they were going to die, at least they'd die free and together.

They dashed through the doorway. Arman only caught a glimpse of the carnage—not all the guards were dead—one was aiming right at him, crouched behind a scorched stretcher. A bullet whizzed by Arman's ear before Rostami shot the man dead, then they were across the hall in relative safety.

Arman looked back at the man who just saved them. Rostami was IRGC, but in the end, he realized where his allegiances truly lay. Arman prayed for a miracle that would allow him to escape, but he knew it was unlikely. Perhaps Rostami had come to terms with everything he'd done over the years and realized that, while he could not save those he'd terrorized in the past, he could save these few who might go on to save still more.

And that was exactly what Arman intended to do.

38

Imam Hospital, Iran

ZHINA FLINCHED AS the sounds of gunfire escalated behind them.

So much death.

"Keep running!" Arman tugged at her arm, but she was already going as fast as she could.

A bullet hit the wall beside her, and she skidded to a stop, pulling Arman and Ârash into a window alcove that once housed a Ficus tree that was now long dead.

"What are you doing?" Ârash clutched the gun to his chest, his hand shaking.

Zhina closed her eyes. They had to keep running, but it would be suicide. "This is a long straight corridor—we're sitting ducks if we run down it."

An angry shout filled the hall they came from. "Cowering are you?" The sound of a slap echoed off the tiles. "Those *bisharfha* just killed General Moradi!"

Arman paled. "Islami. I'd know that voice anywhere."

Zhina cringed. Arman had confided in her about some of the unthinkable tortures the man had perpetrated on him. He'd probably be hearing that monster's voice in his dreams for many years to come.

Ârash saw Arman's reaction and his face hardened. "You will not hurt anyone else I love!"

He stepped out and fired the gun twice. A dull *thud* sounded and Ârash's eyes widened. Zhina yanked him back into the alcove.

When no more sounds came from the hall, Arman yelled, "Come on!" He pulled them from the alcove, rushing to the end of the hall and around a corner out of the direct line of fire.

Arman slowed, his chest heaving. His brow creased in pain. Zhina supported him, pausing for a small moment so he could catch his breath. Ârash cast wary glances behind them, though the other guards weren't following… yet.

"Which way do we go?" Arman asked.

"This way." Zhina set off, both men following. The exit light glowed at the end of the hall like a beacon of hope. She allowed herself to let out a breath. They were going to get out!

Four strides away, the door opened, revealing two guards. Zhina skidded to a halt, Ârash slammed into her from behind.

"There they are!" the guard yelled.

Ârash shoved Zhina aside, raised his gun, then fired three shots that missed, the guards sent diving for cover back out the door.

"Come on!" Zhina yelled, dragging Arman down the next hall. There were other exits that could lead them to the beach. With all the confusion, it was unlikely the IRGC were watching all of them, but every moment that passed it became more and more likely the hospital was locked down. There were exits few knew of, but they weren't easy to get to. She ran around another corner and opened the door to the laundry room. They slipped inside and Zhina bolted the door behind them. Ârash placed his back against the wall and slipped to the floor, resting his forehead on his knees and holding the gun atop his head. He rocked forward and back, not making a noise.

Arman sat beside him. "My friend, I know this is hard."

"I just killed someone." Ârash continued to rock. "I killed someone. I killed someone. I killed someone."

Arman grabbed his shoulders. "I need you to be strong. If you let this into your head, we could all die."

Ârash blinked, looking up. "I don't want to lose you, too."

"Then I need you to get up! The only way for us to live is if we work together and get out of here. Sitting on the floor is asking for death. It's letting them win."

Arman pointed at his friend and then curved his finger.

Ârash stared before nodding slowly. "Yes. I'm with you. Forever." Ârash hooked his finger with Arman's before Arman pulled him to his feet.

Arman looked around at the old, dented light-duty machines and the four solid brick walls. "There's no way out."

"We're trapped," Ârash whispered.

Zhina made for the far wall. "No. There's a chute to send bulk laundry down to the lower level." She pushed on a swinging door about two feet square set in the wall. "We joked that we could probably fit a person in there."

Arman peered down into the darkness. "How far down?" The hole in the wall echoed with his voice.

"One floor," Zhina said softly.

"What would we land on?" Ârash asked.

Someone in the hall outside tried the door, shaking the handle when it didn't open.

"Whatever we land on will be safer than getting shot," Arman said. "Let's go." He held open the swinging door. "Ladies first."

"*Now* you decide to be chivalrous?" Zhina muttered, swinging one leg into the chute.

"It had to happen someday or another."

"Wish me luck."

Arman gave her a quick kiss, and she dropped herself into the chute. Darkness engulfed her as she slid down a long, narrow tube. Her hair dampened, humidity and the stench of vomit and urine engulfing her until she crashed to a halt in a pile of blankets. A moment later, automatic lights flickered on and the room was cast in a soft, yellow glow.

She scrambled out of the pile of filthy laundry. "It's okay!" she called back up the chute. "Come on!"

Ârash came down first, and she quickly helped him out of the pile. Arman came tumbling down a moment after. He hit the soft material with a grunt and then rolled out, holding his injured leg.

Zhina ran to him and helped him up. "Are you okay?"

He gritted his teeth, his face red. "I'm fine."

The sound of guards banging on the laundry door and shouting echoed down the metal chute from the room above. Eventually, they'd break down the door, and it wouldn't take them long after that to figure out where their prey had gone.

Zhina needed to take advantage of every moment and find a way to get away while they still could. Her gaze swept over the stacks of linens, detergents, and machines until she spied a door on the far side of the room.

She pointed. "That has to lead to the street. We can slip out from there and find a way to blend in until we're clear."

They sprinted over, and as she placed her hand on the door, a metallic clang reverberated through the air—the guards had forced their way into the room above.

Zhina pushed the door open, revealing a dimly lit corridor.

"I thought it was an exit?" Ârash said.

Zhina gulped. "I thought it would be."

The chute clanged as someone slid down it.

"We have to go!" Arman said, pulling them both through the door. He slammed it behind them before they hurried down the narrow passage.

Zhina's lungs burned as she tried to think. "W-we're on the east side of the building. If I'm right, there's a maintenance tunnel ahead. It leads to an underground storage area. We can lose them there."

As they entered the tunnel, the sounds of pursuit faded, but to her despair, the tunnel twisted in the opposite direction. Zhina's stomach sank—there weren't any basement-level exits on that side of the building. Still, they had no choice but to keep moving forward.

They emerged into a cavernous storage space filled with crates and machinery, much of it labeled for recycling. It was what the maintenance men called "The Pit of Despair," where they sent old machines to die. Zhina only hoped it wouldn't be their death.

Arman grabbed her arm and pulled her between a stack of crates. She ducked as shadows moved through the room, cast from waving flashlights, the beams lancing the air over their heads.

"We're trapped," Ârash whispered.

Arman looked up, squinting at the ceiling. Zhina followed his gaze and traced the massive ventilation ducts overhead.

"Can we get through those?" she asked.

"It'll be tight and probably filled with dust and bugs. Don't think it's like in the movies."

Ârash gulped. "We have to try."

Truer words had never been spoken. When the last of the flashlights disappeared, Zhina climbed up onto one of the crates. "Someone help me."

Arman laced his fingers together and Zhina stepped onto his hands so he could hoist her up onto his shoulders. Arman swayed, and Ârash caught him.

Zhina steadied herself on the ceiling tiles, looking down at him. "Are you okay?"

Arman grimaced. "J-just go. I won't let you fall."

Even with his injury, she found she trusted him completely—he wouldn't let her fall. Luckily, there was an access point for maintenance and it was easy to remove—finally one thing in their favor.

Ârash gave her an extra shove, and she pulled herself through the opening and into the tube. The thin metal material clanged, buckling with her weight, but it seemed solid enough to hold.

She could hear Ârash struggling to get up into the tube behind her. She winced as the vent buckled further but held firm. Which made sense—the maintenance workers normally inside these ducts likely weighed far more than any of them.

"Come on, I've got you," Ârash said.

Arman grunted as Ârash helped pull him up. "I've never been much of a climber," he panted when he was safely in the vent. "That was not easy."

He'd been tortured for far too long, his only exercise his therapy sessions with Zhina—it'd been a good decision to send Ârash first to pull Arman up.

The men followed as Zhina dragged herself through the tube. "Ugh." She pulled cobwebs from her face, praying the spider wasn't still there.

"You're doing fine," Arman said from behind.

"Thanks for the vote of confidence. Luckily, there's only one way to go—straight." She squinted. "At least, I think so."

Dark wasn't the word for it. Past the entrance, she felt blind and didn't even want to think about what she might be dragging her body through.

A gravelly voice sounded from below. "What was that?"

Zhina froze. A few more voices murmured, along with shuffling footsteps.

"Let me check," another voice said.

The ductwork several feet in front of her bulged, letting out a *clang* as someone pushed on it from below, and then another as it was released. She prayed they were pushing on it with a broom handle, but she knew it could just as easily be a rifle.

The duct bent in again, this time a foot closer.

Clang-clang.

She could hear stifled panting behind her from Ârash. She wanted to tell him to shush, but even that noise might be too much.

Clang-clang.

This time, it was only inches from her face. The next time they pushed on the duct they'd feel her weight. Could she arch her body and avoid it? If she could, would the men be able to do the same?

Zhina heard the scraping of metal below her chest as the vent bulged against her, even as she tried to hold herself above it.

This was it. They'd be discovered. They'd shoot her and the others through the ducts and leave them there to die or for the rats to eat. No one would ever know what had happened to her.

"Come on," someone called from below. "They want us to check outside."

Zhina's heart drummed madly against her ribs, as if trying to free itself. Sweat matted her hair to her forehead and more trickled down her face, but she didn't dare move. The pressure against her chest fell away. Someone mumbled below, and then a door shut.

She placed her forehead against the cool metal below her, ignoring the dust and grime. How had she gone from being an accomplished therapist to a fleeing criminal so quickly?

The aluminum sheets surrounding her buckled, and she lurched falling towards the floor.

"Zhina!" Arman screamed.

Fluorescent lighting blinded her and the world spun as she fell face-first toward a white-tile floor. She shrieked, covering her face before she jolted to a sudden halt, pain shooting through her leg.

Zhina swung several feet above the floor. She looked up and found Arman held her by the ankle, his eyes bulging and face red, his arm shaking with exertion.

"Ârash—" he began but never finished.

The rest of the duct squealed and Zhina resumed her race toward the ground. She held her hands out, jamming one wrist as she crashed into the tiles. She wheezed, the air knocked out of her lungs as Arman landed on top of her and Ârash atop him.

Ârash rolled off his friend as Arman groaned. Zhina vomited yellow bile over the tiles, her head spinning. Slow, steady breaths eased the pain slightly as a long table came into fuzzy focus. She'd barely missed cracking her head on the edge when she fell.

Arman's face hovered over her. "Are you okay?" He offered her a hand.

"I think so," she said as he helped her up. "Are you? You look like you're about to fall over."

Ârash was staring to the side, his nose bleeding again, a purple bruise forming around his eye. "I can't believe it!"

Zhina blinked away the last of her fog and saw what caught his eye—four large windows and a door with a bright exit sign centered between them.

"Come on!" Arman bolted for the door, dragging her behind him.

As crazy as it was, she couldn't stop thinking like his therapist—how did he move so fast with his injuries? It had to be adrenaline, and when it wore out, he would probably collapse and need another hospital stay. She just had to hope his strength lasted until they were safe.

Zhina followed, trusting his lead as her head continued to spin. She couldn't be the weak link in this escape. Arman wouldn't leave without her, and Ârash wouldn't leave without him. If she faltered, all were as good as dead.

They burst through the door into hot night air and some sort of sunken cement alley. The sounds of the sea called from the left, overshadowed by the shouting of guards above them.

"There!"

Gunshots rang out, and Ârash fired back blindly as they all ran with no real goal in mind aside from *away*. The pavement beneath her feet sloped down—possibly a delivery entrance.

"No! Not that way!" a young voice shouted. "Mr. Arman! Come this way!"

Arman skidded to a stop and turned. A boy with a patch over one eye peeked from behind a thick hedge, beckoning to him.

Arman ran for him. "Bâbak! What are you doing here?"

"Saving you like you saved me! Come. This hole is big enough for us both." He ducked into a break between two thorny bushes.

Arman waved the others over. "Come on! We can trust him!"

A bullet screamed past Zhina's ear and she ran. Stopping meant death. Thorns scraped her arm as she squeezed through and stumbled into a partially lit street. The scent of sea air wafted around her, and a dull drumming sound echoed through the street, so loud it rivaled the shouts of the guards. The Zaar ceremony!

"Come, Mr. Arman, Come!"

The child led them past long rows of open-air street vendors. Three old men sitting on their haunches holding plates of food watched as they ran past in the dusty streets.

The drums grew louder. They were free, but they were far from out of danger.

"Come on!" Zhina grabbed Arman's hand. "We're almost there!"

39

Qeshm Coast, Iran

ISÂ STOOD IN the sand as moonlight glistened on the waters of the Persian Gulf. Evening was always the most peaceful time to look over the water. Some days, he liked to bring his boat out just to enjoy the silence, but tonight there was none.

Drums filled the air behind him, and the voice of the Baba Zaar rose, followed by many others. The Baba Zaar held his staff high as he walked across the sand, dozens of people following him. The Baba smiled at Isâ as he passed, probably to remind him that he was doing the right thing. But as he looked out at the still-calm, pristine waters, Isâ had to wonder if this was all for naught.

Where are the Americans? If the ceremony passed the beach and the soldiers weren't ready, all of this planning would be for nothing.

People streamed from huts and in moments, the crowd doubled. Isâ had never seen so many come so quickly, especially since this hadn't been planned. Had the Baba arranged this somehow?

The drums grew louder, the incessant, staccato beat grating against the increasing rhythm of Isâ's own heart. The sea still sparkled, tranquil in the moonlight. But no Americans. He'd failed. No one was coming.

Someone tapped him on the back, and Isâ jumped.

"Greetings, my friend," a man said in flawless Farsi. "I did not mean to frighten you."

Isâ spun, holding his chest. Behind him stood the soldier named Scotty, wearing a sturdy, earth-colored shirt common amongst the men of Isâ's village.

Isâ gaped, looking out at the sea and then back to the soldier. "How?"

Scotty adjusted something hidden under the long, loose clothing—his gun, no doubt. "A story for another day."

Three men walked past, two beating drums, the other chanting. The one chanting was the soldier called Nichols, who'd sounded excited at seeing the Zaar ceremony. How long had they all been here?

Scotty scanned the people, including at least three more of his soldiers, walking calmly with the group—being respectful, thank goodness. "Where's the hospital?" he asked.

Isâ pointed through the crowd. "Up that hill, then down the street and past the vendors on the left."

A man moved behind Isâ, the one they called Techie. "I don't like it. Not enough cover, and it'll call attention to us if we break off this early in the ceremony."

"What do you mean?" Scotty asked.

"Nichols filled me in. These people will stay here for the duration, which could be all night. We'd have to have a good reason to leave. Even then, it would still be odd, and anyone watching would notice."

Isâ nodded in agreement. The IRGC looked at Zaar ceremonies as a nuisance because they couldn't control them, and no non-believers wanted to deal with the noise that lasted through the night.

Nichols moved closer, chanting and carrying a traditional drum. His voice carried through the crowd in perfect rhythm. The ceremony was solemn, but the soldier seemed to be enjoying himself. Right behind him came the Baba Zaar.

Nichols circled them, doing a fairly good job with the chant, maybe trying to cleanse his partners of any jinn that may have attached themselves to them before the Baba Zaar tapped Isâ on the back and headed up the hill with the entire procession following.

The soldier called Scotty gaped, watching as the once-empty pathway filled with people, and more than enough cover to hide their approach. "I can't believe it."

Carnegie laughed. "Believe it. Nichols is a crazed bookworm, but it looks like he got them to pave our way."

As they went up the hill, even more people joined. Voices rose, chanting into the night as the growing crowd funneled through a narrow street lined with open-air shops leading up to the hospital peeking out over a cement wall in the distance.

A small figure entered the procession, weaving in and out of the taller shadowed forms. Isâ froze, recognizing the slight limp. *No. It can't be!* He pushed forward, pressing through the men banging their drums. "Mona!"

His daughter spun and smiled at him.

Isâ grabbed her shoulders. "What are you doing here?"

"The Baba Zaar called for anyone sick. He said this would be the largest healing anyone has ever seen!"

As the crowd pushed past them, Isâ had no doubt that he was right. "That's no matter. You are too young for a Zaar! Go back to our hut."

"But, Father, everyone is here!"

The glint in her eyes was infectious. The Zaar was lively, but it was still a solemn ceremony. It was not a place for children… especially if things went wrong.

Isâ crouched and looked into her eyes. "I'm sure the Baba didn't intend for children to show up. Please, go home."

She frowned. "You are here to help Dr. Zhina. I want to help, too."

Isâ stared in shock. How did she know? Not that it made a difference—she couldn't be there. He pointed back to the beach. "Go home."

"But—"

"Go home now! I told you this is no place for a child."

Mona stuck out her lower lip but nodded, allowing the crowd to pass her. Isâ wanted to give her the world, but he also wanted to keep her safe. None of these people understood that they were here to hide enemy soldiers preparing to rescue a man who their government considered a threat—being here was not safe.

As they grew nearer to the hospital, Isâ's heart lifted. For years, he hoped for a way to repay Zhina for all she'd done for his daughter. He just hoped these Americans truly could save her friend.

The chanting increased, but other sounds filled the air— voices not in time with the music and popping sounds not in sync with the drums. Isâ frowned, craning his neck to look up the path. Light shone down the hill from the hospital, illuminating three silhouettes racing toward the procession. Two men and one woman. Behind them, lights flashed, and a faint smell of smoke carried on the breeze.

Scotty shouted something and raced ahead. Nichols handed his drum off before weaving through the crowd, following. The rest of the Americans sprang to life, spreading out among the throng and moving to the front of the crowd.

The Baba Zaar lifted his staff and turned the crowd down the last street before the hospital, raising his voice and continuing the chant. Isâ stared at the soldiers running up the hill, rapt. Scotty pulled the gun out from beneath his shirt and fired. The silhouettes ducked but didn't slow as more light flashed behind them—Isâ realized now they were muzzle flashes. The guards were shooting at them even as they ran. Nichols fired back and the smoky smell of gunpowder filled the air. The Baba appeared again and Isâ's breath hitched. *What is he doing?* It wasn't safe!

Isâ's gaze met one of the people coming toward him. Her eyes widened as she screamed.

Zhina!

Another round of gunfire erupted behind her. The Americans fired back over Zhina and the two men with her. Something punched Isâ in the shoulder, then the chest. He stumbled back, falling against the cold ground and stared at the distant stars above.

40

Outside Imam Hospital, Iran

ZHINA'S CHEST BURNED as they ran down the dirt street leading from the hospital. Vendors dove into their shops as bullets sprayed the street and people screamed. Arman limped along beside her, his face flushed and brow furrowed in pain. They needed to get off the streets before the IRGC caught up with them but the beach was still a quarter mile away—it may as well have been a hundred miles. Their chances were slim.

Ârash grabbed Arman's arm. "Keep running, my friend. I can hear the water."

"Yes, yes!" Bâbak said. "The beach is just down this hill!"

He was right, but as the shouting behind them grew louder, the path seemed longer and longer. They needed to find a place to hide, but if they stopped they'd be found. Ârash was right—their best chance of survival was pushing through to the beach.

They passed a cross street and the boy skidded to a stop, looking down both alleyways before turning to Arman. "Dr. Arman. You go to the beach. I will distract them."

Arman shook his head, panting. "No. You come with us."

"No, Dr. Arman. If we all go down that street we will be shot." He pointed in the direction of the beach. "It's just like in the prison. It's a small hole, but you can get through."

"So can you!"

"No, Dr. Arman. I stay behind so you can go free, just like you did for me. Don't worry. I got away from them the first time. I'm fast and hide good. Now go!"

Bâbak ran back up the hill toward the soldiers, waving his arms. "Dr. Arman Pirouzi! Don't leave me! I see you over there! I'm coming!" he shouted as he ran down a side street.

Zhina pulled Arman and Ârash into the alcove of a shop as the guards shouted, giving chase to the boy.

"Go with God," Ârash whispered. He tugged Arman's arm. "Come, my friend. Let's not waste the head start he just gave us."

Arman watched the street where the guards had disappeared with horror. "What have we done?"

"Come on," Zhina said. "We can make it. Don't make his risk for nothing." She had no idea who that boy was, but he was the bravest person she'd ever met.

Arman finally pushed away from the building. "All right." He grimaced, limping with each step, moving glacially slow.

Up ahead, Zhina saw a crowd of people appear, flooding the street in seconds. *Isâ's Zaar ceremony! Thank the skies!* Many held drums, and their voices rose in slow, rhythmic chants. They would definitely be a good distraction and good camouflage, but the IRGC wouldn't hesitate to shoot into the crowd if they thought the escapees were there. Zhina's heart ached at the thought of these poor, innocent people being cut down. The man holding a long walking stick in front of the procession nodded at her, smiling, before turning down the last street before the hospital. The people behind him started following.

Zhina puffed out a quick sigh of relief just before shots rang out behind her. She flinched as several people in the procession pulled weapons from beneath long shirts. Zhina stared in shock, too stunned to dive for cover as they opened fire. She screwed her eyes shut and waited for the impact, but none came.

The men continued to fire, the bullets whizzing over their heads and she heard shouts from the IRGC soldiers as they took cover.

"Dr. Arman Pirouzi?" one of the men shouted in a Texan accent. "We're here to get you out!"

"Who are you?" Ârash stammered.

The man with the gun grabbed Arman, shoving him behind himself. "Doesn't matter. We're not the ones trying to kill you."

342

It truly didn't matter—they were Americans, and they were clearly here for Arman.

More gunfire filled the air. Zhina ducked, running in the direction the Americans waved her as some of them kneeled and returned fire.

A man down the street from Zhina turned and was struck twice, red bursting from his chest and shoulder. As he fell, his wide eyes met hers, and her heart ripped in two.

"Isâ!" she screamed.

One of the soldiers grabbed her arm. "Don't."

Zhina dug her heels into the soft earth as the man tried to pull her down the street. "Isâ!"

She twisted free as the man swore, running for her friend and dropping to her knees beside him where a pool of blood had already turned the earth black.

"Dr. Zhina?" Isâ whispered.

She grabbed his hand. "I'm here."

A soldier appeared beside her and took Isâ's pulse while Carnegie pointed a gun over their heads and shot up the hill. "Pick up the pace, Nichols. We need to get these people to cover!"

"Two minutes!" Nichols checked the wound. "Are you really a doctor?"

She nodded. "Yes."

"He has a ruptured spleen. There's nothing we can do."

"Then we gotta go," Carnegie said. "Now!" He fired again and swore as a bullet ripped past close enough Zhina could hear the crack.

"We can't leave him!" she shouted.

Isâ squeezed her hand. "Yes, you can. Take care of Mona for me."

Zhina wiped tears from her eyes. "No. *You* will take care of her. Mona needs her father."

Mona crawled out from a nearby stall, her eyes widening with fear and horror when she saw them.

"Baba!" She ran from the shop as bullets flew down the street, then threw herself down on her father, skidding in the dirt on her knees. "Baba! Baba!"

Carnegie continued to provide cover fire. "We're out of time! I'm sorry, but we have to go, *now!*"

Isâ wiped back Mona's hair. "You shouldn't be here, but for this one time, I'm glad you were stubborn." He smiled, touching her hair, her face. "You're a good girl. You need to go with Zhina now. She will take care of you."

"No, Baba!"

Isâ looked at Zhina. "You heard this man. I'm not going to see the next sunrise. Go now and live. Just take care of my precious *khanoomi.*"

Carnegie grabbed Zhina and yanked her to her feet. "We're done."

"No!" Zhina clawed for Isâ's hand. They couldn't expect her to let him die alone!

"Go!" Isâ pushed Mona toward her.

The child scrambled back, sobbing as she reached for her father. "Baba!"

"I love you! Go now and live!"

"Come on!" Nichols clutched Zhina's arm hard enough to bruise, and she barely had time to grab Mona and drag her along… leaving her friend and Mona's father behind in the dirt, illuminated only by the sparks of gunfire bearing down on him.

41

Qeshm Coast, Iran

ARMAN DUCKED HIS head, running as fast as his injured legs would carry him. His stomach knotted at the sight of the man lying on the ground behind him. Zhina's friend had helped him when he'd never even met the man. He'd been a good person, and he'd gotten caught in the crossfire.

The Zaar ceremony appeared again, as if they'd gone down the side street only to turn around and once again put themselves in harm's way. What were they doing?

The man with a long walking stick—the Baba Zaar, Arman assumed—ran forward and threw a white cloak over Mona and Zhina. It was smart—there was no better way to conceal them in a Zaar healing ceremony than in a cloak like those being treated. Hopefully Zhina and Mona knew enough about Zaar that they would move like one possessed with a jinn dancing to the music.

The Baba ran to Arman with another cloak. "Take this and stay together. Follow me and I will get you out."

"Yes, yes," Arman panted. He moved forward, following the sound of the Baba's voice as people milled around them. He hoped Ârash was also hidden, although his native clothing would conceal him better than Arman's prison attire.

The sound of gunshots filled the night again.

People started screaming, and some around him started to run. The Baba Zaar picked up his pace but continued to chant, leading Arman, Mona, and Zhina down the street.

"Here we go!" one of the Americans shouted.

The sheet was pulled off Arman's head, and he found one of the SEALs standing there. "Run for the beach. We'll cover you."

Arman nodded, then looked back at the Baba Zaar. "Thank you."

The Baba nodded and Arman ran. Mona and Zhina had already started down the path ahead of him, Zhina holding up the white sheet so she could see.

"Come, my friend!" Ârash grabbed his arm, pulling Arman faster.

Behind them, someone yelled, "Fire in the hole!" and an explosion lit up the night.

"Go, go, go, go, go!" One of the SEALs grabbed Arman's arm and pulled him down the hill.

Dust kicked and filled the sky, diffusing a fiery orange glow. Something was burning, and the wind carried the stink of singed fabric and plastic.

Arman's leg exploded anew in pain with each step, but he used the gravity of the slope and the soldier's shoulder to keep going. He needed to push through the pain just a little longer, then he could rest. He had to live—not just for himself, but for Zhina and Ârash. For that little girl who seemed so important to Zhina. For his cat, who hopefully had been eating, for his mother, waiting for him at home. He'd lost track of time and had no idea if he'd missed her birthday, but he'd bring that cake to her, no matter what. He was her son. He owed her everything, and he refused to break his promise to come back to her.

The little girl fell and rolled out from under Zhina's white sheet.

"Mona!" Zhina screamed as bullets peppered the sand around her. One of the SEALs threw himself on the girl and grunted as he got hit.

"Carnegie! Nichols is hit!" the man holding Arman screamed over his shoulder.

"On it!" Carnegie took a knee, pulling him off the girl. "Nichols, you good?"

"Yeah. You know me," Nichols said, groaning as Carnegie helped him up. "I gotta be the hero."

"Let's try to keep you from being a dead hero!"

Carnegie picked up Mona and ran down the hill, while another soldier helped Nichols. Two other Americans took places on either side of the path and shot at the IRGC, keeping them at bay as everyone else rushed to the beach.

As Arman's bloodied feet hit cold sand, someone behind them yelled, "Fire in the hole!" again.

"Go, go, go, go, go!"

Three explosions lit up the night and the Zaar ceremony disintegrated into complete pandemonium as people screamed and ran. The Baba Zaar, looking unconcerned in his long robes, held his walking stick high as he chanted his song, slowly walking a man with a sheet over his head. The patient's body gyrated to the sound of the Baba's voice. The older man smiled, inclining his head to Arman before he steered the white-shrouded man into an outcropping of tall grass and out of immediate danger. The Baba seemed completely unfazed by the danger literally exploding around him. Arman wished his own faith was as strong.

The soldiers led them farther down the beach before flashing a light at the water. Another light flashed back three times.

"That's our ride." The soldier holding Arman pulled him toward the breaking surf.

"Wait." Arman's heels dug trails in the soft sand. "My friends!"

"We got them out of harm's way. We're only cleared to extract you."

Arman backed away and pointed up the hill. "The IRGC will kill them for helping me."

The soldier frowned, chewing the inside of his cheek.

Arman shook his head. "You can't ask me to sacrifice them. You know the information I have is critical or they wouldn't have sent you. Saving a few more people will be worth it."

"That's not for me to decide."

Zhina stepped up, the little girl clinging to her leg, looking up at the soldier with puffy red eyes. "Please help us," Zhina said. "You know what they'll do to her."

They might be merciful to Mona and kill her quickly. Zhina, on the other hand, would face a torture before her death. These American soldiers had probably witnessed atrocities most couldn't stomach, but the reality of living under IRGC rule was something even they might not fully comprehend.

"All right. We act now and ask for forgiveness later." The soldier pointed to another American. "Get them all on the boat."

Ârash limped up to Arman as one of the soldiers led Zhina and Mona into the water. "Marjan is on her way to the Pakistani border. Will I be able to get to her?"

Arman gaped. "What do you mean?"

"My friend smuggles people over the border. He was there the night the IRGC came for me. He was trying to convince us we should leave—that both Niki, and then you, being questioned would make us a target."

Arman lowered his gaze. He'd obviously been right.

Ârash continued. "When the IRGC banged on our door, my friend jumped out a window and told us he'd smuggle out whichever one of us they didn't take."

Arman nodded. "That's a good friend." He'd heard of many instances when a wife or husband had been tortured to try to get a confession from their spouse. And if Ârash escaped, they definitely would have gone after his wife if she were still there.

"Come on, gentlemen." The soldier held out his hand to the empty seats in the boat.

Ârash paused, the surf lapping at his feet. "Can you help my wife get out of Pakistan?"

"Not us, but Pakistan is an ally. If your friend makes the right connections, she can get out." Another boat silently moved toward the beach. "Right now, we need to get you all to safely."

Ârash went pale.

Arman placed his hand on his friend's shoulder. "You'll have the best chance of seeing her again if you're both alive. You need to come with us."

Ârash nodded as he made his way to the water. Arman gulped, watching the last two soldiers lying on the sand, their weapons pointed up the hill, shooting anyone who came down the path. Nichols, the soldier who'd thrown his body over Mona, walked slowly to the beach, leaning on another soldier.

Nichols clutched at his chest. "Techie…"

"Come on," Techie coaxed him, "we're almost to the boat, just a little further."

"Can't…breathe…" Nichols wheezed, then fell to his knees, slumping to the sand.

"Nichols!" Techie yelled, rolling him over.

Arman cursed under his breath and ran over, ignoring the cries of the soldier loading Ârash into the boat.

"Where were you hit?" Arman asked.

Nichols patted at his chest. Arman could see a dark stain at his side. "Can't… g-get a full…"

Arman ran his thumb over the soldier's distended neck vein, then placed his ear on the man's chest. There was no air entering his right lung.

"Tension…" Nichols wheezed.

"Tension pneumothorax," Arman said. "Shit." He glanced to the other soldier. "You—run to the high grass. Pull up as many reeds of different sizes as you can and be back here in thirty seconds or your friend is going to die."

Techie cursed and sprinted for the grass.

Arman went to remove the man's armor and Nichols grabbed his hand, shaking his head. He pointed weakly at the boat and mouthed *"Leave me."*

"I took the Hippocratic Oath," Arman said. "I can't leave you here to die."

Techie skidded into the sand beside them, carrying a fistful of reeds. "Here."

"I need a sharp knife," Arman said, quickly sorting through the reeds and finding the best candidate.

Techie pulled a knife out of his boot and handed it over. Arman cut the ends of the reed, creating a straw.

Techie looked down at his suffocating friend. "Don't die on me, bro. You hear?" He grabbed the man's head and looked into his eyes. "I'm getting you home."

A fresh burst of gunfire raked the beach, kicking up sand and Arman flinched. The two soldiers watching their backs returned fire.

"Any chance we can do this on the boat?" Techie asked.

Arman shook his head. "He'll be dead before we get him there." He held the reed up to the dim moonlight. Hopefully it would be enough. He wiped the knife on the edge of the soldier's shirt. "I wish I could make this sterile, but your clothes are probably cleaner than mine." Arman looked at Techie. "I need to drive this reed into his chest to vent the air trapped there."

Techie cursed. "Then he'll be able to breathe?"

"Yes."

Arman pressed his fingers to Nichols' chest until he found the second intercostal space, the textbook place to insert a chest tube—or, in this case, a reed. Arman placed the knife against his skin. "Here we go."

Nichols twitched as Arman made the incision.

"Here comes the vent." Arman placed the reed in the hole and pressed. He waited for the sound of air, but nothing came.

A bullet whizzed by and Techie swore again, lifting his own gun from the sling and firing a quick burst back up the hill. "He good?"

Arman shook his head. "Damn." This was no time for him to make a bad call! Any one of them could take another bullet at any moment. "We'll have to do it again."

He felt along the ribs until he hit the fourth intercostal space. Nichols' lips were turning blue, his skin pale—the man had no more time for error. Arman shifted down to the fifth intercostal space. "Here we go."

Nichols didn't react as he made the second incision, which was a bad sign. Arman pulled the hollow reed from the first incision and placed it into the second. He applied pressure until he heard a hiss, like opening up the valve in a tire.

"There," Arman said.

"Good?" Techie asked.

Nichols drew in an unsteady, painful breath, but he drew it in nonetheless and gave a weak thumbs-up.

"We good to move him?" Techie asked.

"Not really, but we have no choice. This is only temporary. We need to get you to an actual hospital."

Arman got on one side and Techie got on the other, hoisting Nichols from the sand. The other soldier from the boat appeared, taking the burden from Arman.

"You need to get into the Beaver, Dr. Pirouzi We're leaving ASAP."

"Beaver?" Arman asked.

"The boat! The boat!"

One of the soldiers from up the hill ran down, grabbing Arman by the shoulder. "Time to go, Dr. Pirouzi."

The soldier ran down the beach, practically dragging Arman along with him. They splashed three steps into the water before the soldier lifted Arman and threw him into the boat.

The other two soldiers lifted Nichols in next and placed him on the bench beside Zhina.

One tapped the side of the boat. "Go! Go! Go!"

Zhina held a cloth to Nichol's forehead as they sped out into the dark sea, moonlight glistening off the black water.

Once they'd cleared the beach, one of the soldiers on the shoreline shot at the IRGC still coming down the hill as the others jumped into another boat. They started the engines and the last man dove in behind them as they pulled away, engines roaring as they opened them up fully.

Mona clung to Zhina's arm, sniffling. The poor girl had lost her father. Arman wasn't sure how well the child knew Zhina, but now she was being ripped from her home and headed to a country that didn't speak her language. That was a lot for a child, but Arman was only a little older than her when he came to the United States. It was hard, but he left a shadowed future for one filled with hope and limitless possibilities. Hopefully, Mona would look back at this as the first day of the rest of her life, rather than the day her life had fallen apart.

She pointed back to the shore. "Look!"

Torches lined the beach. Small flashes of light sparkled in the night, followed by *pops* carrying on the breeze. Voices raised in song—not unlike the cadence of the Zaar ceremony—as a throng of people stormed toward the IRGC. More gunfire lit up the beach, and some townspeople fell, but there were far more good citizens willing to risk their lives for what they believed in than there were IRGC.

The crowds overtook the guards, and the gunfire stopped, replaced by silence.

Arman smiled at Zhina. Qeshm Island was small compared to the rest of Iran, but hopefully, the IRGC would not be able to squelch the news of this one small victory. If more good citizens realized they could stand up to oppression, perhaps Iran would have the chance to one day be free.

Arman turned from the beach and looked out across the vast ocean. The water sparkled in the moonlight, a calm, tranquil contrast to the uprising on the not-too-distant shore. A few hours ago, they faced almost certain death. Now, an unlimited destiny awaited all of them.

Arman reached out and took Zhina's hand. If this was the start of their new lives, he promised himself not to waste a single moment.

42

Eglin Airforce Base, Emerald Coast, Florida

ARMAN SQUEEZED ZHINA'S hand as the helicopter circled the landing pad below. Their first stop had been Germany for a debriefing and the handover of the false tooth to the CIA. The United States allowed Zhina into the country as a continuation of her previous student visa—an unheard-of concession—and allowed her daughter, Mona, to come with her, making note in the paperwork that Zhina had been unable to grab the documents that could prove the little girl was her true daughter. Arman could barely believe how quickly the government could cut through red tape that normally would have taken months, if not years—not to mention their willingness to bend the rules in Arman and Zhina's favor.

Ârash's wife was detained at the Pakistani border, probably terrifying for poor Marjan, but that delay ended up making it possible to easily find her. Ârash just as quickly received political asylum and was negotiating her extrication to the United States with the help of the CIA.

Mona clung to Zhina, closing her eyes as the helicopter landed. Arman hugged them both as a flurry of people circled the craft on the tarmac.

"Hold on a few moments." The pilot took off his headgear and smoothed back his short, black hair. "We'll come and get you when it's safe." He looked at little Mona before stepping off the helicopter. Judging by the picture taped to the dash, he was a father and understood the loud noise made things even harder for the child.

As the group stepped out of the helicopter, Agent Zarabi approached with a large bundle of white fur in his arms. Arman's eyes flooded with tears. "Anâr!" Arman collected the cat and hugged him close. Anâr pretended to look away, aloof as always, but accepted the cuddles. Arman just hugged him closer. "I missed you too, my friend." He stroked his fur, surprised that the cat seemed fit and full. For as long as Arman had owned him, Anâr would only eat food if Arman prepared it. Apparently, Agent Zarabi was right—he *did* have a way with animals.

Arman crouched and showed the cat to Mona. "This is my good friend, Anâr. He loves children." Anâr snorted and looked away from her, but didn't complain when she smiled and stroked his fur.

"He's pretty," Mona said.

Arman smiled. "You are welcome to come and pet him anytime." In fact, he hoped their visits would turn into something more permanent. He hadn't really thought about children, but Mona had become important to him over the past week since leaving Iran, and Zhina was dedicated to making sure the girl had the best future.

Arman left Anâr in Mona's arms and stood, looking over the crowd. The one smiling face he hoped to see wasn't there. He turned to agent Zarabi. "Where's my mother? Didn't anyone tell her I was coming home?"

Agent Zarabi lowered his eyes. "Dr. Pirouzi, your mother wasn't well enough to join us at the airport. She's waiting to see you at a hospice nearby."

Arman grabbed Zhina's arm to keep from falling. *Hospice...* meaning there was nothing else the doctors could do for her. They were making her comfortable until her body finally gave up. How long had she been there? How long did she have? Had he missed the last moments of her life?

He screwed his eyes shut, his lungs burning for air.

Zhina squeezed his arm. "We should go to her."

Arman nodded, gasping in a breath. "Yes. Yes, we must."

The hospice loomed like a somber fortress against the evening sky, casting long shadows that seemed to reach out and claw at Arman's heart. Mona shifted beside Zhina. "Is this the hospital?" she asked in Farsi.

Zhina nodded. "Yes, it is a hospital for those who are very sick."

Mona reached up and took Arman's hand. "I'm sorry your mama is very sick."

Arman choked down the painful ball building in his throat.

The child smiled sweetly, holding up the box containing Ânâhid's favorite Persian roulette cake. "But this will make her feel better, yes?"

Arman couldn't help but smile at her innocence. "Yes, I'm sure it will."

He looked up at the building. Ânâhid had been sick when he left, but still very much alive. Tired, but still a free spirit willing to take on the world. What would he find inside these walls? How far had the cancer progressed? Would she be in pain? Would she know him? He closed his eyes and wiped away a tear. Part of him wished he'd never left her. But if he hadn't, Iran would certainly have tasted the bite of another war. Countless innocents would have died, and Zhina, Mona, and Ârash would still be cowering beneath the whims of the IRGC.

Of course, Mona would still have father. That was one piece of this puzzle Arman wished he could erase. He'd never met Zhina's friend Isâ, but he must have been a fine and courageous soul to risk so much to save a man he didn't even know.

Zhina placed a hand on his elbow. "Are you all right?"

Arman cleared his throat. "I suppose I'm as okay as I'll ever be."

She held his arm as she led him into the Hospice. The walls were cold and white. Down the hallway, a woman screamed, "You're not my daughter! Where's my daughter?" Arman's stomach turned. He dearly hoped his mother would recognize him—he didn't think he could handle it otherwise. He stopped outside her door and took a deep breath.

Zhina squeezed his arm. "I'm here for you. We both are."

Mona looked up at him, smiling and nodding.

Arman gulped down the ball in his throat. "I know, but I think I'd like to go in alone. At least at first."

The woman at the end of the hall started screaming again.

Zhina pulled Mona close and nodded. "I understand. We'll wait out here until you say it's okay."

As Arman entered the dimly lit room, the scent of antiseptic mingled with the faint aroma of the sweet cake in Mona's hands outside. Ânâhid lay on her bed, frail and pale, yet her eyes sparkled with life as they fell upon Arman.

"Oh! My boy!" She held up a thin arm. "I knew you'd come back."

Arman burst into tears. "Oh, Mom!"

He stumbled toward her and pulled her into his arms. Her body weighed barely more than the white blanket laying over her. She stroked the back of his head. "There, there, my boy. What's all this crying?"

"I-I was afraid I'd never see you again."

"Don't be silly. I told you I'd be here, waiting."

He pulled her tighter. "It was so bad, Mom. More horrible than I ever could have imagined."

She pressed her weak hands against his chest until he leaned up.

She looked into his eyes. "You look a little thinner. I guess the *Aabghoosht* in Iran isn't as good as it used to be."

Arman laughed, then choked out a sob, burying his head in her hair. "I missed you so much."

"Well, now you are back. I want to hear all about your adventures." She smiled. "Did you save the world?"

He wiped away his tears. "For now, I suppose."

"Well, *for now* is all we needed, right?" She placed a cool palm on his cheek. "Tell me what happened."

He placed a hand over hers, desperate to warm her up. "Not today. Today is for celebration."

"I do love a good celebration."

He managed a smile. "And what good would a celebration be without guests?" He released her and opened the door. His mother's eyes lit up when she saw who was waiting outside.

"Zhina!" She lifted her arms for a hug. "I knew the last time you left would not be goodbye. Come here, child!"

Zhina's eyes filled with tears. "Hello, Ânâhid."

"I knew you'd be back someday." Ânâhid grabbed Zhina and Arman's hands. "I felt it in my heart that you two were meant to be together."

Zhina's smile dazzled. "Yes, I think I always knew, too."

Ânâhid looked around them to the small child lurking in the doorway. "Who do we have here?"

Arman waved her in. "This is Mona."

Mona took a tentative step inside and held up the box. "Happy birthday, Bibi. We brought you a cake."

Ânâhid smiled. "You did?" She opened the box. "Look at that! It's my favorite!"

Mona beamed, nodding. "Dr. Arman told me."

Ânâhid straightened her blankets. "Well, Dr. Arman has known me for a long time."

"Yes, his whole life!"

Ânâhid laughed. "Yes, in fact he has. You are such a smart girl!" She looked up at Zhina. "She's yours?"

Zhina nodded. "She is now."

Arman placed his arm around her shoulder and the other around Mona, letting his mother know that Mona calling her "Bibi" was more than an honorific, that this was his new family, and his mother now had the grandchild she'd always longed for.

"You need to eat the cake!" Mona said.

"That sounds like a good idea." Ânâhid tapped the bed beside her. "How about you come up here and help me?"

Mona's smile grew wider as she climbed onto the bed and Ânâhid offered her the first bite.

"No!" Mona said. "It's *your* birthday. You should have the first taste."

Arman smiled. It wasn't his mother's birthday anymore, but he was glad that Ânâhid didn't correct the child. Mona was far too excited, and she needed some joy, some *normalness*, in her life.

Ânâhid scooped the cake into her mouth and rolled the pastry over her tongue. She sighed with her eyes closed. "Delicious. There is no better taste in the world."

Mona clapped her hands. "Now me! Now me!"

Ânâhid laughed, giving the child a scoop And Mona's eyes widened. "It *is* good!"

Ânâhid smiled, looking past her to Arman. "I am proud of you, and I can see the happiness in your eyes." Her gaze settled on Zhina. "I'm glad you found love again."

Arman closed his eyes and looked down, trying to cover his tears. "I'm just happy I was able to get home." The words *in time* hung in the air, but he didn't want to utter them and ruin the moment.

Ânâhid squeezed his hand. "Thank you for making this old woman's heart so full."

Tears streamed down Arman's cheeks as he leaned over and kissed his mother's forehead. "No… Thank *you* for being the best mother anyone could ever ask for."

Zhina leaned in as well, planting a tender kiss on Ânâhid's cheek. "Thank you for raising such an incredible man. I promise to cherish and love him forever."

Ânâhid's smile lingered for a moment before she closed her eyes. "I'm a little tired. I'm sorry. It's all these medicines."

Arman gave her a hug. "It's okay. We'll let you rest. I'll be back tomorrow to see you."

His mother nodded. "That will be nice."

Mona hugged her tight. "Good night, Bibi."

"Good night, sweet joojoo."

Arman stared at his mother as they left, knowing well that every goodbye now might be his last, but he planned to make the most of their visits until that time came. She deserved that much.

43

The White House, Washington D.C.

MONA SQUEEZED ARMAN'S hand as she looked up at the massive, white stone columns on either side of the wide, pristine steps. "This is a house? Why is it so big?"

Zhina smiled. "This is the White House. The President of the United States lives here."

Mona pushed herself into Zhina's leg. "Is he going to hurt us?"

Zhina frowned, hugging her. "No, joojoo. We're safe here. The American leader isn't like that. We're here for a grand dinner in a ballroom."

"Like a princess in the movies you showed me?"

Zhina laughed, hugging her again. "Yes, very much like that."

"It sure looks like a palace," Mona said as they stepped inside.

Arman nodded. It certainly did.

Their footsteps echoed through the grand corridors as guards led them down a hallway. The atmosphere was tense, a sense of anticipation hanging in the air, but as they stepped into the main hall, their attention was drawn to the large TV screens mounted alongside the stage.

Gasps and murmurs filled the room as men in tuxedos and women in long gowns watched scenes from the streets of Iran. People clad in green, white, and red liberty colors filled city squares, shouting and raising their fists. Some held up photographs of the Azadi freedom tower in Tehran with a tattered flag on top, the symbol of the woman's movement. Beneath the news footage, white words scrolled by with a rough translation as the people's voices rose in unison: "Game on, mullah gone." That wasn't *exactly* what they were saying, but it was close enough, and possibly more meaningful to an American audience than the actual words.

Several young women draped in loose hijabs held pictures of those recently killed by the IRGC for standing up to tyranny. Brave souls who paid the ultimate price for their defiance. Among those pictures was Niki's, whose sacrifice ignited a fire of rebellion. Arman's heart swelled that his goddaughter had risen from death as a martyr for the cause she felt so strongly for. At least her death hadn't been in vain.

As the camera panned across the sea of protesters, Arman's heart skipped a beat. There, amidst the sea of faces, were signs bearing his own image and the words "We are not alone!" It felt surreal, as if his two worlds—the life he left behind in Iran and the life he now led—converged in an astonishing display of unity and hope. The weight of his actions, his sacrifices, and the price paid by those back in the country of his birth bore down on him, and he fought to contain his emotions. Zhina and Mona stood by his side, their eyes glistening with tears, a mix of pride and concern etched on their faces.

On the screen, a young protester with a patch over one eye shouted right into the cameras, holding up a picture of Arman. Arman gaped at the familiar face. "Is that Bâbak?" Zhina asked.

"Yes, it certainly is." Arman wiped a tear from his eye. "You made it out," he whispered. "I see you, my friend."

The last question eating away at Arman's soul had now been answered, and he would finally be able to sleep at night. His heart still clenched, though. No one at that protest was safe. The IRGC would come down on them just as assuredly as they had come down on others.

Bâbak knew that, though. Protesting was what sent him to prison the first time, yet he was still there, risking everything for the possibility of a better future.

Arman's heart swelled for him, and for all of them.

The screens all cut to a stage where a young girl in her early teens stepped up to the podium. The caption read: *Masoumeh Moradi, orchestrator of the largest civilian protest in Iranian history, and daughter of recently deceased Iranian General Naser Moradi, speaks in public for the first time.*

Arman gaped. Could the daughter of a man so bent on controlling the people have turned on the government her father strived to control?

The young woman's eyes swept across the crowd. "We unite with a single purpose." She pointed at the cameras. "The eyes of the world are on us, and I am here to tell you that the youth of Iran will not stand for persecution and oppression any longer. You may torture us and shoot us, but like a swarm of ants, there will be more and more to replace us. We will keep coming, increasing our numbers until we have achieved our goal." She looked directly into the camera. "We will have our *freedom*."

Arman felt a burst of hope, but he also ached inside for the young woman. Her family name would not be enough to protect her. Hopefully, that swarm of ants she referred to would be willing to pull her from that stage and hide her from the IRGC. Still, the Moradi name was one that struck terror into the hearts of good people. For her to come out in opposition to everything her father stood for was a major development. Hopefully she could rally the people into an army without guns, able to overwhelm the IRGC with simple numbers rather than military might.

The room remained captivated by the events unfolding thousands of miles away. The power of the people's will, the collective yearning for freedom, was palpable even through the screen. In that moment, Arman realized his mission was far from over. He had achieved much, but the struggle for Iran's liberation was ongoing. The support of the international community, the unity of nations against tyranny, and the resilience of the Iranian people were crucial elements that would determine the nation's ultimate fate.

The world outside might still have been fraught with danger and uncertainty, but within the walls of the White House, in the presence of loved ones and allies, Arman felt a glimmer of hope. The journey was far from over, but he was ready—ready to stand alongside the Iranian people, to fight for justice, and to ensure the sacrifices of Niki, Isâ, and countless others would not be in vain.

The screens grew dim as security led Arman, Mona, and Zhina to a table near the front of the room. Mona giggled, seeing a laptop screen perched on the table with a clear view of the stage. Arman's mother smiled on the screen, waving from her bed in the hospice. Mona waved back, clapping her hands. Arman blew a kiss to his mother. He'd rather have had her there in person, but this was the next best thing.

The East Room of the White House buzzed with anticipation as distinguished guests and government officials filled every corner of the opulent space. Arman never imagined his journey would lead him to this moment—it all felt a bit surreal.

The lights dimmed, and a voice boomed over the speakers. "Ladies and gentlemen, the President of the United States."

"Hail to the Chief" played as the President, flanked by security personnel, made his entrance. A wave of applause followed him as he stepped up to the podium and raised his hands for people to sit.

"Ladies and gentlemen," the President began, "we are gathered here today to honor an extraordinary individual; a man whose actions have shaped the course of history and exemplified the spirit of selflessness and heroism."

As the President continued his speech, he recounted the harrowing tale of Dr. Arman Pirouzi's journey into Iran, his courageous efforts to bring back critical information, and the risks he'd taken to ensure the safety of the Iranian people. The audience listened with rapt attention, many staring in Arman's direction with stunned looks on their faces.

"But his mission was not just a personal quest," the President proclaimed, his gaze locking with Arman's. "It was a mission that united many nations and peoples against tyranny and oppression. Thanks to Dr. Pirouzi's selfless acts and the invaluable information he brought back, today, we stand united against the Iranian regime—a regime that has trampled on the basic human rights of its people for far too long."

The president paused, his gaze carrying over the room, before returning to Arman.

"I am proud to declare that the United States, together with our European allies, will support the Iranian people in their quest for freedom and justice," the President declared, his voice firm. The crowd cheered, and Arman squeezed Zhina's hand.

The President lifted an arm, quieting the audience. "The countries of the European Union have agreed to take significant steps. The IRGC will be declared a terrorist group, the EU embassies in Tehran will be closed, and Iranian diplomats will be asked to leave European countries immediately. Furthermore, all trading contracts with the Iranian government will be put on hold until the current regime is no longer in power."

A murmur of astonishment and approval swept through the audience. This was a moment that would reverberate across the world, signaling a monumental shift in international relations and support for the Iranian people's struggle.

Arman's heart fluttered, and he took a deep breath, trying to calm himself. His actions had set in motion a chain of events that would reshape the future of his homeland, and none of it would have happened if he hadn't agreed to speak to the CIA. A wiser man might have stayed home, played it safe, and let someone else take the risk. But Arman stepped forward.

Of course, heroic acts were never without consequences. Isâ paid with his life, the greatest sacrifice of all. Arman still walked with a slight limp, but it was nothing compared to the guilt he felt for the loss of Zhina's friend and Mona's father, even though Zhina told him Isâ believed his life was a small price to pay to save countless other Iranians.

The President gestured at Arman. "May I present the man we are here to honor tonight—Dr. Arman Pirouzi."

A spotlight shined on Arman's table, and the audience rose to their feet and applauded. Arman's cheeks flushed as he stood, waving to the room and shaking hands as he approached the stage and was directed up the steps by security.

Trembling, Arman shook the President's hand. "Thank you, Sir."

The President smiled. "On the contrary. Thank *you*, Dr. Pirouzi." He reached over and took a medal with a white star surrounded by gold from a velvet pillow held by a man in a stiffly starched military uniform. The President placed the long blue ribbon over Arman's head. "Please accept this Presidential Medal of Freedom, the highest civilian honor available in recognition of bravery and selflessness."

The audience roared, applauding again, and Arman's eyes burned. All those days in his cell, and through all the countless struggles, the one thing he held on to was the idea of *home*. He had desperately wanted to get back to the United States and give his mother the cake he promised her. He wanted to return to the medical profession and save lives. He wanted to make sure his cat was okay, and so many other things he'd taken for granted or, at one time, considered a burden... but never had he dreamed of getting a medal.

The weight of the ribbon and heavy metal pendant centered him. Somehow, it felt right, like he'd been meant for this. As a doctor, he'd sworn an oath to save lives—but maybe that oath had a wider reach than just his patients.

He had a clear view of the laptop sitting at his table, where his mother wiped tears from her eyes on the screen. Arman held his head a little taller. Of all the praise in this room, hers meant the most. She'd given up her life and friends in Iran to give him the opportunity of a new life. Knowing he helped spearhead a movement that would give the same opportunities to others meant everything to him.

He turned back to the President and nodded. "Thank you, Sir."

The President shook his head. "No. Once again, thank *you*." He held his hand out to the applauding crowd. "This is all well deserved."

Arman shook the President's hand and returned to his table. Zhina gave him a hug, and Mona threw her arms around his waist. A deep sense of safety overwhelmed him, maybe for the first time in his life. For years, he'd searched for who he was, and who he wanted to be. Zhina and Mona completed something he didn't realize was lacking.

Everything was good and right, and he'd never let it go.

EPILOGUE

Queens, New York

THE LIGHTS IN Memorial Hospital seemed brighter than he remembered, and the walls seemed even cleaner. He wondered if it was a figment of his imagination, or if he was just relieved to be home.

He headed down the hallway to the meeting room. He was oddly excited to find out more about their plans for the new wing—the funding having come from the generous donation the CIA had given under the guise of a gift from the Iranian Society of Cardiology. He'd already sent in his requests and suggestions and was looking forward to seeing their final decisions.

Inside the presentation area, Dr. Smith stood in the front of the room with a projector remote in hand. "And, as you see, we will barely even be losing any parking with this plan. Plus, the addition of the solar panels on the roof will help with our electrical bills for years to come."

Arman gaped, seeing the name of the new wing. "The Owen Smith center?" He asked as he walked toward the front of the room.

Doctor Smith's eyes widened. "Why, yes. The council met yesterday, and the decision was nearly unanimous."

"Nearly unanimous? Who did you pay off?"

Dr. Smith smiled, folding his hands. "Now, Dr. Pirouzi, there's no reason to be uncivil. I've been at this hospital a very long time, and everybody thought it was fitting that my name should be on the new wing."

"Your name, or an American name?"

Dr. Smith frowned. "Now, let's not make more of this than it is, Dr. Pirouzi. We just made a decision based on seniority."

"You made a decision on naming a building you wouldn't have been able to fund without me." Arman looked around the room. "The money for this wing came as a donation for me going overseas to teach doctors in the Middle East. You all know what I went through over there, and this hospital quickly jumped on the marketing when the President of the United States put a medal around my neck. But you couldn't even grant me the simple request of what to name the building?"

"It's just a name." Dr. Smith moved the pointer from one hand to the other. "This wing will still be a significant presence for cancer research. You have to be happy about that."

"For that, yes, I am happy, but frankly, Dr. Smith, I'm sick and tired of your rhetoric and your prejudices, not just against me, but every foreign doctor working in this hospital. You should be ashamed of yourself, and I refuse to work in the same building as you any longer."

Chief Executive Officer Murray stood. "Dr. Pirouzi, what are you saying?"

"I'm saying that I quit. There are plenty of hospitals in this city that would be thrilled to have me. I don't need to put up with this anymore."

"But this is ridiculous," Dr. Smith said. "The name you wanted on the building isn't even yours. And what is that word anyway it sounds, so... so..."

"Iranian?" Arman asked.

"Well, yes. What does that word even mean?"

"Ânâhid means purity—something you know nothing about."

Dr. Smith wrinkled his nose. "Purity?"

Arman lifted his chin. "It's also my mother's name. And you will never, *ever* find a stronger name for the symbol of the fight against cancer." He turned and walked through the door.

Chief Executive Officer Murray chased him down. "Dr. Pirouzi, this really isn't necessary."

"Oh, I think it is."

They all expected him to be the same person he was when he left, but he wasn't. He refused to let anybody walk on him ever again.

"But Dr. Pirouzi, I wanted to talk to you about that promotion."

Arman turned. "Promotion?"

"Head of Interventional and Endovascular Surgery?"

Arman frowned. "Head? No one ever even wanted to make me a *senior* interventionist."

"Well, that was a mistake, one I would like to now make right. We don't want to lose you."

"And the cancer center?"

"I think the *Ânâhid Pirouzi Cancer Center* has a wonderful ring to it."

Arman nodded. "And Dr. Smith?"

Dr. Murray looked to the side before returning his gaze to Arman. "There's an opening in our Harlem branch that I believe Dr. Smith would be a perfect fit for." He held out his hand to Arman. "What do you say, Dr. Pirouzi? Will you stay?"

Arman stared at his hand but didn't shake it. "I'd like to see the plans for the *Ânâhid Pirouzi Cancer Center* in your office tomorrow morning. Eleven sharp." He started walking again. "And then we'll discuss the details of either my promotion or my resignation."

Dr. Murray gaped. "You don't know which?"

"I'll let you know tomorrow."

Arman smiled as he walked down the hall. All he'd really wanted was to name the cancer center after his mother, but if he could get a promotion and get rid of Dr. Smith at the same time, he was going to take it.

Arman eased into his seat at his kitchen table as he and Zhina finished singing the birthday song. Mona clapped her hands as Zhina placed a cake in front of her with seven candles on top. "What are the candles for?" Mona asked.

"For your special day." Zhina turned the cake so Mona could see her name. "We light one candle for every birthday we've already celebrated and one for today."

Mona's eyes widened. "You must need a *really* big cake on your birthday!"

Arman laughed as Zhina tousled the girl's hair. "Just blow out the candles so we can eat."

Zhina and Mona were spending more and more time at Arman's place. In fact, it started to feel empty whenever they left. Mona started school and was picking up English ten times faster than Arman had when he'd come to the USA for the first time, and Zhina found a job at a local physical therapy center. Her dreams had always been bigger than that, but it was a good start. In no time, she'd find the funding for all the research she dreamed of, and she'd have a team of her own.

He couldn't wait for her dreams to come true and couldn't think of anyone more deserving.

"You can do it!" Zhina clapped her hands as Mona tried to blow out the candles for the third time.

The child wiped her brow with the back of her hand. "This is hard!" She took an exaggerated breath and blew, leaning over the table on her tiptoes.

When the last candle finally winked out, they all cheered. It was a small victory, but the first of many for this little girl who now had a lifetime of opportunities ahead of her. Zhina cut the cake and handed each of them a piece.

Mona took a bite and smiled; her lips coated with white icing. "It's good!"

Arman sat back in his chair. It certainly *was* good. Having Mona in the house filled a void he didn't even realize existed until she became a part of his world.

Anâr jumped on the table and sniffed the cake before backing away, sneezing.

"It's not for you, silly kitty." Mona laughed. "It's for people!"

Zhina picked up the cat and placed him on the floor. Anâr stuck his nose in the air and left the room with his tail high, like he'd never been interested in the first place. Some things never changed, and Arman wouldn't have it any other way.

His phone rang and he went to silence it until he saw the caller—"Anâr's Best Friend." Arman shook his head. Agent

Zarabi insisted on typing his number into Arman's phone, then he put some sort of encryption on it so Arman couldn't change the name. The CIA agent had an odd sense of humor. Walking into the living room, Arman answered. "Agent Zarabi, what can I do for you?"

"Dr. Pirouzi! I hope you're taking good care of my cat."

Arman smiled. "Yes. He tells me every day how much happier he is. He said your apartment stinks."

"He did not!"

Arman laughed. "Did you really just call to check up on him?"

"Well, not exactly. I'm glad you asked. We have a little something we need help with. We think you'd be a great fit."

Arman frowned. "In what way?"

"Classified. We'll need you to come down to the CIA to discuss the details."

Arman's eyes widened as he looked back to the kitchen, where Zhina was handing Mona another piece of cake. Having them here with him was so perfect. So right.

He was finally home. Finally *safe*.

He could hear Agent Zarabi shift on the other end of the phone. "What do you say, Dr. Pirouzi? Ready to save the world again?"

The End.

ABOUT THE AUTHOR

DIAKO HAZHIR is a medical professional and a writer of gripping political thrillers. As a member of the Iranian diaspora, he brings a deeply personal perspective to his storytelling, drawing from 27 years of lived experience in Iran. Many of the events in his novels echo real-life moments he has witnessed, blending authenticity with high-stakes intrigue. Through his writing, Diako Hazhir explores themes of resistance, espionage, and the resilience of the human spirit in the face of oppression.

MORE...

For more about this book and the author, upcoming releases and other works, and to find out more about the cause for Iranian freedom visit www.DiakoHazhir.com.

NOTES

[i] Moin B, Khomeini: life of the ayatollah, 2000, p. 208.

[ii] Nasiri S, Faghfouri Azar L. Investigating the 1981 Massacre in Iran: On the Law-Constituting Force of Violence. *Journal of Genocide Research*. 2022, 26 (2): 164–187. doi:10.1080/14623528.2022.2105027.

[iii] https://www.iranrights.org/library/document/106.

[iv] https://www.womensvoicesnow.org/irans-women-revolution#:~:text=%E2%80%94%20Shakib%20Lolo%2C%20Iranian%20Protestor%20Living,United%20for%20Iran